Robyn Annear is an ex-typist who lives in country Victoria with somebody else's husband. She is also the author of *Bearbrass, Nothing But Gold, The Man Who Lost Himself,* and *Fly a Rebel Flag.*

A CITY LOST & FOUND
WHELAN THE WRECKER'S MELBOURNE

Robyn Annear

Black Inc.

Published by Black Inc.,
an imprint of Schwartz Publishing Pty Ltd
Level 5, 289 Flinders Lane
Melbourne Victoria 3000 Australia
email: enquiries@blackincbooks.com
http://www.blackincbooks.com

The National Library of Australia Cataloguing-in-Publication entry:
    Annear, Robyn.
    A city lost and found : Whelan the Wrecker's Melbourne.

    Includes index.
    ISBN 1 86395 389 2.

    1. Whelan the Wrecker Pty. Ltd. 2. Construction industry –
    Victoria – Melbourne – History. 3. Melbourne (Vic.) –
    History. 4. Melbourne (Vic.) – Buildings, structures, etc.
    – History. I. Title.

994.51

Cover design Thomas Deverall
Text design Anna Warren, Warren Ventures Pty Ltd
Printed in Australia by Griffin Press

Dedicated
to the memory of
Myles Whelan,
1932–2003

~ also to Jean Whelan,
'the crane to his wrecking-ball'
(in the words of their son, Patrick)

~ and to Keith Dunstan
who introduced me to Whelan the Wrecker

On the one hand, there is the simple perception that if places, objects and customs are not preserved, then they are lost, and that therefore preservation efforts must on balance be a good thing. But there is the more sophisticated knowledge that to preserve things deliberately, for the sake of doing so, is to lose them in another way, and to risk keeping the shell of a world at the expense of its meaning.

GILLIAN TINDALL, *CÉLESTINE*

TABLE OF CONTENTS

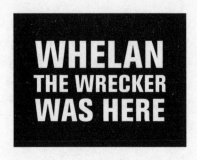

WHELAN
THE WRECKER
WAS HERE

PREFACE

I was born under the sign of Whelan. Not literally: so far as I know, the Alfred Hospital stood unassailed in June 1960. But near by, in the heart of Melbourne, the WHELAN THE WRECKER sign was rampant. The wind coming from that quarter (unusually for June), some speck of pulverised brick must have carried from the wreckage of the Eastern Market and lit on me as I first drew breath.

And so, with Whelan in the ascendant, it was my destiny to grow up charmed by demolition and impervious to dust.

The 1960s and '70s, my formative years, coincided with Whelan the Wrecker's heyday. And I wasn't the only one under their spell. Almost daily, the newspapers ran stories of their exploits – WRECKER IN FULL CRY, BRICKS FLY AT THE MINT, DOWN WITH HISTORY, BEGINNING OF THE END – with pictures of beaming Whelans amid the bones and rubble of gutted city landmarks. It never occurred to me that their business was destruction. It was revelation, surely – bringing hidden things to light. A kind of archaeology with gusto.

What was happening, of course, was that Melbourne was being remade. It was always being remade, but from the mid-1950s the city was falling over itself in pursuit of progress. To make way for new buildings, old ones had to go. Whelan the Wrecker's job was to dispose of the bodies.

The Whelan family wrecked for almost a century, until 1991. It's no stretch to say that they changed the face of Melbourne in that time, demolishing hundreds of buildings in the central city alone. In this book I use their demolition sites as portals, to explore layers of the city laid bare when Whelan the Wrecker was here.

CHAPTER 1

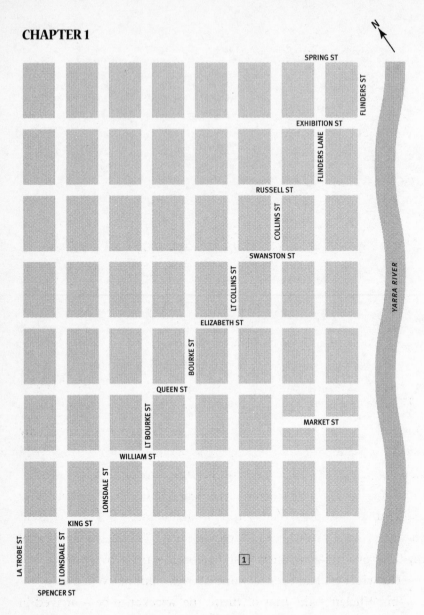

SPRING ST

FLINDERS ST

EXHIBITION ST

FLINDERS LANE

RUSSELL ST

COLLINS ST

SWANSTON ST

LT COLLINS ST

ELIZABETH ST

BOURKE ST

QUEEN ST

LT BOURKE ST

MARKET ST

WILLIAM ST

LONSDALE ST

KING ST

LA TROBE ST

LT LONSDALE ST

SPENCER ST

YARRA RIVER

1. *609-611 Little Collins Street*

Two Pounds in his Pocket

Stawell to Melbourne ~ Whelan becomes a wrecker ~
first city demolition

You've heard, of course, of Marvellous Melbourne, boom metropolis of the 1880s. In upthrust and modernity it rivalled New York and Chicago, and among cities of the British Empire only London outranked it. Old-Melburnian, William Westgarth, travelled from the eye of the Empire to visit his one-time home at the peak of the boom, 1888. Thirty-one years had passed since he'd seen the place and, 'I now wandered,' he wrote, 'through countless streets without encountering a single recognisable object … The old Melbourne of my time, of a full generation past, had been entirely swept away …'

The wreckers had been at work, all right. But not Whelan's.

Jim Whelan – the first of them, the wrecker-to-be – arrived in Melbourne in 1884 from the Western District town of Stawell. Tall and brawny at twenty, he'd been earning wages since the age of ten: horse-and-dray work mostly, in connection with the Stawell gold mines, plus a spell as a boundary rider. He was second-born of a brood of eight belonging to James and Mary Whelan, immigrants from Ireland at the height of Victoria's gold rushes. The Whelans' first wreck (Jim would later joke) was the fortune his father made and lost on a mining venture in the '70s. Now, after years working underground, James snr. was gravely ill with 'miner's complaint', his lungs shredded by quartz dust from the rock-drills. Clearly the deep mines of Stawell were no place for a young man who loved daylight and his life. In Melbourne – Marvellous Melbourne – there were fortunes to be made much nearer the surface. With his parents' blessing and £2 in his pocket, Jim Whelan set off for the boom town.

Family ties drew him to Brunswick, at that time the most Irish of Melbourne suburbs. In the early '80s, with the old city being remade and new suburbs built from scratch, Sydney Road was worn to ruts by the constant traffic of laden drays. City-bound, they carried bricks warm from the kilns or bluestone from the Merri Creek quarries; returning, they bulged with firewood for the brickworks. When the railway reached Brunswick in 1884 (the same year as Jim Whelan) the welter of cartage traffic subsided. But there was still work enough for Jim to find a living with horse and dray.

Not his own horse and dray, mind you. That would take the kind of money he didn't have – yet. He worked for a Brunswick carter, hauling not bricks or stone, but timber: from docks and railways to the timberyards, and from timberyards to building sites. At first, he sent most of his wages home to Stawell. James Whelan snr. died within a year of his son's leaving, and in 1887 the rest of the family joined Jim in Brunswick. By the end of the '80s, he'd saved enough to buy his own horse and dray, and was one of the busiest carters on the Melbourne docks.

Most days, Jim would end up with odd scraps of timber on his dray, picked up on city building sites on the way home. According to Whelan family legend, it was from just such scraps that he built his first house. In any case, he soon accumulated a surplus of the stuff and began sidelining as a timber merchant – from his backyard to start with; then from his own woodyard and carting depôt in Brunswick Road.

It was 1892, and Melbourne was a boom city no more. The great land boom had burst, with banks caught short and so-called permanent building societies gone in a puff of smoke. Thousands of speculators, large and small, lost their own and others' fortunes in the collapse. The frenzy of building activity had ceased; even so, the city was over-stocked with floorspace. The boom-era buildings of seven and eight storeys were short of tenants, while in the suburbs whole streetsful of brand new houses stood blank-eyed and empty.

Many a small tradesman, during the '80s, had been spurred to reck-lessness by the availability of easy credit. On as little as £10 deposit, a building society would advance him the means to buy a tract of suburban land, knock up an estate of tidy terraces, and make a killing. It sounded easy. But even before the bust, Melbourne's suburbs were oversupplied with spec-built cottages and villas. In 1891 almost ten per cent of houses in Brunswick were unoccupied.

Thirty-eight of those empty houses stood on the Thule Estate, the speculative venture of a Scotsman named Alexander Sturrock. A timber merchant with a sawmill in Brunswick Road, he'd bought the land, a mile distant, on the usual 'easy terms'. Sturrock subdivided the '19 Villa Residence Sites' to fit two weatherboard cottages apiece – most of which, however, never found occupants. By 1892, with his stillborn estate beset by vandals and vagrants, Sturrock decided to cut his losses … and the cottages began disappearing.

Sturrock's neighbour in Brunswick Road was – you guessed it – Jim Whelan. The carting business being slack and building scrap in short supply, Jim 'saw any opportunity' and was quick to recognise one in the unloved Thule Estate. Paying Sturrock £10 each for the cottages, he broke them up – it took months; maybe longer – carting all the materials back to his yard to sell. 'And that,' he would say, 'was the beginning.' Whelan was a wrecker.

Not that anybody, even Whelan, gave their trade as 'wrecker' or 'demolisher' in those days. It wasn't considered a trade in its own right, more a sideline. It was a recycling job essentially, salvaging the

Jim Whelan dressed for his wedding, 1897.

used building materials; and that it was called 'removal', not wrecking, implies a degree of care in the process. Jim Whelan's deal with
Sturrock was typical in that the remover paid the building's owner,
not vice versa. Profits lay in the re-sale of materials, and big, bluff Jim

Whelan was a born dealer. Palings, roofing iron, mantelpieces, doors – even during the slump, he shifted the lot. And Sturrock's weren't the only surplus houses he dismantled around Brunswick in the '90s. What had begun as a sideline became his mainstay, built from ruins of the land boom.

But though Whelan made his start as a wrecker in the suburbs, it was in the city that he would make his name.

As variously related in future years, Whelan's first city job was a couple of shops, a tin shed, or stables. Probably there were elements of all three, if you counted outbuildings. The main structure, though, was a long and narrow conjoined pair of two storeys in brick. Built in the 1860s, they'd since been occupied by a leather merchant, the Church of England Mission Rooms, and several incarnations of eating house.

Before that, this spot had lain within the grounds of the Immigration Depôt, where assisted female immigrants were kept and processed upon arriving in Melbourne. From the 1840s until the early '60s, the government shipped in female domestic servants 'of good moral character' in an effort to counter the colony's testosterone imbalance. About 2,500 women were imported each year during the 1850s, every shipment being met at the Immigration Depôt by a mob of would-be employers and wooers.

The whole area now bounded by Spencer, Bourke, King and Collins streets had been commandeered for 'public purposes' back in 1836. Not far from the centre of the compound was built the settlement's first courthouse – earthen-floored and just four metres square, with walls of wattle branches and mud, heaped over with reeds for a roof. Actually, it served as a police office for all but that hour most mornings when Police Magistrate Lonsdale sat at a packing-case bench to hear the previous day's misdemeanours. The police office and court moved to slightly smarter premises in 1838, taking the door with them and leaving the old structure to the weather.

In 1901 the site of these successive obsolescences – 609–611 Little

Whelan's men wreck the burnt-out shell of Watson's Chambers, Flinders Lane, 1911.

Collins Street – provided Jim Whelan with his biggest job yet.

Back when he started in the wrecking game, he'd had just one lad working for him. To tackle his first city job he had a gang of twelve, among them Mick and Mark Quinn, Boomer Woods, Pat Kennedy, Ginger Farmer, and a fellow known as 'The Crow'. By now, Whelan had plenty of experience in breaking up timber cottages. But had he ever knocked down brick walls two storeys high?

Demolition of a city building was – still is – an exercise in containment. On this job, like most, the building was hemmed in: attached to its neighbours on both sides and its front wall breasting the footpath. Jim Whelan, right from the start, practised a distinctive style of inner-city demolition. Where most wreckers knocked a building down one storey at a time, he would take off the roof and gut the interior, leaving the brick shell standing to its full height. Then he'd range his men along the top of the walls and they'd break them down, brick by brick, from under their own feet, knocking the rubble inwards. Their tool was a wrecker's pick: a long, slender adze-head fixed to a handle like an axe's. The curve of its handle meant that the pick pierced the mortar between brick courses with a clean, horizontal strike, whence the wrecker levered upwards, breaking apart the brickwork. Working from above gave him gravity's benefit, the pick falling in a loose arc to meet the wall beneath his feet. But gravity menaced him, too: without a head for heights and nimble footwork he might easily join the tumbling masonry.

Down below waited the rest of the wrecking crew. At a signal, they'd dart out and shovel like crazy to clear away the fallen brickwork before the next cascade shattered it. Remember, Jim Whelan's livelihood depended on the re-sale of materials from the dismembered building. Intact bricks fetched good money; broken ones (brickbats) he could hardly give away. A skilled wrecker knew how to lever out masonry so that it fell just where he wanted it, with a minimum of bounce and damage – to materials or man.

Record-keeping wasn't Jim Whelan's strong suit. The little that's known of his early wrecking career is based on recollections set down at distant dates. That two-storey brick pair in Little Collins Street featured in the Whelan canon only as his first city job, so there's no saying whether it took him a week or a month, or how much he learnt in the process about party-walls and the manners of falling bricks. All that can be said for certain is that it led to bigger things.

BUILDINGS TO BALLAST

There was a neat – or, let's be honest, an untidy – circularity to the demolition business, Whelan the Wrecker's in particular.

At the time Jim Whelan started wrecking, Melbourne was largely confected from local landstuffs – hewn into blocks, cast into bricks, ground into dust. Basalt, or bluestone, from quarries in the (now) Flagstaff and Fitzroy Gardens formed the foundations of many of the town's early buildings. Bluestone in quantity, for the likes of St Francis' Church and bond stores by the Yarra, came from quarries north of the city – as far afield as Kilmore and the Keilor Plains or nearer by at Brunswick. The thunder-grey basalt was abjured as too gloomy and workmanlike a fabric for entire buildings, though, and its use was generally limited to foundations and dressings.

More characteristically Victorian, if less distinctively Melburnian, was the sandstone used for most of the city's landmark nineteenth-century buildings, including Parliament House, the treasury, post office, and customs house. Early Melbourne builders sourced a coarse, iron-tinged sandstone close to the town, on the south side of the Yarra and west of the Saltwater (Maribyrnong) River. Now only the resurrected St James' Old Cathedral survives of the 'ugly brown' sandstone generation. More pleasing to the eye, and a favourite for Victorian facades, was the golden, fine-grained sandstone quarried not far from Stawell.

The sign, 'For Sale – Whelan' tells the story. The source of salvage on this occasion was the rambling Melbourne Benevolent Asylum in North Melbourne, wrecked in 1911.

For a sharper effect, granite from Harcourt, near Bendigo, was the building stone of choice. A glinty, dappled grey, it supplied the classical facades and ornamentation for enumerable city banks and commercial premises. Melbourne stonemasons loved the stuff, lauded it as the best splitting stone in the world. Its only flaw was that, after long exposure to the city air, Harcourt granite acquired a brownish taint. But then, who doesn't?

By Jim Whelan's time, most city buildings had, at best, facades of stone and were otherwise built of brick. In Melbourne's earliest days, bricks were scarce – brought over from Van Diemen's Land – and their use confined to chimney-building. Soon though, brick works were established across the Yarra, proximate to St Kilda Road. Besides supplying Melbourne with sturdy building stuffs, the Brickfields district harboured a good deal of the town's villainy. In 1849, the brickmakers were evicted from Southbank and their operations shifted to the claypits of Brunswick. The building surge sparked by the gold rushes quickened the demand for bricks, but they continued to be made by the old methods – pressed into moulds by hand – until the 1870s when mechanical production took over. Output increased tenfold during Melbourne's boom decade but strained, even so, to meet demand. Bricks were sent to building sites still hot from the kilns, causing disfigurations that no amount of stucco could hide.

As well as solid stone and cooked clay, a wrecker in Edwardian Melbourne would've carted away loads of timber: not just slabs, palings and shingles from knockabout old buildings and outbuildings, but fancy joinery of oak, cedar, jarrah, even Huon pine. There'd have been stacks of roof slates and, with luck, tons of valuable lead pipe and guttering. Besides all that, there was no end of galvanised iron – from the ubiquitous roofs and verandahs, of course, but also from buildings clad entirely in iron. For a time during the 1850s, with building materials in short supply, there'd been a craze for 'portable' iron buildings: shops and houses, imported in parts – the kit-homes of their day. The last of the type in the city, on fashionable Collins Street, was pulled down in 1920.

All this left Jim Whelan with an awful lot of stuff in his yard and on his hands. 'Pulling down is nothing,' he said, 'it's the taking away that wants careful organising.' Some of it he could sell readily enough. Galvanised iron was always in demand for roofing, repairs and chook sheds. Good timber would go for building, the rest as firewood. Machine-made bricks were re-used for foundations, paths and paving, while the old hand-mades were popular with house builders – their porous surface made for a firm hold and fewer cracks in the stucco. Lead was wrecker's manna. It fetched a high price for recasting. As for the stonework, for all its curlicues and fine finish, it was hard to find a home for. Monumental masons would take an amount of granite or marble off the wreckers' hands, to refashion as headstones. Some stone was bought by the Roads Board or local councils, to be crushed for road-making. But much of the unhoused building stone was returned whence it came, to holes in the ground.

If a quarry needed filling in, or a swamp, Whelan's had (some of) the stuff that'd do it. Wreckage from city buildings helped firm up the West

Melbourne swamp and give Coode Island its footing. Out at Brunswick, close by Whelan's yard, were stone quarries and brick pits whose day was done and were howling out to be plugged with superfluous building rubble.

And so, by meandering route, we return to the point: the circularity of the wrecking business. Jim Whelan came from Stawell; so did Melbourne's favourite sandstone. Stawell stone built the city; Whelan's wrecked it. Bluestone and bricks were dug out of Brunswick; Whelan's put them back there.

Brickclay to brickbats, basalt to bluestone, buildings to ballast.

CHAPTER 2

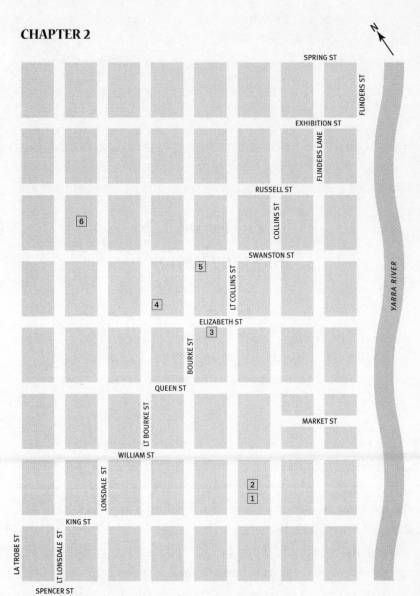

1. McCracken's City Brewery
2. St James' Old Cathedral
3. McLean Bros and Rigg
4. Myer's site
5. Leviathan Store
6. Melbourne Hospital

CHAPTER 2

Bigger Things

McCracken's City Brewery ~ St James' Old Cathedral ~
McLean Bros. and Rigg, making way for Myer's, Leviathan store,
Melbourne Hospital

Exactly a block east of Whelan's first city job stood the massive works of McCracken's City Brewery. Sprawling over four inner-city acres was everything required for brewing ale and stout: stores of malt and hops, tun-room, ice-works, bottling plant, cooperage and stables, all underrun by cellars.

The main brewery building facing Collins Street had three lofty storeys with barley sugar trim, and a flounced, showy rump at its Little Collins Street end. In between, all was business-like and reeky. Smells varying from sharp to sweet to plain beery combined, out of doors, to give the whole neighbourhood a burnt-toast-and-apples tang. A local oddity was the tall brick smokestack which shook whenever a tram approached, westbound, down Collins Street. To the west of the main building and rearwards over Little Collins were the older parts of the works.

Brewing began on the site in 1851 and the gold rushes broke out that same year, causing McCracken's to increase their output many-fold from the initial four barrels a day. By the 1880s, McCracken's was well-fixed as one of the colony's principal brewers, with production and profits – and their west-end city premises – growing year by year. The McCracken heirs sold out at the height of the boom and in 1890 the City Brewery, now a public company, outdid all past successes. Then came the slump. Within four years, demand for McCracken's beverages – Australian bitter ale, pale ale, 'ordinary running ale', and stout – had halved and the company shouldered loss after loss after loss. The brewery was fully refitted in 1900, but its fortunes were never restored. In 1907, Jim Whelan had the job of pulling the place down.

The only recorded account of the demolition runs to a bare fifteen words – 'Another substantial job was that of razing McCracken's Brewery in Collins street, some years ago' – related by Jim to a reporter in 1932. So there's no saying exactly how he went about it. It's safe to suppose, though, that his crew numbered many more than twelve and that, on such a large site, there was less concern about containment during the wrecking process. Away from the street frontages and the worry of passers-by or close neighbours, Whelan's wreckers could afford to whack the masonry harder and drop it faster – their own safety permitting. And drays could be driven onto the site and loaded direct from the wreckage, without the mediation of barrows.

Most of the buildings on the McCracken's brewery site were of brick, fronted and quoined with bluestone. Taking just the Collins Street frontage, there were more than sixty windows, plus fanlights, and ten pairs of substantial doors. There'd have been a couple of acres of roofing iron, besides the slates from the cupola above Little Collins Street. And bricks … beyond reckoning, except by the drayload. There must have been 10,000 or more in the shuddery smokestack alone.

Despite the roominess of the McCracken's site, Whelan's men wouldn't have toppled the big chimney in too dramatic a fashion.

Bombs aweigh! Wrecking a smokestack behind the GPO in 1924, Jacky Thorp drops a hefty coping-stone.

The concussion of a 100-foot chimney hitting the ground would have shattered windows all over the city's mercantile district. Instead, one man with a pick would have started at the top, climbing up either by rungs set inside the chimney or ladders pegged without. As he chipped his way down and the chimney broadened out, he'd have been joined by another wrecker or three. Only after reducing its height by more than half might Jim Whelan have used heavier persuasion to pull or knock over the remaining stump without startling the neighbours too much.

Soon, if not on this job, Whelan would call on Jacky Thorp (a.k.a. 'The Cat') whenever a case of chimney-wrecking was in the offing. A steeplejack, Thorp was renowned as the most surefooted aerialist outside of a circus tent or monkey cage. Crowds would gather to watch him at work and there'd be a 'feeding time at the zoo' atmosphere when Thorp stopped work at midday to hoist up his lunch in a bucket. He caused a panic one lunchtime when – tiring perhaps of the public's gaze – he lay down for a nap on the inner lip of the chimney he was wrecking. Invisible from the street below, he was supposed to have dropped to his death and woke to an uproar.

In pictures of McCracken's City Brewery, smoke from its tall chimney invariably gusted to the east, half-obscuring the tower of St James' Old Cathedral. St James' and McCracken's were neighbours for fifty-six years, and the old cathedral would outlast the brewery by

McCracken's City Brewery, 1883, casting its habitual smokescreen over St James' Cathedral.

another six. Sixty years later still, in the 1970s, Jim Whelan's grandson, Owen, would chance to meet a white-haired woman who'd lived, as a girl, not far from St James'. She recalled how, arriving home from school for the holidays, she'd been shocked to learn that 'her' church was being pulled down. 'I loved that church,' she told Owen, 'and I was so distressed that I ran down Collins Street and there it was, being demolished!' She'd pressed her face against the iron fence railings and wept. 'And a lovely old man, one of the workmen, came over to me and said, "Now what are you crying for?"' On hearing the cause, he'd reassured her that the old church was to be rebuilt near by. 'Come on,' he'd comforted, 'dry your eyes,' and he offered her a peppermint.

'And I reckon,' says Owen Whelan, 'it was probably my grandfather, because that was one of his great passions in life: he *always* had a packet of peppermints.'

The 'old' man with the peppermints was a year shy of fifty when he won the contract to dismantle St James' Old Cathedral in 1913. He still gave his profession as timber merchant, with wrecking merely the means of keeping his yard* well-stocked with secondhand building stuffs. On most demolition jobs he still paid for the right to wreck and remove. But not at St James', where – as he told the weeping girl – he was moving the old cathedral, not removing it. That made it a cash-down job.

It was called the old cathedral because it *was* old, being not much younger than Melbourne itself. But it was old, too, in the sense of 'former'. The city had long-since outgrown its original Anglican cathedral.

Before Melbourne's streets were even drawn on a map, there was a church on the site of St James'. A slab hall with shingle roof and dirt floor, it was built in 1836 on what was then a portion of John Batman's sheep-run. When streets were laid out a year later, the church found itself at the corner (more or less) of Collins and William streets, on part of a reserve set aside for the Church of England. It continued as an ecumenical place of worship until 1838 when the Church of England laid claim to it and drew up plans for its own church on the site.

The original design shows a plain, stone-built rectangle facing William Street, with a spire at its western end. But funds ran short, and when St James' Church opened for worship it was far from complete and crowned by a squat octagonal tower – derided by newspaperman, Edmund Finn, as an 'unsightly deformity' – in place of the spire. The church walls, of iron-stained sandstone ('ugly brown', a guidebook called them), were set on limestone foundations so crumbly that they had to be replaced within ten years.

St James' became Melbourne's first cathedral when the town was made a city in 1848. Height and embellishments were added to the tower three years later, resulting in 'another abortion', wrote Finn, 'not

---

* Whelan's yard was by then at its permanent address: 605 Sydney Road, Brunswick.

quite so bad as the first'. Townfolk christened the landmark 'Palmer's Pepper Pot', in (dis)honour of Dr Palmer, head of the church building committee.

The building's completion coincided with the mad inrush of gold seekers, and St James' congregation outgrew it in no time. The cathedral had been built with a smaller city in mind – the city that Melbourne had been shaping up as before 1851. Now there were far more trouser seats than pew-room in St James' of a Sunday. Soldiers attending services had to be crammed into the organ loft – until, that is, some disgraced their regiments by scratching graffiti on the organ casing.

The Church of England's original Melbourne land grant had been a whopping five acres, running from Collins to Bourke along William Street and thence halfway to King Street. St James' itself, set well back from the Collins Street corner, took up only a small portion of the church reserve. The two acres on the Bourke Street side were occupied by the St James' school and parsonage, as well as, in the early years, the parson's extensive cabbage garden. Shrubs and flowerbeds hedged the cathedral all round, and there were gravelled paths, lawns and spreading trees. A real oasis, it was, at the western end of the city.

The neighbourhood of St James' had been deemed 'decidedly the healthiest' part of the town back in 1840, by a visitor who predicted its future as 'the select spot for fashionable residences and gay promenades'. (That was before McCracken's set up shop next door.) Two years later, at the first meeting of Melbourne's town council, a portion of the St James' reserve, between Bourke and Little Collins, was mooted as the ideal site for a town hall – but the Church declined to part with it.

Under the State Aid Abolition Act of 1872, however, St James' lost most of its gardens and its prominent position when the government reclaimed and sold the valuable land fronting Collins and William streets. Melbourne's Anglican cathedral was reduced to a Little Collins Street address, boxed in by grey commercial premises. It was further overshadowed after the Church leased most of its remaining land on the Bourke Street side, to be built over by the massive St James' Buildings – stores, warehouses and offices, many of them connected with the tea trade. The neighbourhood once destined to be healthful, fashionable and gay was now 'the Mincing-lane of Melbourne'.

The writing was not just on St James' organ now, but on the wall. Before a decade had passed, St Paul's Church, on swampy but open ground at the other end of town, was chosen as the site for a new cathedral, more befitting the city that Melbourne had become. With the opening of St Paul's Cathedral in 1891, St James' was relegated to parish church status and the grudging title of 'old cathedral'.

Along with its land and standing, St James' had lost its congregation. Of a Sunday around the turn of the century, the streets at the western end of the city were practically deserted – the tea merchants' cargo hoists along St James' Street all swinging idle and even McCracken's chimney stoppered. Hardly anyone lived about those parts any more, and what city-dwelling Anglicans there were mostly favoured St Paul's or St Peter's on Eastern Hill over the old brewery-smelling church in the warehouse quarter.

And it leaked – so badly that, on one occasion, the organ pipes filled with water. In May 1913 came the headline in the *Argus*: HISTORIC CHURCH DOOMED. Investigating damp stains on one of the inside walls after heavy rain, a builder had discovered that the arch over the chancel wasn't an arch at all, but a flimsy lath and plaster screen. Supporting the bogus arch (barely) was a rotten oregon girder which rested, in turn, on a layer of crumbling mortar. Judged to be 'in imminent danger of collapse', the building was condemned.

There was an outcry at the prospect of Melbourne's oldest church being demolished. Friends of the old cathedral found it ridiculous that, with rent from the St James' Buildings amounting to £7,000 a year, the Church couldn't afford the cost of repairs. But it was hard to ignore the fact that here was a church with almost no parishioners, occupying more than an acre of valuable city land. As a compromise,

The bells from St James' tower, unbelfried and awaiting removal.

it was agreed that the old cathedral would be removed to a site on the edge of the city, in King Street, West Melbourne. The cost of relocation was on a par with the likely repair bill, and money from the sale of the old St James' site would be used to establish a new city mission – so that, in a way, the old cathedral would go on serving an inner-city congregation.

It was Jim Whelan's task to dismantle the church and cart it in pieces to the new site, less than a mile away. The solid stones of the outer walls were kept – each one carefully numbered for re-erection – but the inner walls, of compacted shells and rubble, were replaced on the new site with reinforced concrete. Changes were made, too, in the old cathedral's design. The ceiling was lowered, supporting columns omitted, and the tower altered once more, this time to improve the peal of the bells – it was a long time since it had been safe to ring them.

One stone that didn't make it to the new site was the foundation stone of the old St James'. Charles La Trobe, newly landed Superintendent of the Port Phillip District, had laid the stone in 1839. There being no monumental mason in the town at that time, the foundation stone had gone unmarked. The words that ought to have been inscribed thereon were read aloud by La Trobe from a parchment which, along with a few coins, was poked in a bottle and thence into a niche in the foundation stone. Seventy-five years later, neither bottle nor foundation stone came to light. It was supposed that, being unmarked, the stone had simply escaped notice in the course of relocation and its contents been lost – or else, that both had been missing since 1850 when the original foundations were replaced. In 1929, however, the then-minister of St James' claimed to have discovered the truth of the matter.

> *I found that the carter who transferred the material to the new site was responsible for destroying the foundation stone. He accidentally broke it and then threw the parts on the rubbish heap and gave the contents to his friends, keeping the most valuable himself.*

Had the carter unburdened himself, I wonder, or been unburdened on?

Aside from his fee, Jim Whelan didn't carry much away from the St James' job. The only lasting trace would be an in-house joke, that ran like this – One of Whelan's men wrote to his folks in Ireland: 'Australia's a great country. Back home we wreck Protestant churches for nothing; here, they *pay* you to do it.' Years later, an alleged relic would occupy pride of place at Whelan the Wrecker headquarters. It was a wrecker's bar with the inscription: 'Used for wrecking Protestant churches.'

Contemporary wrecks

McLean Bros. and Rigg, ironmongers (139–149 Elizabeth Street), 1911

Demolition ended with a midnight session, complete with festive crowd. The head office of the State Savings Bank replaced it.

Even after midnight, Whelan's drew a crowd. Demolishing McLean Bros. and Rigg by spotlight.

Three shops (314–320 Bourke Street), 1911

Drapery and shoes had been the staple wares of this neighbourhood since the 1850s. Before that, this was the site of a slaughteryard. Jim Whelan uncovered no end of sheep and cattle bones when he cleared the ground for Myer's first Melbourne store.

Leviathan store (south-west corner Bourke and Swanston), 1912

Lewis Sanders, senior partner of the Leviathan Clothing Company, on the eve of the store's demolition, said:

> The Leviathan was considered a good building – that is, for
> those days [mid-1850s]. The contractor afterwards boasted that
> he had brought 20 barrels of lime with him, and that he had
> carried 20 barrels of lime away when it was erected.

It was replaced, in 1913, by the new Leviathan Building, still standing at the corner of the mall.

Melbourne Hospital (Lonsdale Street, between Swanston and Russell), 1909–12

The original portion of the hospital, dating back to 1846, was by now lost in a mass of extensions. Over several years, Whelan's wrecked the rambling assortment of old hospital buildings, to make way for uniform red-brick structures.

CHAPTER 3

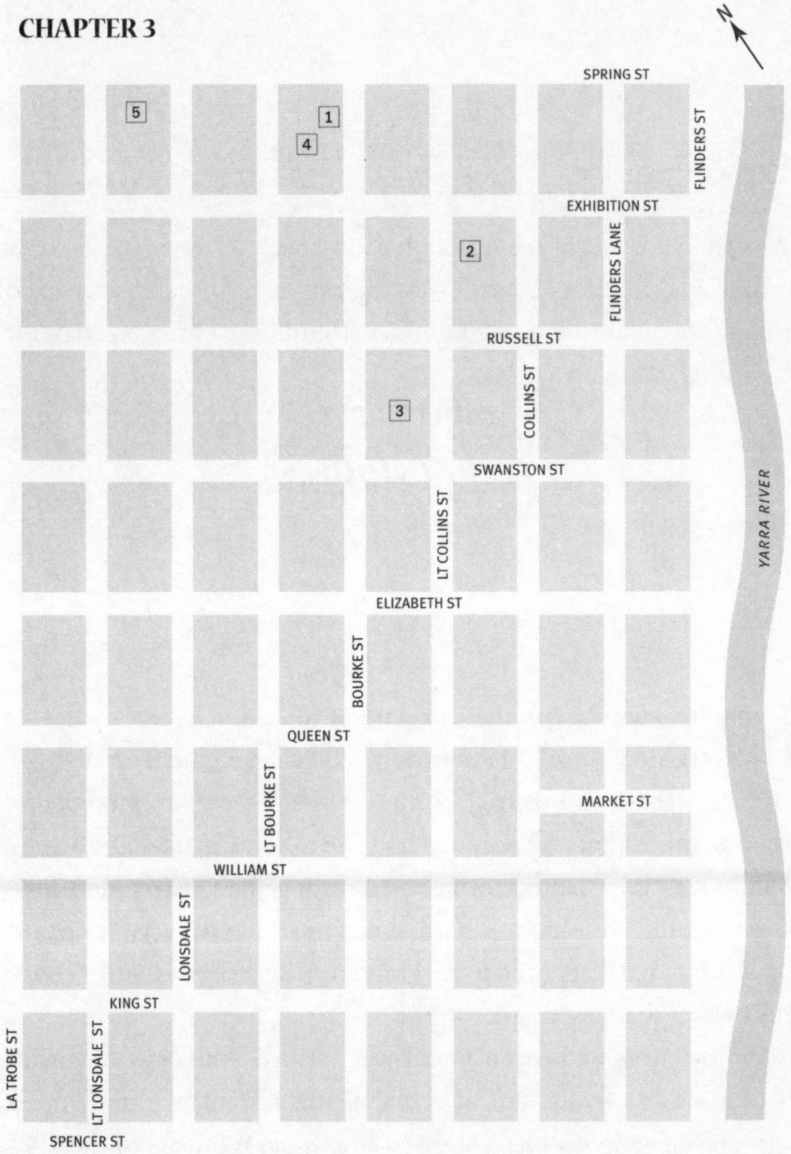

N

SPRING ST

FLINDERS ST

5

1

4

EXHIBITION ST

2

FLINDERS LANE

RUSSELL ST

COLLINS ST

3

SWANSTON ST

LT COLLINS ST

YARRA RIVER

ELIZABETH ST

BOURKE ST

QUEEN ST

LT BOURKE ST

MARKET ST

WILLIAM ST

LONSDALE ST

KING ST

LA TROBE ST

LT LONSDALE ST

SPENCER ST

1. *Hotel Douglas*
2. *Paddington Hotel*
3. *Palace Hotel*

4. *Bilking Square*
5. *Little Lon*

CHAPTER 3

Out of Hiding

Hotel Douglas ~ Palace Hotel ~ Bilking Square ~ Little Lon

Time-travellers expecting to find a pub on every corner in nineteenth-century Melbourne would scarcely be disappointed. In the mid-1870s, no district of Victoria had less than one hotel to every 150 inhabitants (children included); in some parts of the colony, the ratio was 1:30. Hotels proliferated during the toast-happy 1880s and, even after a decade of hard times, just about every tuppenny grog-shanty that had ever been granted a licence was still serving drinks when the new century broke.

The Licences Reduction Board was formed under the Licensing Act of 1906, with the aim of reducing the extent of drunkenness and social calamity in Victoria by cutting hotel numbers to the 1885 level. By 1922, there were roughly 500 fewer hotels in metropolitan Melbourne, and the total number of Victorian hotels had been nearly halved, to just over 2000.

The majority of hotels to lose their licences were unadorned pot-houses, offering no accommodation, no parlour or dining room, no niceties whatsoever. Some licences were withheld over shortcomings

Hotel reduction, Whelan-style – the Duke of Rothsay, 24–26 Elizabeth Street, 1914.

or infringements, others were relinquished voluntarily – gratefully, even – in return for the cash compensation. Whether the hotel closures reduced alcohol consumption is debatable. Drinkers who lost their old 'local' seldom had to stagger far to a new one.

Jim Whelan didn't mind a drink, but he gained more than he lost by the dealings of the Licences Reduction Board. In fact, the Board and Jim Whelan were by way of being in the same line of business. *They* removed the licence, *he* removed the rest – not in every case, of course, but often enough for his grandson Myles to reckon, ninety years later, that Whelan's must have pulled down 400 Melbourne hotels, at least.

Among the city pubs given a shove was the Hotel Douglas at the top end of Bourke Street, wrecked by Jim Whelan in its 62nd year on tap. It was 1914 and Whelan's eldest son, another Jim, had just joined the family firm. That was the year, too, in which Whelan senior's ubiquity first won him the attention of the Melbourne press and the tag 'Whelan the Wrecker'.

The Hotel Douglas sat on the front part of a long, broad block that stretched back to the Princess Theatre's scenery store. It was a typical city hotel of the middle size: three storeys in brick, with fourteen bedrooms upstairs facing Bourke Street or the yard, food and drink departments at street level, billiards room at rear, and cellar beneath.

The name Hotel Douglas was a new one, or newish. For forty-odd years until 1901, it had been the Excelsior. During the '80s it belonged to William Stutt, a Canadian – one-time bullock driver, twice member of parliament – who cast his vim and personality over a succession of city hotels. At the Excelsior, hard by Parliament House (where Stutt no longer had a seat, but presumably still had friends), he made food the ostensible drawcard, devoting almost half the ground floor to a restaurant. Years earlier, in the pick-swinging '50s, the hotel's cellar had been rented out as a 'night restaurant' under the classy appellation, the Chop Cellar.

Back then, the hotel itself still went by the name it was born with: the National. It must have been built toward the end of 1852, when Melbourne hardly knew itself, so strange and sudden had been the changes sprung by the gold frenzy. The National Hotel got its licence in the new year, and Frank Harris commenced to solicit for patronage of his 'Commodious Hotel, Which will be found unsurpassed for comfort and moderate charges by any house in Melbourne'. Advertisements stressed the 'very superior' nature of the sleeping accommodation, 'every *gentleman* being provided with a Separate Bedroom' – presumably the rabble had to be content with the usual two-to-a-bed-and-five-on-the-floor style of Melbourne hospitality. The hotel's position on the Eastern Hill commanded twenty-mile vistas, from 'the Romantic Yarra' out over the Bay, and away to Richmond or Williamstown and beyond. What the adverts didn't mention was the immediate view – and ruckus – of the Salle de Valentino next door, a vast canvas dancehall with resident polka band.

By the end of 1854, the National Hotel was under the management of Tom Mooney, proudly Irish and of nationalist persuasion. Legend tells that Mooney harboured the injured rebel leader, Peter Lalor, in an attic room at the National 'for months' after the clash at Eureka stockade in December 1854. A more plausible account of Lalor's months as a fugitive puts him at Geelong, shacked up with his fiancée. After all, what full-grown man – even one with a reward on his head and an arm shot off – could endure a Melbourne summer stuffed inside a roof-cavity? For, as Jim Whelan found when he prepared to take the roof off the Hotel Douglas in 1914, the attics under the shallow

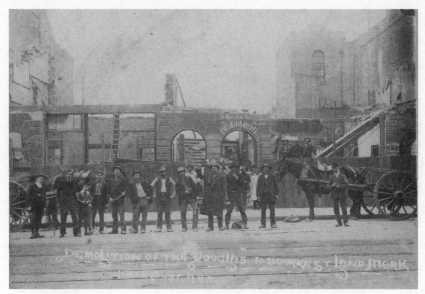

'The Happy Gang' (as Whelan's crew was known) on the Hotel Douglas site.

mansard slope were just four feet high. A person, particularly one of Whelan's six-foot-plus stature, had to bend nearly double to fit inside. He'd not heard the story about Peter Lalor; what shocked him was that the rooms had lately been occupied as servants' quarters.

The Hotel Douglas site was built over by the National Theatre, renamed the Palace in 1919 and modified for moving pictures. Nowadays the same building, much altered, is a nightclub.

When Whelan's wrecked the delicensed Paddington Hotel in 1912, to make way for one of the city's first motor garages, the man who knocked out the ceilings had been amazed to find a dozen silk belltopper hats inside the roof-space. 'There was great joy among my men for a while,' Jim Whelan recalled. 'Each one wore a belltopper while he worked.' When that novelty wore off, they kicked the tall hats up and down Little Collins Street, eventually reducing them to ruins.

How twelve belltoppers had got inside the roof was anybody's guess. The Paddington had never been a fancy hotel, situated as it was at the rear of the seedy Eastern Market. Nor had its position given it

Jim Whelan (in bowler hat) and men amid the ruins of somebody's parlour.

the ghoulish cachet it might have acquired had it survived until 1921 and the Gun Alley murder.*

It must've been about that time that the mystery of the Paddington belltoppers was finally solved. The story of their discovery having done repeated rounds of Melbourne's pubs, it was bound eventually to meet the ears of one who could supply the missing facts. It did, and they were these: the hats had belonged to a touring English cricket team back in the 1870s. Whether the players had lodged at the Paddington or merely gone there carousing wasn't clear. But somebody (a spin-bowling prankster? a disgruntled waiter?) had spirited their hats away, stowed them in the attic ceiling – and then, apparently, forgotten all about them.

Since gold-rush times, it had been practically mandatory in Victoria to ridicule any man who wore a tall hat in the bush or sporting circles. A belltopper, in those settings, was the sure mark of a new

---

* The body of 12-year-old Alma Tirtschke was found in Gun Alley, just a hat's toss from the Paddington Hotel.

chum needing his edges roughened. Look at any photograph of visiting English cricketers after the 1870s and you'll notice that, whether in their cricketing kit or out of it, they're wearing boaters or bowlers – never belltoppers. Fashion? Perhaps. Either that or the legacy of the Paddington hatnapping.

One-and-a-half blocks west, fronting Bourke Street, the Palace Hotel was deprived of its licence, most unwillingly, at the end of 1914. The Palace was on a far grander scale than either the Paddington or the Douglas. It had seven storeys served by elevators and three hundred bedrooms piped with hot and cold water, plus several bars. The hotel occupied the first to sixth floors, above the Gaiety Theatre and an arcade of shops at street level.

As a police prosecutor told the Metropolitan Licensing Court in 1913, the drinking portion of the Palace Hotel was 'a pretty hot place'. He was opposing the transfer of the hotel licence, just as he would argue for its cancellation the following year. The Licensing Court heard of the conduct of 'certain barmaids' in the American Bar at the Palace – 'lying on lounges in front of the bar, whistling after men, and fondling them, and taking familiarities that no respectable house would tolerate'. Three of them had been fined in 1910 for using indecent language in the bar, the magistrate singling out the oaths of May Davidson as the most reprehensible: 'Even in the lowest quarters in the city worse language could not be indulged in.' Reminded of that occasion three years later in the Licensing Court, one of the Palace's proprietors rejoined, 'Yes, but she was a perfect lady otherwise.' The police prosecutor's questioning continued –

– *Were barmaids frequently drunk?*
– *They were not drunk and incapable.*
– *Oh, they were drunk and capable?* (Laughter)

The Licensing Court also heard of robberies and hooliganism in the arcade beneath the Palace. In the decade before the First World War,

Bourke Street East teemed with roisterers and street gangs. The street came alive by night, strung both sides with the dazzle-and-shade of music halls, theatres, late-night bars and all-night 'supper rooms', along with the Eastern Market and its sleazy satellites. One gang made the street its own: the Bourke Street Rats. Their repertoire ranged from larrikinism – bad language, rough-housing, kicking in windows – to shop-breaking, robbery (both of the sly sort and with violence), race-fixing, and extortion. The craftiest member of the gang, the flashest Rat, was Leslie Taylor, twenty years old and better known as Squizzy. And their headquarters? You guessed it: the Palace Hotel.

The long-time owner of the Palace, John Wilson, had a reputation not just for tolerating bad behaviour, but for making his premises a haven for hoodlums. According to the police prosecutor in 1913, under Wilson's stewardship the hotel's character had been 'exceptionally bad; there was nothing like it in Melbourne'. Repeatedly he had promised, and failed, to reform. The deprivation sitting of the Licences Reduction Board in 1914 was the end of the line.

Though the Palace lost its liquor licence, several witnesses had assured the Board that the hotel was 'a satisfactory and comfortable place to stop'. It continued to accommodate guests for fifteen years, then was locked up and idle for another five. By the time Whelan's got to it in 1934, memories of the Palace Hotel had so dimmed that the press had to remind readers of the 'reasons for its decline'.

Memories of the bad old days were further revived when the wreckers discovered a secret room – palatial compared to Peter Lalor's reputed bolt-hole – in the hotel basement. Squizzy Taylor by that time was a Melbourne legend: racketeer, alleged murderer and outlaw, and dead in a gun battle seven years since. The hide-out in the Palace basement, it was claimed, had been his, for those times when 'he wasn't inclined to leave the city'.

Squizzy's supposed benefactor, John Wilson, had owned the hotel since 1882. He bought adjoining land and enlarged the hotel outwards and upwards, renaming it the Palace in 1889. Before that, it was the Academy of Music Hotel and Café, built in 1876 as an adjunct to the Academy itself.* How different its character and reputation from that which the Palace would acquire; and how indifferent its success. Emphasising fine food and good breeding – in keeping with the Academy of Music's own exalted aspirations – the hotel offered separate dining rooms for ladies and gentlemen. But after six years, both hotel and Academy had failed to flourish and were sold to Wilson, who took a less rarefied, more animalistic view of what the public wanted.

If the wreckers found animal bones under the floor of Squizzy's basement retreat, well, so what? They'd have supposed that there'd once been a butchery next door (there had), or that inhabitants of the Palace Hotel's predecessors had buried, or simply tossed, their chop bones under the floor (as nineteenth-century people certainly did). But had they looked closely at the bones turning up in the topsoil, Whelan's men might have noticed a preponderance of horse, scored with toothmarks such as no person, or their dog, ever made.

Before the Academy of Music, from 1861, the City Buffet Hotel stood on the site, kept by the same William Stutt who later ran the Excelsior. In the yard behind the City Buffet was a tea garden, and in the tea garden was a cage, and in the cage were two lions. Wallace was the lion's name – 'the finest and largest caged lion in the world at present', or so his owner claimed. Besides Wallace and his mate ('a truly fitting companion for this noble monarch'), Stutt's Bourke Street menagerie included an Indian bear, a cheetah, some monkeys, and an aviary of songbirds, 'unsurpassed in their several kinds'. That tea garden must have been both noisome and noisy, not at all the spot for a restful shandy. Perhaps apprehending as much, Stutt in 1867 sold his 'specimens of animated nature' to the Acclimatisation Society, to form the basis of 'the menagerie in the park' – that is, the Melbourne Zoo.

---

*   For more on the Academy of Music, see the Bijou Theatre (also wrecked by Whelan's in 1934), Chapter 5.

In Little Bourke Street, not far from the Hotel Douglas, the Berlin Hotel had its licence renewal knocked back in 1871 on the grounds that it was frequented by thieves and 'women of ill-fame'. That wasn't to be surprised at, since the hotel stood at the corner of Juliet Terrace, which, with its neighbour, Romeo Lane, formed a sink of harlotry and lowlife. Off Juliet Terrace, a crooked footway led to the *ne plus ultra*, the dunghill in the mire – Bilking Square.

Romeo Lane and Juliet Terrace were rechristened Crossley and Liverpool streets during the 1880s, in an effort to put their infamy behind them. Bilking Square ... well, on the evidence of street maps and city directories, Bilking Square never existed. Yet everybody knew it: police, magistrates, clergymen, the newspaper-reading public. For all that it appeared on no map, Bilking Square served as a handy purgatory with which to admonish wayward Melbourne girls.

Too late, however, for Annie Banneith, 'a respectable looking young girl' who was enticed into a Bilking Square brothel in the winter of 1872. A policeman finding her there 'spoke to her kindly, and cautioned her against the life which she seemed to have entered upon', to which she retorted that she would do as she liked. A fortnight later, she faced court for 'the most indecent conduct in the public streets', a police witness observing that Banneith had become 'almost incorrigible in a very short time'.

'Bilking' was the ruse of getting a man trouserless, then running off with his wallet. An 1878 Select Committee on the prevention of contagious diseases ought to have been pleased with the evidence of a Bilking Square witness who stated with pride that 'she did not give way to men now as she once did', but made a living instead by 'taking money from men and running away'. The beauty of it was that most bilkees were disinclined to summon the police.

No policeman, anyway, would enter Bilking Square alone. Not that temptation was their only cause for caution. Besides the saucy likes of Annie Banneith, all manner of crookdom felt at home in the Square: pickpockets, pimps, thieves, magsmen – murderers, even. There was one among the shambling wooden cottages in which murder was said to have been done and £700 in ill-gotten cash concealed.

Sometime around the First World War, the wreckers were called in to Bilking Square. Its heyday – if you could call it that – was long past; in fact, even the name was on its way to being forgotten. But Whelan's men found themselves attended by a keener bunch of onlookers than would normally have been drawn to such a prosaic pulling-down. No cash was found, nor human bones. 'There was an eerie atmosphere about the place,' Jim Whelan conceded, 'but we didn't dig up one ghost.' What they did turn up was a cache of 'brummy' (counterfeit) jewellery – enough to fill a cart, or so the story goes. Can't you picture a dray rattling up Sydney Road piled high with tin-and-paste brooches and bugle beads, bound for … where? A brick pit needing fill? Or Whelan's yard, where they just might catch the eye of some amateur-theatricalising tradesman?

Sister locale to Bilking Square was Little Lon, a disreputable tangle of laneways off Little Lonsdale Street's upper end. Whelan the Wrecker took several swipes at Little Lon over the years. On his first outing there, not long after Bilking Square, Jim Whelan kept as souvenirs four sets of knuckle-dusters he found under the floor in one of a row of disreputable cottages. Two generations later, in 1958, Whelan's wiped out a whole slab of Little Lon, clearing the way for Commonwealth government offices.* In the process, they struck a bonanza of old coins – sovereigns, half crowns, even a silver dollar. They were inside the walls, under floors; some had got there by accident, some apparently by design. According to Trevor Turner, one of Whelan's men, the ground itself was 'lousy with coins'. The crew put in many extra hours on that job, painstakingly sifting debris and topsoil through a wire mattress so as not to miss a single coin.

---

* Best, if not fondly, known as the Green Latrine, now itself demolished.

MELBOURNE'S 'AGE OF STEEL'

Melbourne is being rebuilt. Until a year or two ago the city had
undergone very little change ... since the feverish days of the
land boom. Then gradually it began to wear a new expression.
Its buildings began to take a different shape; its street frontages
assumed a brighter appearance. This was the commencement
of the era of rebuilding which is likely to last for a long time.
Melbourne, from the point of view of its buildings – their
structure, their appearance, their utility, and their comfort – is
being modernised.

~ *Argus*, 1912

*It was about 1910 when Melbourne began to show signs of emerging
from its post-boom torpor. Just a few years earlier, a British traveller had
likened the city to an age-worn beauty: gone was 'the sparkle, the anima-
tion of other days. Yet, whatever it has lost, it has retained its conscious-
ness of former prosperity.'*

*Towards the end of that decade, Melbourne felt the first stirrings of
the town planning movement, the 'City Beautiful' campaign in the USA
broadcasting notions of civic design and whole-city planning. Melbourne's
leading architects went abroad to study the latest in office and department*

store design, and a succession of visiting experts followed them home. In the light of advances in building materials and design, Melbourne City Council began the long process of reviewing its antiquated building by-laws.

The hottest new trend in building was the steel frame. Actually, it wasn't so very new. Melbourne had got its first steel-framed building in 1889. But with the withering of the local building scene soon after, the potential of the steel frame went largely unexplored in Melbourne until the city's fortunes began to rally in the years following Federation.

Steel's main attraction was that it provided strength without bulk. Without steel framing – and its partner in progress, steel-reinforced concrete – a multi-storey city building required supporting walls to as much as two metres thick. A steel-framed structure might rely on supporting pillars less than half that thickness, with hardly any wall between them. The result was more floorspace and higher returns for the landlord. State and Federal land taxes, brought in with the new century, had property-owners seeking, more than ever, to maximise the value of their city land-holdings. Steel construction was the key to tall, spacious buildings and – most importantly – more square-footage to let.

Without the need for bulky supporting walls, steel and concrete buildings were light and airy compared to their predecessors – 'no longer utterly dependent on artificial light in the middle of the day'. Moreover, many new buildings were faced with pale ceramic tiles as an antidote to Melbourne's habitual 'grey and sombre' palette. Allan's music-sellers published drawings of their proposed new premises in Little Collins Street, a pale, svelte structure of the latest sort. The site had hitherto been occupied by 'a very substantial five storey bluestone structure, strong enough to stand for centuries, but modern conditions warranted it being swept aside for the concrete pile shown here'.

'Fire-proof', 'earthquake-proof', and, as nearly as may be, 'time proof'. These are the conditions asked for today in our new buildings. And so it will come about that the Melbourne of

tomorrow will be a marked advance upon Melbourne of to-day
and yesterday.

*The year was 1914 and the outlook steely bright. But then came the
Great War and shortages of manpower and materials – steel most of all
– brought city progress to a halt. The airy and economical ten-storey
towers had to wait a while longer. The war lasted four years, but by 1925
the clatter of the pneumatic riveter almost drowned out the noise of trams
in Collins Street. Melbourne's 'Age of Steel' had arrived.*

CHAPTER 4

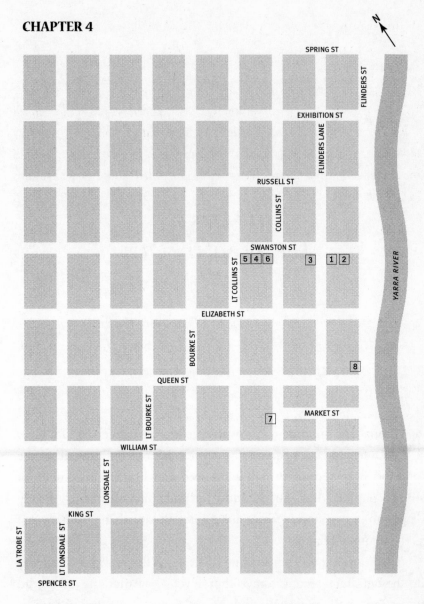

1. Monahan's Building
2. Alexander's
3. Champion's Hotel
4. Capitol Theatre site
5. Royal Oak Hotel
6. Stewart Dawson's
7. Temple Court
8. Peterson's Building

CHAPTER 4

The Face of the City

*Monahan's Building ~ Alexander's ~ Champion's Hotel ~ Capitol
Theatre site ~ Royal Oak Hotel ~ Stewart Dawson's corner ~
Temple Court, Peterson's Building, Yarra Bend asylum*

Monahan's Building had a Swanston Street frontage and a Flinders
Lane address. A square, five-storey slab of a building, it set the
tone for Swanston Street: big-windowed and brash. This stretch of
street – populated by grocers and wine and spirit merchants, mostly
– had run to two storeys, three at best, before Monahan's went up just
as the boom fell flat.

The year after its completion, 1893, 'Four floors vacant' summed
up the building's tenants above shop-level. Over time the offices did
fill, mainly with importers and agents tied up with the rag trade.
Entrance to the upper floors was off Flinders Lane, where the long
slit of a lightwell – the ghost of a laneway, Hotham Place – divided
the building into two wings. There was a café called Dolores in the
basement.

Now it was 1925. The remaking of the city, interrupted by the war,

40

'Humorously referred to by their employer as "Whelan's Birds",' said the Argus, 'the men who are engaged in demolishing Monahan's Buildings ... fearlessly pick the bricks from under their feet, four storeys above the pavement.' (Parapet circled above.)

was underway again, with gusto. While the *Age* wondered deafly, 'Is there a Boom?', the *Herald* not only heard the noise but identified it as 'the thunder of the building wrecker'.

... old landmarks fall in nearly every block ..., and the face of the city is changing so rapidly that the time is not far distant when a search for a building 50 years old will be in vain.

The pulling down of Monahan's Building, nowhere near fifty years old, caused some of the mightiest rumbles. Substantially built of brick, the structure also contained a good deal of concrete and served as Whelan's introduction to that stubborn material. The basement walls had been made six feet thick to support the weight of the upper storeys.* Walls on the ground floor were hardly less staunch and, though they slenderised floor by floor, the Monahan Building's dense walls made it less spacious and airy than it seemed from outside. Jim Whelan called its demolition his biggest feat yet.

It wasn't the bulwarky walls that posed a problem – at least, not much of one. In all probability, those hefty basement walls were given a nocturnal 'shake-up' by Frank Bock, a powder monkey mate of Whelan's whose day job was blowing up stumps out in the bush east of Melbourne. In fact, much of the heavy wrecking on the Monahan's job had to wait till after dark, for the building stood less than a block from Flinders Street railway station. Every weekday the Swanston Street footpath coursed with commuters in their hundreds of thousands. And Whelan's 'birds' were wrecking overhead.

Then there was the practically adhesive presence of the Alexander Building, next door in Swanston Street. A five-storey contemporary of Monahan's, it was an elegant sliver by comparison, and looked as if it wouldn't stand too much of Frank Bock's shaking-up. Alexander's had been named for its first owner, a tobacconist, and kept his name though it passed through several hands, including those of a Reverend Ah Cheong and John Wren, the racketeer. It was built on the site of an 1850s hotel, called the Beehive and later Bell's, which all its life had played poor relation to the Princes Bridge Hotel (Young and Jackson's), a few doors down the street.

The massive south-facing wall of Alexander's, looming over its two-storey neighbours, was the original billboard at the city's gateway. Travellers approaching by Princes Bridge were welcomed, for years,

---

* The 10-storey, steel- and reinforced concrete-framed building replacing Monahan's would be supported by base columns just 2½ feet thick.

by a painted fob-watch advertising James Henry & Co., watchmakers. Alexander's north wall had been a billboard too – the enormous letters SAPOLIO (a brand of soap) visible all the way from Carlton – for the year or two before Monahan's Building obliterated it. In 1925, with Monahan's gone, the dusty SAPOLIO again saw the light of day. But not for long. Built in Monahan's place was the ten-storey Nicholas Building: solid, stately, and named for its owner, the Aspro millionaire.

But still it was the south wall of Alexander's – five storeys shorter but decked out now with illuminated beer signs – that dominated the Swanston Street vista. Was it to shift attention to his namesake that G.R. Nicholas would, in 1937, buy Alexander's Building and have Whelan's demolish it? More likely it was hard to find tenants for the dingy rooms of Alexander's. With its vast side walls all brick (except for an odd sash window apparently knocked through by tenants desperate for air), how sunless and stuffy must it have been for the needle-pullers of Bowley & Son, tailors, on the dim third floor? A two-storey Coles store would replace Alexander's, and it's the flashing south wall of the Nicholas Building that has grabbed the gaze ever since.

Monahan Place appears to run off the wrong side – the north side – of Flinders Lane; Monahan's Building was on the south. But Thomas Monahan once owned property on both sides of the Lane. The building that bore his name was never actually his; it was built by the trustees of his estate after he died a millionaire in 1889.

The property on the north side of Flinders Lane was Monahan's original holding, and Whelan's would wreck there twice, sixty-six years apart. In 1906 the Monahan Estate redeveloped the property, tearing down Champion's Queen's Arms Hotel at the corner and a straggling rank of two-storey shops along Swanston Street. In their place arose the new Champion's Hotel – a majestic six storeys, plus turret – with Champion House alongside. The red-brick pair had pressed-metal ceilings and 'continental' touches like oriel windows and balconettes.

If the property belonged to the Monahan Estate, who then was

Champion? Elizabeth Champion was licensee of the Queen's Arms Hotel. With her late husband, Ben, she'd been there since the 1850s, and Champion's (as it was known) was one of only two hotels in Victoria in 1906 to have been kept by the same family for fifty years or more. Before the Champions, it was licensed to Elizabeth's uncle, a Mr Hawkins. And before that – in the first place – the Queen's Arms had been run by Thomas Monahan himself.

Monahan built the hotel at the Swanston Street–Flinders Lane corner in 1845, but there'd already been a building on the site when he bought it. The previous owner, John Peers, had built it in 1839 as a makeshift chapel for Melbourne's Wesleyan Methodists, of whom he was one. Made of bricks from the Southbank kiln of Horatio Cooper, the poky shed served the Wesleyans for just a couple of years before they outgrew it. But Monahan, when he took possession, thought it too good to pull down. Instead, he incorporated the chapel into his hotel. Backing onto the right-of-way at the rear of the block (now Monahan Place), it became the kitchen of the Queen's Arms and, though the hotel changed and grew around it, Melbourne's cradle of Methodism would continue in such 'ignoble' use until 1906, when the wreckers came.

After presiding for a decade over the palatial new hotel, Elizabeth Champion passed the licence to her son. Just seven years later, Champion's Hotel closed when Thomas Monahan's old properties were sold at last. The State Savings Bank converted the hotel to banking chambers, and in 1972 paid third-generation Whelans to knock the whole lot

Champion's Hotel kitchen, originally a Methodist chapel, shortly before demolition.

A postcard view of Swanston Street, c.1905, is framed by the twin towers of
Alexander's Building (left) and the Talma (distant centre).

down. In place of the quondam hotel and Champion House they put
up a thirteen storey ice-tray, outstripping – yet not outfacing – the
Nicholas Building, across the Lane.

Postcard views pre-dating the copper-roofed turret of Champion's Hotel
show the Swanston Street skyline neatly bookended by Alexander's
Building and its near-twin, the Talma, opposite the town hall. Just like
Alexander's, the Talma Building was a skinny five storeys with a roof
like a rosebud, crowned by a cast iron coronet. But unlike Alexander's,
the Talma was spared by Whelan's – just.*

At the first sale of Melbourne land, in 1837, Captain Henry Howey
had paid £120 for all four allotments – two acres – at the Swanston
Street end of the city block hemmed by Collins and Little Collins
streets. Though practically on the town's outskirts at that time, by
the 1880s Howey's land was at the epicentre of Melbourne's marvel-
losity. But the captain didn't live to see that transformation. He was

---

* Spared, but not untouched. The Talma's interior was completely remodelled in
1922 – and guess who did the wrecking?

lost at sea with his family in 1841 – not merely sunk but really lost, somewhere off the coast between Sydney and Melbourne. It was years before Howey's death was declared a certainty and the estate settled on his brother, who subsequently entailed the Melbourne property on the males of the Howey line. In that way the original landholding remained intact until 1914 when, with the city building scene gathering steam, portions of the Howey estate changed hands for the first time. Over the next twenty-five years, every building on the captain's two acres – all but the Talma – was laid low by Whelan the Wrecker.

A Colonel Wilson '(formerly of South Africa and England)' bought from the Howey heirs in 1914 a suite of three-storey buildings in Swanston Street, on the Talma's south side. Announcing plans to put up a ten-storey building at 109–117 Swanston Street, the new owner told the *Argus* –

> *I was struck on arrival here with the waste of building space in the heart of so important a city. Many of the buildings in Collins and Swanston streets have only two storeys. This state of affairs would not be permitted to continue in America.*

But then came the war, and it was 1921 before Jim Whelan got his teeth into Colonel Wilson's waste of space.

The Colonel's Swanston Street properties were occupied by a café flanked by a couple of shoe shops and Reg Williams's boot-shine parlour, with assorted offices and studios (music, dance and photographic) on the upper floors. This part of Swanston Street – like the Collins Street 'Block', close by – had long been favoured by artists and jewellers seeking the patronage of Melbourne's moneyed elite. The Talma Building was originally Buxton's Art Gallery, and now was named for its principal tenant, Talma & Co., 'vice-regal photographers', whose studios took three whole storeys.

In keeping with the neighbourhood's social standing was Lucas's Town Hall Café, dead-centre on the block. Antony Lucas had come to Melbourne from the island of Ithaca in 1886 and, like many Greek immigrants of the period, set up first as a fruit-seller. He branched from there into cafés and, by the turn of the century, was proprietor of two of the city's grandest. A café then was not a café as we know it now: it was a dining establishment on a sumptuous scale. Lucas's Town Hall Café filled all three floors of its double frontage and, with rooms for dining, luncheon, tea, supper, and smoking, could accommodate 650 patrons at a sitting. Window displays of fresh fruit and confectionery tempted the take-away traffic and, by the outbreak of the first war, Lucas's incorporated a Milk Palace – a kind of milk bar, to the power of ten.

Whelan's took a big bite out of Swanston Street in 1921, clearing the way for a picture theatre surmounted by Colonel Wilson's long-planned ten storeys. The theatre, variously called the Central or Town Hall during its construction, opened in 1924 as the Capitol, boasting a spectacular Burley Griffin design and a seating capacity more than three times that of the erstwhile Lucas's café.

One of the upstairs tenants at 117 Swanston Street had been Miss M. Franck, photographic artist, and it was in the ruins of her old darkroom in 1921 that Whelan the Wrecker's famous sign was born. During his sojourn there with a pick, one of Whelan's crew chiselled into the remaining wall the words WHELAN THE WRECKER IS HERE. The plaster-white words hovered, practically luminous, against the black-painted background. A day or two later they were gone – wall and all – but the slogan lived on as Whelan's calling card.

Within just a few years, WHELAN THE WRECKER IS HERE (and its triumphal variant, WHELAN THE WRECKER WAS HERE) was acknowledged to be 'the best-known advertising slogan in the city'. Ad men in the side-burned '60s cited Whelan's as virtually the perfect slogan. It was short, sharp and catchy; once seen or heard, never forgotten – the effect being, as Owen Whelan put it, that 'When you think of wrecking, you think of Whelan.' Moreover, Whelan's slogan entered the vernacular even among Melburnians who never had cause to hire a demolisher.

Any scene of disorder – a colleague's desk, a teenager's bedroom, the aftermath of a fondue party – might elicit an exclamation of 'Whelan the Wrecker was here!' And anyone or anything of an accident-prone or destructive bent – a puppy, a toddler, or a dance partner with two left feet – qualified for the nickname 'Whelan the Wrecker', or just plain 'Whelan'.*

And yet Whelan's sign, the original, was an accidental PR master-piece. It was long supposed to have resulted from a bit of lunchtime tomfoolery. Thirty or forty years after the event, though, Myles Whelan got talking with Ginger Farmer, an old Whelan's hand who'd been on the spot that day. According to Ginger, 'It wasn't meant to be clever; it was just a direction for the bloke with the dray.' Lacking a stick of chalk, those words – the advertising apotheosis – were scratched on the darkroom wall as an instruction to an overdue drayman that *here* was the wreckage for carting away.

Another lasting relic emerged from the Capitol site. When Whelan's job was all but done, the builders commenced excavating for the theatre foundations. Four feet down they uncovered the remains of a picket fence and portion of an old corduroy track, both running parallel to Collins Street, with the stump of a chimney buried near by. The building just wrecked had stood there since 1865, and the site had been built over and uncrossed by tracks for long years before that. Jim Whelan souvenired the old section of fence which, being hard-wood, was well preserved even after sixty years or more underground. It stayed in his backyard until he died – all but one post which found its way inside the Whelan house in the shape of serviette rings, intri-cately carved by 'one of the fellows who used to come to the yard'.

Not nearly so well preserved had been the timbers of the Royal Oak Hotel – on the other side, the north side, of the Talma Building – in 1914, the first time Whelan's pulled it down. So rotten were the

---

* Author Shane Maloney acknowledges Whelan the Wrecker as a subconscious influence on his naming of the unwitting Brunswick-based sleuth, Murray Whelan – hapless hero of Maloney's novels which include *Stiff* and *The Brush Off*.

The Capitol Theatre's backers pose for posterity with the picket fence unearthed during excavations.

ceiling joists that Jim Whelan reckoned the second floor had been supported by the brass bar fittings alone. In a wooden lean-to at the back of the hotel, Whelan's men found on an upper shelf several dozen bottles of champagne, of which the licensee, Joe Dillon, apparently knew nothing. Or perhaps he knew better. A few of the wreckers took a swig from one of the bottles and thought themselves poisoned. The story goes that they had never before seen, let alone tasted, champagne. Had none of them been with Jim Whelan on a job at the Exford Hotel a few years earlier? On that occasion the wreckers had found a cache of fluted bottles in a cellar beneath the Little Bourke Street footpath. They'd pulled a cork that time, too, but their curiosity had been curbed and their tasting forestalled when a 'dense mist' arose from the opened bottle.

Whelan's wrecked the Royal Oak for the second and last time in 1926. The hotel had been licensed since 1848 and run by Joe and Mary Dillon for nearly fifty years; since 1914, they had owned it. After

Joe Dillon's death, the Royal Oak closed and was sold to the Aeolian Piano Company, which put a building of seven storeys on the site. When the property changed hands again in March 1929, it fetched the highest per-foot frontage price ever seen in Melbourne. The city was on the up and up.

The up and up stalled with the stock market crash in October that same year. But the severity of the downturn not being immediately apparent, 1929 was toasted as the busiest year on record for Melbourne's building industry.* 'The 1929 peak' was talked of with reverence for years to come, as the city – like everywhere else – plunged into, then crawled out of, the Great Depression. At the lowest point, 1931, building activity sank to just 15 per cent of the 1929 level. But the building industry in Melbourne began showing signs of recovery ahead of most other areas of business – let alone most people. In fact, even with the depression at its deepest, the industry was trumpeted as the engine of the city's regeneration. And Whelan the Wrecker was part of it.

> A few minutes before midnight last night a small group of
> men assembled in one of the rooms of the old Stewart Dawson
> building, at the corner of Collins and Swanston Streets. They
> were engineers and business men gathered to see the beginning
> of the first great building job of 1932 in Melbourne. In the street
> below, a group of unemployed workers stood, hoping against
> hope for the chance of a job.
>   The bells rang out the Old Year and rang in the New, over a
> scene in which pathos, enterprise, and confidence in the future
> were strikingly mingled.
>
> ~ HERALD, 1 JANUARY 1932

---

*   That record was based on the value of building permits issued by the city council. But since the permit system had been in existence only since 1916, the 1929 record took no account of the 1880s building frenzy.

Stewart Dawson's Goes

Demolishing the Depression – work begins on Stewart Dawson's, New Year's Day, 1932.

At the midnight strike of the town hall clock, while Jim Whelan joined the building's owners and contractors indoors to 'baptise the work', his gang of fifteen began tearing off the iron roof and verandah of Stewart Dawson's corner.

Back when Stewart Dawson, a city jeweller, bought the building in 1914, the expression 'Stewart Dawson's Corner' was already lodged deep in the Melbourne argot, his shop having occupied the ground floor since before the turn of the century. Its wide, scalloped verandah opposite the town hall clock made it a favourite rendezvous for Block promenaders. In fact, as a meeting place, Stewart Dawson's rivalled 'under the clocks' at Flinders Street station.

Like Colonel Wilson further along Swanston Street, Dawson had envisaged a new, taller building on the site – 'a very poem in architecture rising in the face of the Town Hall' – but his plans too were halted by the onset of war. Afterwards, he found the cost of the scheme beyond him. His hopes rallied fleetingly when the building caught fire in 1927, but the fire-fighters were 'dreadfully efficient' and little damage was done. The following year, at the age of eighty, Stewart Dawson relinquished his corner, and his dream, to the Manchester Unity Independent Order of Oddfellows, the richest friendly society in Australia. Their intention, like Dawson's, was to replace the existing building with one 'worthy of the site'.

At just four storeys high, Dawson's corner was now dwarfed by its neighbour, the Capitol building. Its single-storey predecessor had been, for forty years, the grocer's shop of Germain Nicholson. No doubt Melburnians waxed sentimental when Nicholson's was pulled down in 1882; and so it was with the Stewart Dawson's demolition, fifty years later. As the *Herald* wrote, 'No longer will sweethearts and husbands … stand there, anxiously consulting the Town Hall clock' –

> *Such is progress; but it means the disappearance of a Melbourne landmark and regret which will not be relieved by the knowledge that on the old site there will soon arise something bigger and more magnificent with better and more convenient appointments. Sentiment is rarely in step with the march of progress.*

And progress marched at the double on the Stewart Dawson's site. The owners and contractors were out to show Melbourne a thing or two about getting a job done fast. With a depression on, they had more willing workers than they could use, and not a whiff of union strife. By special permission of the Arbitration Commission, work on the site proceeded around the clock, seven days a week. Whelan's were given a month to complete the demolition – but it took them just twenty days. WRECKERS WIN ran the headline.

5·5·34

J.P. Whelan, in a characteristic pose.

They did it with a workforce of fifty men, working across three shifts. Lightweight materials – plaster, ceilings, internal fixtures – were removed by day, while the heavy stuff was dropped at night, to minimise public risk and the annoyance of dust. There was plenty of heavy stuff to drop, too. Dawson's building must have been one of the earliest in Melbourne to depend on a skeleton of steel and concrete. Its concrete floors were as much as two feet (60 cm) thick, and Whelan's men broke them up by muscle-power alone. It wasn't that the jackhammer hadn't been invented; it had. But it was Jim Whelan's firm belief that 'The machine isn't made than can outwork a man.'

The blaze of publicity surrounding the Stewart Dawson's site launched Whelan himself into the limelight as a 'character'. The press loved him. Now sixty-seven years old, the 'big man with a stoop'* was hailed as 'the oldest and most consistent wrecker in Melbourne' –

In the last 40 years he has demolished over 1000 buildings, and he looks forward to adding several hundred more to his list before he retires.

For a man who (on the authority of his telephone listing and business card) was still a timber merchant, Jim Whelan had strayed a long way from his brief. It wasn't just that there was barely a stick of wood in the whole of Dawson's building; he estimated that 98 per cent of the city buildings 'displaced' during the past forty years had been wrecked by his gangs. 'Others come and go like flies,' he boasted to the *Argus*, 'but I always remain at the job.'

All three of Whelan's sons – Jim, Joe and Tom – were now with the firm, but they never got much of a look-in when their Pa was holding court with the press. He did, though, point out some of his 'star wreckers'. There was Bill Lodge, foreman on the Dawson's job, and Tom Sheridan who, along with Jika and Gerry Henderson, had joined Whelan's after the police strike of 1923 when, like their 600-plus fellow strikers, they'd been refused reinstatement to the force. There was big Ted Riley, a rigger with diamonds in his teeth, and George Parker, who could shift anything with a block and tackle. And, of course, there was 'The Cat', Jacky Thorp – 'Where the least foothold and the most nerve are required, there will he be climbing.'

---

*   He was described elsewhere as 'a grim little man with a lame leg', though it seems to have been generally agreed that, but for his infirmities, he'd have stood at least six feet tall.

*Many people think our men get their training at sea. That is not
so. Most of them are Australians who have never been to sea.
There was a time when I wouldn't go 10 feet in the air myself.
But when you go higher, you begin to lose your nervousness.*

Jim Whelan's stoop and uneven gait were the legacy of a couple of
falls: his from a wall and a wall's onto him. Those were just two of the
dozen or so serious accidents he'd survived during his career to date.
In 1911 he was struck on the head by a brick dropped from a height of
six storeys. 'That night he spat blood,' his son Jim recalled, 'but three
days later he was back on the job.' Photos from that period show him
wearing a bowler hat, reputedly stuffed with cotton wool as a cushion
against the next flying brick.

After Whelan's shovelled the last rubble of Stewart Dawson's into
trucks and drays, the builders moved onto the site. The superstruc-
ture of the new Manchester Unity Building's eleven floors and fluted
tower went up at the incredible rate of one floor a week between May
and July 1932. At the grand opening on 1 September, Melburnians
clamoured to try out the city's first escalator. In two hours that afternoon, it carried an estimated 12,000 'escalatees' between the ground
and first floors. The Manchester Unity Building was declared the
'travel postcard centre' of Melbourne and, in a triumph of progress
over sentiment, Stewart Dawson's Corner was hardly spoken of again
– except by the Whelans.

Contemporary wrecks
Temple Court (424 Collins Street), 1923
A three-storey building of some grandeur, the old Temple Court formed
a long, narrow 'arcade' through to Little Collins Street, housing barristers' chambers, stockbrokers, shipping agents and the like. Built in

1859, it was panelled throughout in blackwood and cedar, some of which, forty years after its removal, would be used to line the hallway of Whelan the Wrecker's office in Brunswick.

Peterson's Building (east corner Flinders and Bond), 1930

At seven storeys, this was hailed at the time as the largest building wrecked in Melbourne. According to the *Herald* in June 1930: 'Whelan the Wrecker has just finished … the work of pulling down a seven-storey cement and brick building at the corner of Bond and Flinders Streets, City. It is a coincidence that, forty-two years ago, Mr Whelan helped to cart the timber used in its construction.'

Yarra Bend Lunatic Asylum, Abbotsford, mid-1920s

The asylum opened in 1846, on land now occupied by Yarra Bend Golf Course. Originally a single bluestone structure, the asylum expanded over the years to a staggering eighty-three buildings, some of them as big as city blocks. It took Whelan's eighteen months to demolish the lot.

THE RAGGED SKYLINE

The skyline is 'ragged' owing to the numbers of old shops,
relics of the early settlement, which have been suffered to
remain cheek by jowl with tall and stately modern temples of
commerce.

~ *Argus*, 1927

The problem (as seen by the Argus *and others) was that the allotments
occupied by such relics were too narrow to carry new buildings of
sufficient height 'to do justice to the street' and harmonise with their
loftier neighbours.*

*The overhaul of the council's building regulations, culminating in the
Melbourne Building Act of 1916, had set a maximum height limit for
the city of 132 feet (roughly 40 metres). That was based on the height
of the Equitable Building in Collins Street (built 1892–96), judged to be
'the best proportioned building in the city'. In 1928, one of those derided
relics of old Melbourne – a tiny furrier's shop, with dwelling above – still
cowered in the lee of the Equitable Building's passenger-liner bulk. But,
as in Aesop's fable, the lion had cause to be grateful to the mouse. Tenants
on the west side of the Equitable Building had the insignificant furrier's
shop to thank for their access to daylight. A structure of more harmonious
dimensions would (and eventually did) sink them in permanent shadow.*

A Committee of Public Taste was proposed as one solution to the irregularity of the city's streetscapes. Paris already had such a committee – exercising 'a jealous supervision of street designs, so that none may clash' – so why not Melbourne? A proposal to introduce a minimum building height was applauded by the Herald. *'It is a good thing that the City Council should provide for the gradual elimination of the unsuitable and anachronistic' – of anything, in fact, at variance with the 'graceful towers of colour and harmony reaching to the astounded sky'.*

'Skyscraper' originally was slang for a tall man, a stovepipe hat, or a high-flying hit in baseball or cricket. Only in the 1880s was the term first applied to buildings. The US cities of Chicago and New York led the way, with ten-storey structures already commonplace by the early '80s. Chicago thrust higher, faster – until 1893 when the imposition of a height limit halted that city's ascent. Then New York raced ahead, surpassing two hundred feet, then three. At the turn of the century the world's tallest commercial structure was the Park Row Building, 391 feet (120 m) high. Advances in building technology saw New York's height-record almost double within a decade, then culminate in 1913 with the 792-foot, 55-storey Woolworth Building. And there the record rested for

The 'insurance end' of Queen Street, c.1920, displayed the uniformity of height desired (by some) for the rest of the city.

*Holeproof's 'Skyscrapers' range of neckties on display at the Leviathan Store,
Bourke Street*

more than twenty years after new zoning laws, passed in 1916, put a lid
on the New York skyline.

Returning after a twenty-year absence, the writer Henry James likened
New York City's skyscrapers to 'extravagant pins in a cushion'. He was
accustomed to the London skyline, dominated by the dome of St Paul's
and the modest 'pins' of parish church steeples. London's tallest private
building was the 151-foot (46 m) Queen Ann's Mansions, and even that
was considered beyond the pale. The outcry at its erection (overlooking
Buckingham Palace) had led to the London Building Act of 1888, limiting
the height of buildings to just 80 feet or the width of the street on which
they stood.

At 153 feet high, Melbourne's tallest building was on a par with London's.
During its construction, the Australian Building (at the Elizabeth Street–
Flinders Lane corner) was flagged as the world's tallest; but by the time
it was finished, in 1889, American giants had overtaken it. Up until the
Great War, though, no Melbourne building came near its height and, with

the introduction of the 132-foot limit in 1916, it looked as if the Australian Building would hold on to its record indefinitely.

Originally planned to be even taller, the Australian Building had been constructed to the utter limit of 1880s know-how and materials. Steel beams were used to bolster its lower floors and one-twelfth of its total cost was spent on elevators. It was a marvel in its day. Yet the height limit set nearly thirty years later seemed to indict the Australian Building as too tall. Indeed, many had condemned it as such from the outset. The problem was that no ladder or fire-hose existed that could reach an outbreak on the building's upper floors. Calamitous city fires were a regular occurrence well into the twentieth century, and it was the limitations of fire-fighting, as much as anything, that dictated 132 feet as the maximum feasible height for a Melbourne building.

Light and ventilation were also considerations. In the years between the wars, most of the world's major cities adopted height limits based on street-width. The usual 'ideal' was one-and-a-half times the width of the street that a building faced. The purpose of such equations was to maximise daylight and airflow, not only within buildings but at street-level. In New York the upper limit was two-and-a-half times the street-width – more, if the building was set back from the footpath – but, of course, the Woolworth Building and its contemporaries far exceeded those limits.

Compared to most cities, Melbourne's height limit was stunted: just one-and-a-third times the width of its expansive main streets. Sydney, with its much narrower streets, permitted buildings 150 feet tall. In 1928, the Royal Victorian Institute of Architects proposed an increase in Melbourne's height limit to match Sydney's. Then came the New York horror stories, of wind-ripped chasms and office workers like moles. Moreover, according to opponents of the RVIA proposal, 'It is now widely agreed that the herding together in one building of many thousands of workers has proved a false economy.' Some workers in New York skyscrapers, they claimed, were forced to leave their offices as early as 3 p.m., 'so that the footpaths will not be congested by the simultaneous discharge of thousands of workers *late in the afternoon'. Even so, rush hour brought such a crush that multi-level footpaths must soon become a necessity.*

The city council said 'No' to the architects' 1928 proposal, but the push for a taller city continued on right through the '30s. On the eve of the Second World War, an opponent of the latest building-height sortie argued that skyscrapers would be the target of hostile aircraft. The limit of 132 feet remained in place for nearly twenty more years. As for the city skyline, though – by 1939 it was more ragged than ever.

It wasn't those cowering 'relics' that were the culprits, but the ornamental towers which, under a council amendment of the early '20s, could be built to an unlimited height in addition to the 132-foot maximum. In the 'craze for towers' of the 1920s and '30s , architects designed many a splendid target for enemy aircraft. The tower atop the Manchester Unity Building, soaring to 210 feet, was just one – and not the tallest – of them. So much for uniformity: one critic condemned Melbourne's skyline as a 'scrap-heap'.

As was the case in London, though, the tallest structures in Melbourne were still the spires of its churches. The main spires of St Patrick's and St Paul's cathedrals outreached by 100 feet or more the swizzle sticks of their commercial counterparts. But even as early as 1928, the city council foresaw that the low-lying St Paul's might one day be blocked from view by skyscrapers on the city approach. 'The day would come when only the tips of the spires would be visible from the south.'

CHAPTER 5

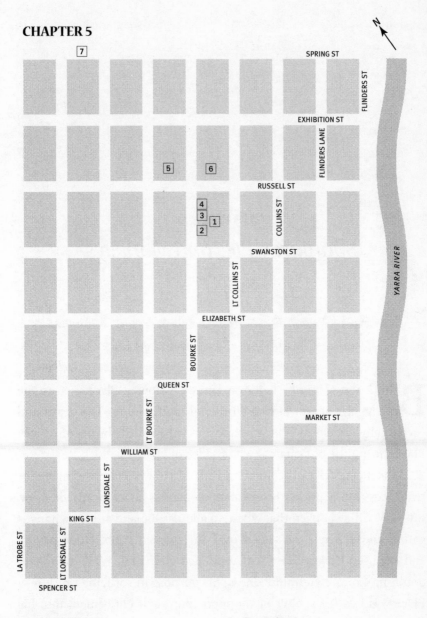

1. Cole's Book Arcade
2. Rubira's Hotel
3. Bull and Mouth
4. Britannia Theatre
5. Theatre Royal
6. Bijou Theatre
7. Model School

CHAPTER 5

Spaniards, Pies and Monkeys

*Cole's Book Arcade ~ Rubira's Hotel ~ Bull and Mouth ~ Britannia
Theatre ~ Theatre Royal ~ Bijou Theatre ~ Model School*

Behind the Capitol Theatre a laneway, Howey Place, marks the extent of Captain Howey's original landholding. The drays and (eventually) trucks of Whelan the Wrecker became habitués of Howey Place during the old estate's two decades of change.

Like most Melbourne lanes and alleys, Howey Place was made for rear access to the properties thereabouts. It was never meant for show. But E.W. Cole changed that when, in about 1906 and at his own instigation and expense, he sealed over the uneven cobblestone paving and enclosed Howey Place with a pitched glass roof. While there's no doubting Cole's civic-mindedness, his purpose in sprucing up Howey Place was less the shelter of shoppers than their enticement into his Book Arcade.

Cole's Book Arcade is a Melbourne legend and was, even in those days. Professing to be the world's largest book store, it must certainly have ranked among the most eccentric. In that, it was a reflection of Cole himself, a man of unstemmable energy, enterprise and curiosity – a true original. As a young man, he'd hawked lemonade on the goldfields and travelled the length of the Murray as an itinerant photographer. He made his start in Melbourne selling pies from a barrow, which gradually transformed into a book stall at Paddy's Market* in Bourke Street. Besides secondhand books, Cole sold pamphlets of his own with titles such as *Mental Freedom* and *Religious Sects of All Nations*. In 1874, he moved to a shop in Bourke Street proper, above Russell Street – his first Book Arcade.

From his earliest days as a bookseller, Cole had employed novel means to attract customers. His first, and enduring, slogan – originally painted on the barrow – was: READ FOR AS LONG AS YOU LIKE. NOBODY ASKED TO BUY. Once established with a street address, he embarked on a campaign of newspaper advertising, filling an entire front-page column of every day's *Herald* with his distinctive brand of bombast, quack philosophy, riddles, jingles, doggerel, and straight-out huckstering. Idiosyncratic they may have been, but Cole's adverts were effective. His serial stunts found an eager following, and in 1875 he even used the daily column to advertise for a wife – within a month, he was married. Cole regularly struck bronze promotional 'medals' and had his shopboys scatter them in the streets. They could be exchanged for pencils at the Book Arcade, but more often people kept them as souvenirs.

In the flourishing early '80s, Cole began to hanker for a *real* arcade, with a skylit glass roof, right in the heart of Bourke Street.† He found what he wanted – or the makings of it – in the old Spanish Restaurant, a Bourke Street fixture since 1860 but by then on its last legs. Set between two roaring hotels, it appealed to the abstemious Cole as just the spot to offer a different kind of fun – the wholesome and 'improving' fun of his Book Arcade. He went ahead and leased the

---

*   See Chapter 10.

†   That meant the stretch between Elizabeth and Swanston – nowadays the Bourke Street Mall.

building from Matt Cantlon, who'd owned it since the 1840s and now gave Cole *carte blanche* to make it the arcade of his dreams.

It was three storeys high and ninety feet (nearly 30 m) wide, built of brick on a bluestone foundation. Cole had the roof replaced with glass, and wide balconies (or galleries) built in place of the upper storeys so that daylight could penetrate all the way to the ground floor. In fact, to pull off his dream, the whole structure had to be sub-stantially rebuilt – underpinned, shored up, and tied to the crooked walls of its neighbours. To finish off, the entrance was overarched with the Book Arcade's trademark, a magnificent painted rainbow.

In the latter weeks of October 1883, Cole's daily column in the *Herald* showed a lot more white space than usual. Instead of the usual close-printed manifesto, it carried just fourteen words, stretched out to the length of the page –

COLE'S

NEW

BOOK

ARCADE

WILL

OPEN

SHORTLY

The

Grandest

Book

Shop

in

the

World

For the opening, Cole chose the first Tuesday in November – Melbourne Cup Day – pitching his gala to the 'intellectual non-racing' public as an alternative to the hoopla at Flemington. As it turned out, Melburnians (intellectual and otherwise) availed themselves of both spectacles, flocking to the Book Arcade after the Cup was run. A great attraction was the 'elegant parlour lift' that ran every two minutes to the Arcade's top gallery. There, jam-packed under the glass roof, was Cole's Ornament Exhibition, billed as 'The Prettiest Sight in Australia'. Signs overhead showed the way to ornaments for sideboards, mantelpieces, brackets, walls, tables – even 'Ornaments for What-Nots'.* (This, after all, was the heyday of the antimacassar, an era in which no household surface was suffered to remain nude.) By daylight, and even more so by gaslight, the Book Arcade's top floor was a glinting glaze of ruby, frosted, cut and gilded glass, besides china of every shape and superfluosity: moustache cups, jardinieres, urns, artificial fruit, figurines – you name it.

While no longer just a bookshop, Cole's Book Arcade remained a bookshop first and foremost. Cole would stage any stunt or stock any novelty line for the sake of bringing people into his shop and into proximity with books. In his new premises, hundreds of chairs were positioned about the walkways and nooks, in keeping with Cole's policy to allow unlimited reading without obligation to buy. A band played daily on the first floor and, over time, Cole augmented the Book Arcade's attractions with a tea salon, picture gallery, and fernery, complete with aviary of talking birds.

Of course, all this took up space. After a few years, Cole bought the building at the rear and, with the fernery as an intermediary oasis, extended the Book Arcade right through to Little Collins Street, opposite Howey Place. Now, aside from Cole's new entrance, there wasn't much about Little Collins Street that beckoned to shoppers. The neighbours in those days were mostly factories and warehouses and the footpaths ill-made for promenading. Luring customers past the fernery to the 'unfashionable' end of the Book Arcade was Cole's new challenge. His solution was a confectionery department like no other. Its walls were lined with lolly-filled glass panels to a child's eye-level

---

* A whatnot is a portable shelf for displaying ornaments (what else?).

and mirrored above, so that the sweets seemed to go on forever. Best of all was The Hen that Cackles and Lays Eggs, a 'completely life-like' German-made mechanical hen which, when fed a penny, laid a tin egg with a novelty inside.

Never content, Cole next hatched an ambition for the Book Arcade to span two city blocks – all the way from Bourke to Collins Street. During the lean 1890s, he bought the Collins Street frontage that stood in line with the Book Arcade, then, over the space of a dozen years, acquired the intervening properties along the west side of Howey Place. By 1906, he was close to realising his goal. He now owned, or leased, a continuous thread of buildings connecting Melbourne's two premier streets. But still there was an obstacle to the gun-barrel perfection Cole craved for his Book Arcade: it had a dogleg, in the shape of Howey Place.

Unable to wrest the laneway from the city council, Cole did the next best thing, upgrading it to meet his own requirements and renaming it (without official sanction) Cole's Walk. Now the elegant, glass-roofed footway formed a felicitous and dead-straight union between the confectionery department in Little Collins Street and the rear of Cole's Collins Street premises. Along the laneway, the side walls of an old warehouse – now Cole's toy department – were knocked through to make display windows. Tucked away beyond the toys was Cole's printing department, which turned out hundreds of original titles, many of them written by Cole himself, including *Cole's Fun Doctor*, *The 5000 Wisest Sayings in the World*, and *Cole's Family Amuser and Intellect Sharpener*. The most successful, *Cole's Funny Picture Book*, sold more than 400,000 copies.

Though Cole turned seventy in 1902, he still – more than ever – was driven by the idealism evident in his pamphleteering youth. As early as the 1880s, he had advocated federation, not just of the Australian colonies, but of the entire world. He vigorously opposed the White Australia Policy, issuing tracts with titles such as *A White Australia Impossible* and *The Whole Human Race is Mixing and Must Mix*

– Even in Australia. In fact, Cole's belief in universal kinship extended beyond humankind. About 1900, he had a cage built at the Bourke Street end of the Arcade and filled it with monkeys in mated pairs. He intended to make a study of the similarities between human and simian races, even began writing a book on the subject. Cole never finished *The Animal Next to Man*, but his cageful of 'little men' became one of the chief novelties of the Book Arcade.

After Cole's death in 1918, the Book Arcade continued in the hands of his family and long-time staff. But in fast-changing times and without the guiding spirit of its originator, the old Melbourne landmark languished. In 1927 it was put up for sale, not as a going concern but as two parcels of property. A suggestion that the city council knock down the Book Arcade to create a throughway from Bourke to Collins Street (via Howey Place) came to nothing. On a Thursday afternoon in June 1929, the Arcade band played its last tune and Cole's rainbow-fronted Bourke Street store, fount of so many 'quaint and pleasant memories', shut its doors for good. Not long after – you must've known it was coming – Whelan the Wrecker moved in.

Cole's Book Arcade becomes history, February 1929.

Wouldn't you think, in a place of such marvels, that there'd have been some marvels left for the wreckers to find? Not so, it seems. There was a cache of brummy coins – foreign currency, old copper trade tokens – under the floorboards where the cash-register had stood. It looked as if there'd been a hole or chute through the floor into which the cashier, tallying the day's takings, would drop any worthless coins. And there were the slate flagstones underfoot in the old fernery, where, by the time the Arcade closed, the monkeys had been installed, along with the talking birds. Thus it was that in future years 'young' Jim Whelan could state with truth that the slate paving in his Coburg backyard had come from 'the bottom of the monkey cage' at Cole's Book Arcade. When the Coburg house was sold after Jim's death, his son Tony had the flagstones taken up, intending to give them a new life in the house he was building. In the meantime, he stored them at Whelan's tip* in East Brunswick whence they disappeared under metres of mud and silt when the Merri Creek burst its banks soon after. According to Whelan lore, however, that wasn't the last of the Book Arcade monkey cage. The ornamental metalwork of the cage itself is reputed to have ended up part of the decor in a wedding reception place out Essendon way.

There is some talk, too, of the mechanical hen having been part of the wreckers' booty. That remarkable fowl ranked high among the wonders of the Book Arcade, others of which eventually found their way, via the Cole family, to the Melbourne Museum. Nowadays the Hen that Cackles is on display at the Scienceworks museum. Would such a treasure – even with her coin-slot jammed – really have been left for the wreckers?

Not even so much as an anecdote has filtered down from the wreckage of Cole's Collins Street premises, in 1932. On the Book Arcade site in Bourke Street, a six-storey store was built for G.J. Coles & Co. (no relation), whose slogan of 'Nothing over two shillings and sixpence'

*   See Chapter 14.

was more prosaic but just as surefire as anything E.W. Cole had tried. Today Coles has gone and the building is occupied by a David Jones store, whose confectionery department, facing Little Collins Street, corresponds almost exactly – in position, if not splendour – with its phantasmagorical predecessor.

That ought to be history enough for one site; but that's not how Melbourne – nor any city – works. Always there are layers and over-laps, and, peel them back as you will, you can never quite say with certainty, 'The history of this place started *here*.'

The Coles–Cole's site in the Bourke Street mall has, if not a deeper, then a richer subsoil than most. Before the Book Arcade, there was the Spanish Restaurant, opened by Estaban Parer in 1860. The five Parer brothers, emigrants from Barcelona in the '50s, founded a dynasty in the Melbourne hospitality trade. In the 1880s, one branch of the family built a hotel fit for the boomtime, the Crystal Café, a block from Estaban's old restaurant.*

When E.W. Cole refitted the Spanish Restaurant site in 1883, he was much incommoded by the proximity of Hosie's Scotch Pie Shop, his neighbour to the west. Almost every step of the process had to be negotiated with James Hosie, whose premises and Cole's leant against one another. Like the names of Parer and Stutt, Hosie's seems to have attached itself, over the years, to half the hotels in Melbourne.†️ Indeed, the Scotch Pie Shop, far from being the crusty bakehouse it sounded, was a hotel made over by the Hosie touch. Comestibles were James Hosie's speciality, and the dining hall of the Scotch Pie Shop – its menu by no means limited to pies – could feed three hundred at a sitting, besides the bar and counter trade. Born in gold-rush times as the Union Hotel (a name still extant in the lane alongside), the place was run-down in roof and reputation by the time Hosie took it over

---

*   Wrecked by Whelan's c.1961 to make way for Walton's department store – now Village cinemas.
†️   See Chapter 11.

in the 1870s. At the height of the boom he sold it, revivified, to James Rubira, and Rubira's Hotel it would remain until Whelan the Wrecker flattened it, in 1938, for the enlargement of Coles department store.

But before any of that – before Spaniards, pies or monkeys – a theatre, Melbourne's first, straddled the sites-to-be of the Book Arcade and Rubira's. Forty years after its disappearance, when Edmund Finn ('Garryowen') was setting down his *Chronicles of Early Melbourne*, he had no end of trouble in establishing the exact site of the city's original playhouse. The problem wasn't a shortage of informants, but that each one pointed out a different spot. In the end, Garryowen got hold of a contemporary sketch which, he was satisfied, reliably fixed the position of the shortlived and long-gone Pavilion Theatre.

It was put up early in 1841 by the publican of the neighbouring Eagle Inn, to be managed by his barman, Thomas Hodges, an amateur thespian. Tall and narrow and built wholly of timber, the Pavilion was far from being the most stable of structures. 'Whenever the wind was high,' wrote Garryowen, 'it would rock like an old collier at sea.' For a year, the authorities refused to grant the Pavilion a licence, consenting only seldom to a one-night charity performance. On those occasions, the conduct of both theatregoers and the entertainment itself tended to confirm the official view that Melbourne – just six years old and unbreeched – wasn't ready for a theatre. Nonetheless, in 1842 the government granted permission for monthly theatrical performances at the Pavilion. The productions were staged largely by amateurs – many a Melbourne tradesman donning parti-colour or powdered periwig for one night only – supplemented by visiting professionals. The theatre itself was variously billed as the Pavilion, the Royal, and the Royal Victoria. But whatever its name and whatever the playbill, the patrons could always be relied on to act up: bad behaviour was the theatre's only constant. By 1845, the town had a proper theatre, the Queen's Theatre in Queen Street, built of brick, reputably run with 'private constables' to keep order, and licensed to boot. At that stage, the Pavilion–Royal–Victoria gave up calling itself a theatre, instead becoming Canterbury Hall, venue of 'low-class concerts and an occasional pulpit meeting'. Within a few years, its meagre utility long outlived, the creaky white elephant was pulled down.

The unruly character of the theatre's clientele cannot, you would think, have been wholly unconnected with the Eagle Inn, alongside. The publican in those times (the same man who'd bankrolled the theatre) was James Jamieson. A Scotsman, he'd arrived in the settlement in 1840, aboard the barque *Eagle*, and straightaway put up his 'cottage-like hostelry'. A single storey in weatherboard, with detached kitchen at the rear and spacious verandah out front, it was set back some distance from Bourke Street. Jamieson later added a brick room – the main bar – which brought his hotel up to the street-line. As to the actual management of the Eagle Inn, Garryowen wrote that Jamieson, 'though he reigned, did not govern'; his wife, known to all as 'Mother Jamieson', ruled the eyrie. Under her charge, it seems, the Eagle was but one step removed from a bawdy-house. Foremost among the working women on safari in the Eagle's front bar was Jenny McLeod, described by Garryowen as 'not very fascinating, though lively'. (Here the authorities' reasons for refusing to license the theatre next door start to become clear.)

The Eagle Inn changed hands, and name, in 1848. It was known as the Britannia Inn for just five months, however, before the new publican removed both licence and name to premises he'd built up the road, at the Queen Street corner.* The old site had been bought by Matt Cantlon, formerly a Hobart police constable (and, some say, an ex-convict), but now a publican and pioneer Melbourne restaurateur. He replaced the seedy cottage-tavern with the Bull and Mouth Hotel – at three substantial storeys in brick, 'a splendid edifice' by comparison – opening just in time for the gold rushes.† Throughout the spirited

---

* The Queen Street Britannia Hotel was demolished by Whelan's in 1960.
† 'Bull and Mouth' is an archaic misrendering of Boulogne Mouth, where English forces scored a victory over the French in the time of Henry VIII.

Owen Whelan poses in 1966 with a souvenir of the Bull and Mouth demolition, more than thirty years earlier.

'50s, the Bull and Mouth was a popular central staging-point (literally, with the Cobb & Co. coach office directly opposite), offering shilling drinks at all hours and sit-down meals from breakfast till midnight. One familiar with the place described its spirituous atmosphere as 'dense as a Scotch mist'.

The Bull and Mouth underwent alterations sometime in the '70s, increasing its lodgings from twenty to forty rooms in good time for the next boom. Later, the hotel sprouted a fourth storey and had its front redesigned to echo the arch of the Book Arcade's rainbow-striped parapet next door. The Bull and Mouth kept afloat as a city institution until after the Great War, when six o'clock closing and the rise of the department store began changing the Bourke Street scene for good. Not long after the Book Arcade succumbed to the flagship store of G.J. Coles, Woolworths acquired the Bull and Mouth and its easterly neighbour, and had Whelan's knock down the pair of them.

The builders of the Britannia Theatre – and of *its* neighbour, the Melba Theatre – had carried the arch motif still further along the street. In manner and magnitude, the Britannia dominated this part of Bourke Street. A bust of Britannia herself presided from the parapet above the colonnaded upper storey. Over the entrance awning, a broad, recessed arch, like the grinning mouth of Luna Park, seemed to say, 'Step inside.'

The Britannia was one of Melbourne's earliest built-from-scratch picture theatres. On its opening in 1912, it was hailed (admittedly by its owner, the American showman, J.D. Williams) as 'the most luxurious and gorgeously decorated theatre in the world'. At the smaller Melba Theatre, adjoining – in the re-fitted premises of the Victoria Hall, formerly used for vaudeville – there'd hardly been a vacant seat at any screening in the year since it opened. The Britannia not only seated more patrons than its neighbour, but guaranteed them a clear view of the screen. The steeply raked seating ensured that 'not even a picture hat' – which, in 1912, might be as big and untamed as a farm animal – could block a patron's view. On its opening day, the Britannia, with seating for 948, somehow squeezed in 1,200, hats and all, for the first screening. The film was *Christopher Columbus*, and 6,000 tickets were sold that day.

For more than a decade, the Britannia was said to have the highest box-office takings of any picture theatre in the world. But, twenty years after it was built, it was deemed inadequate for the audiences clamouring to see, and hear, the latest films. The effects of the depression on movie-going had more than been offset by the advent of talking pictures. By 1932, picture palaces like the Capitol (which seated 2,000) and the new State Theatre* (4,000) were filled to capacity, while the once-grand Britannia was relegated to 'second release' status, and thence to the wreckers.

Before the Britannia, the site between the Bull and Mouth and Victoria Hall had been plugged by Kitz's Colonial Wine Hall, a tailor's, and a hairdresser–tobacconist's. Peel it back further, to the 1850s, and you'd uncover a hotel and more shops of the hairy-chested sort. Earlier still, there was the fishmongery of Peter Perkins, claimed to be the first to sell oysters in Melbourne and the town's original purveyor of *real* turtle soup. It was Perkins' rival, Henry Clegge of Little Bourke Street, who'd first offered turtle soup for sale; but Clegge's turned out to be 'a heterogeneous home-brewed compound', more mock than turtle. Perkins' genuine article was distilled from a 300-lb (136 kg) turtle, caught and killed off Williamstown in 1845. Not long after, Henry Clegge was charged with stealing jewellery from another small-time celebrity of the Woolworths site, 'a woman named Sutherland, better known as "Jenny McLeod"'.

Whelan the Wrecker's work in this part of Bourke Street began early in 1932, almost a year before the Britannia and the Bull and Mouth shut their doors. It wasn't demolition work this time, but excavation. The Melba Theatre was to continue running as a second-run movie house, augmented by a newsreel theatrette in the basement. Only there was no basement. Whelan's crew burrowed beneath the Melba for nearly two months, shoring up its bluestone and concrete walls as they went. Under the floor they found old coins (one dated 1757) where the Victoria Hall's bar had been, as well as the stubborn stump of a gum tree. And, all the while, the Melba kept on showing films.

When the Britannia Theatre screened its last film in January 1933, the *Argus* mourned the loss of a pioneer: 'The story of the Britannia

---

* Now the Forum theatre.

Theatre is the story of the motion picture industry.' Before commencing demolition there, though, Whelan's first had to pull down a dilapidated chemist's shop in Punt Road, Windsor, where an earlier chapter of the motion picture story had unspooled. Around 1900, William Gibson and Millard Johnson had conducted their pioneering experiments in cinematography in the shop's long back room, while the wall of a nearby building had served as a screen for their first public showings. Gibson and Johnson went on to produce *The Story of the Kelly Gang* in 1906 and to build Australia's 'first luxury cinema', the Majestic in Flinders Street, which opened just ahead of the Britannia in 1912. The *Sun News-Pictorial* in 1933 eulogised the Punt Road chemist's shop as 'an object of historic interest', adding, 'One by one the old landmarks of the State are disappearing.'

The 1930s saw Bourke Street East transformed, as the pleasure palaces that had characterised the street since before gold-rush times were overbuilt by department stores and even more prosaic places of commerce.

East of Swanston Street, at the end of 1933, Whelan's wrecked the Theatre Royal to make way for Manton's – 'a 100 per cent daylight store'. A theatre had stood there since 1855, in two incarnations punctuated by fire. Originally built by John Black with the fortune he'd made from carting supplies to the goldfields, the theatre's character in its early days was in keeping with the racketty, gold-rush times that were nearly over. It opened with Sheridan's *School for Scandal*, and quickly degenerated to staging the racy dance act of Lola Montez and her troupe of imaginary spiders. Before long, the theatre's vestibule was known as 'the Saddling Paddock', prostitutes and their clients assembling there to select mounts. Decent folk forsook the Theatre Royal, and John Black wound up bankrupt.

Under the new management of George Coppin* and Gustavus

---

* George Coppin, 1820–1906 – actor, theatrical entrepreneur, philanthropist, and member of parliament. His Richmond mansion, Pine Lodge, was a showpiece of its time and would be so still, had Jim Whelan not wrecked it, c.1920s.

Brooke, the theatre cleaned up its act. To offset the riff-raffish Royal Hotel, to the left of the vestibule, the right-hand frontage was transformed into the lavish and ultra-respectable Café de Paris. Theatre, café and all were burnt out in 1872 – the inevitable fate of theatres in those times – but were soon rebuilt, incorporating some of the original materials. The vast stage at the Theatre Royal fitted it for some spectacular turns of entertainment. Often these involved livestock, as in a production of *The Derby Winner* in which real horses were galloped down Little Bourke Street and in through the theatre's rear door, for a full-tilt finish at the footlights. One actor and his mount ended up in the orchestra pit.

The old theatre was well beyond its best when it finally closed down in November 1933. A sentimental favourite, *The Maid of the Mountains* starring Gladys Moncrieff, was revived for one last performance. Workmen began carrying out the furniture before the stalls had emptied, and the wreckers weren't far behind.

With the kind of speed made possible by a surplus of labour, it took less than four months for Manton's store to rise on the site of the Theatre Royal. But, 'Though Manton's in their march of progress have swept away the Theatre Royal ... the firm does not intend to allow the passing of the theatre to go unmarked.' A memorial plaque was proposed for the spot where the stage had stood. Underneath, in a lead-lined cavity, would be deposited eight items representative of modern Melbourne life, for which suggestions were invited from readers of the *Sun News-Pictorial*. A motor horn, samples of scientific foods, and an embalmed politician were among the submissions. Most popular with women were a powder compact and lipstick; with men, it was a bottle of whisky. Manton's own nomination was a brick from the Theatre Royal. After all, what could be more emblematic of Melbourne on the eve of its centenary than a specimen of the wrecker's art?

Whelan's lore doesn't relate what became of the iron gates from the front of the Theatre Royal. But the gates from the Bijou Theatre, the Wrecker's next job, ended up at the entrance to a cemetery at

Pleasant Creek, not far from Stawell. They were donated, of course, by that old Stawellite, Jim Whelan. The gates at the Deep Lead cemetery, near by, are said to be a second set from the Bijou – possibly from the other end of the arcade that ran beneath the theatre to Little Collins Street.

The Bijou had charted what seems to have been the typical course for a Melbourne theatre. Opening in 1876 as the Academy of Music, it began with noble ambitions ('the cultivation and development of music and the drama in their higher manifestations') which commercial expediency soon curtailed. The Bijou became Melbourne's home of comedy, its intimate size 'render[ing] every word audible and every gesture visible in every part of the house'. It suffered the usual fate of Melbourne theatres when, in 1889, it became the sixth in a quarter-century to be gutted by fire. Theatregoers had long complained of cooking fumes from the kitchen of the Palace Hotel, adjoining, and it was suspected that the fire had its origins in the same place. Two fire-fighters were killed in the blaze, nearly a dozen injured, and several more disgraced their brigades by making free with the refreshments laid on at the Palace once the worst was over. In fact, the fire at the

Top billing – Whelan's plays the Bijou, 1934.

Bijou triggered an inquiry into firefighting in Melbourne, as a result of which the government finally took over from the volunteer and insurance-company brigades. When the Bijou was rebuilt, it acquired a little sister, the Gaiety Theatre (host to 'entertainments of the higher-class music hall variety'), tucked in under the Palace Hotel on the other side of the arcade.

Both theatres survived the delicensing of the Palace Hotel in 1914 and the advent of moving pictures. By the '20s, though, they were pretty much past it. A plan to replace them with a 5,000-capacity movie house was undone by the depression, and the two were remodelled as second-run talkie theatres – the Gaiety rechristened the Roxy – in 1930. But if the Britannia couldn't compete with the big new picture palaces, what chance did these tiddlers stand? With the seven-storey Palace Hotel now empty, here was a prime parcel of Bourke Street going to waste. In the early months of 1934, Whelan's tore the whole lot down.

Only late in the wrecking did they locate the foundation stone of the original Academy of Music. It had been reincorporated in the building after the fire, but inconspicuously, under the entrance to the dress circle. The usual lead casket was set into the stone, with ten items inside, none of them a lipstick. In fact, compared with those dreamt up by readers of the *Sun*, they made a very dull assortment. Besides five newspapers from May 1876, there were copies of the previous two years' *Statistical Register of Victoria*, and photographs of the then-governor (who laid the foundation stone) and the theatre's original proprietor. Not much there to interest a wrecker. (For them, Squizzy Taylor's hideout in the basement was the monte.)

Sir Benjamin Fuller, head of Fuller's Theatres, swore to re-lay the casket and its contents with the foundation of the new theatre planned for the site. He was a great one for intentions, Sir Benjamin: over the next twenty years, Fuller's would announce a succession of grand plans for the old Bijou–Gaiety–Palace site. In 1934, it was the 5,000-seat St James' Theatre, which would open with a season of grand opera in English ('at popular prices'), but whose design would enable its transformation into a talkie theatre at short notice. As well, there'd be the nine-storey Prince George Hotel, unlicensed (the infamy of the old Palace still staining the site) but with a solarium roof garden and four hundred rooms, each served by its own bathroom. In the basement, Squizzy's ectoplasm would be watered down by an Olympic-size swimming pool – if the authorities would consent to mixed bathing. The whole lot, said Sir Benjamin, would be ready to open in six months, to coincide with Melbourne's centennial celebrations. Six months later, nearly six years later – despite a revised plan, for a 'palatial' block of limit-height buildings that would 'change the face of old Bourke Street' – the site remained as Whelan's had left it.

In 1939, a ten-storey building for the Commonwealth Bank went up on the Palace Hotel portion, bordering Russell Lane. Seven years later, with the war over, Sir Benjamin Fuller announced his latest vision for the rest of the site: a 'complete entertainment centre', with a theatre, cabaret specialising in big floor shows, as well as sideshows and shops. There'd be 'everything', said Sir Benjamin, 'from Punch and Judy to a circus'. But the Bijou site continued flat and vacant until 1954, when excavations commenced at the Little Collins Street end for the multi-storey Grand Central Car Park, 'a kind of glorified coach house for vehicles of the auto age'. Sir Benjamin's aspirations for the site had gone nowhere, and by the time a second ten-storey office block went up on the Bourke Street frontage, the lead casket and its unremarkable contents were forgotten – just as surely as if the wreckers had taken them.

Contemporary wrecks
Model School (Spring and Victoria streets), 1933
Opened in 1854, the Model School was built as head office, teachers' training college, and model for the fledgling National School system.

The Model School, as it was ...

Both boys and girls were taught there – though they used separate classrooms, playgrounds, even entrances. The school had outlived its original purpose by the turn of the century, after which it became one of the first 'continuation' schools, later renamed Melbourne High. During its final years, it was a high school for girls, the forerunner of MacRobertson Girls' High.

For all the enduring elegance of its design, the building had never been very sound, its construction having been compromised

... and in the grip of Whelan's.

by a shortage of reputable materials and tradesmen in the gold-rush '50s. After the school's closure in 1927, the College of Surgeons took possession, intending to refurbish the old building. Their architect, however, advised demolition.

Thousands among Victoria's pioneer generations had attended the Model School, and a surprising number of them were still living – and nostalgic about the place – when it was slated for demolition in 1933. It was older than the university, than the library, than almost any other public building in the city. 'This old building,' wrote one former student, 'should be a venerated monument, the least of whose desserts is an adequate inscription for the benefit of future generations.' Venerated it was not; but it did get an inscription. And so, uniquely, did the wreckers. A plaque outside the Royal Australasian College of Surgeons building reads, in part –

The building was demolished between
August 28 and September 27, 1933.

Archaeologists excavating part of the site prior to building works in 2002 were obliged to Whelan the Wrecker for leaving behind many traces of the old Model School. The basement level, it was found, had been filled with demolition rubble and buried. Amongst the stuff unearthed were two flights of stone stairs and recumbent sections of a stout Doric column, which are now preserved as a decorative feature in the College of Surgeons courtyard.

CHAPTER 6

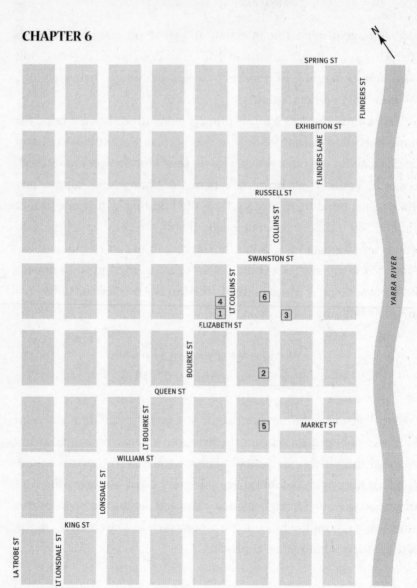

1. Colonial Bank
2. Bank of New South Wales
3. Royal Bank
4. Union House
5. Royal Insurance Building
6. Hotel Australia

CHAPTER 6

Saved From the Wrecker's Pit

Colonial Bank ~ Bank of New South Wales ~ Royal Bank ~
Union House ~ Royal Insurance Building, Hotel Australia site

'Time has written no wrinkles on this 52-year-old architectural gem.' How could it, when the gem was cut from solid
Malmsbury bluestone?

The Colonial Bank (latterly a branch of the National) found itself
acclaimed, in 1932, for its finely sculpted lower facade and 'the most
architecturally handsome doorway in Melbourne'. Those were the
old building's final days. While it had looked like standing forever,
Melburnians seem hardly to have noticed the Colonial Bank, except
as an 'outstanding instance' of gloomy bluestone construction.

Of course, it was Whelan's who pulled it down – or 'dug their
picks into' it, as the papers said. With difficulty, they wrenched out
the bootscrapers mounted either side of the doorway, which turned
out to be made of gunmetal* and weighed a hundredweight (50 kg)
each – a windfall for the wreckers.

---

* A valuable alloy of copper, tin and zinc.

The Colonial Bank doorway in its original home ...

The building had been put up in 1880, replacing the Colonial Bank's old premises on the same spot. At three storeys, and spiked with urns and pomp and statuary, it might have been commanding were it built on a 'Great' street corner. But its situation at Little Collins and low-lying Elizabeth only accentuated the bank's basaltic dinge. The building all but filled its large, squarish allotment; only a tiny rear corner was left bare. Or not bare exactly, for there – 'apparently for sentiment's sake' – stood a fig tree almost as old as Melbourne.

The Colonial was founded in 1856 as a bank for small investors and borrowers. Under the aegis of its first chairman, John O'Shanassy, MLC, the gold diggers' champion, the Colonial was known as the 'Diggers' Bank' or the 'Catholic Bank'. Its final site was also its first.

In those days, the adolescent fig stood at the rear of what had been the Imperial Hotel, a three-storey structure of brick and stone, and less than two years old. In scale and substance, it was a building that bespoke ambition. Who knows what luck – or lack of it – forced the owners to give up their hotel after so short a time? That it acquired some sort of cachet during its brief lifetime, though, is suggested both by its elevation from Imperial to *Grand* Imperial and by its being the lodging-place, in February 1856, of Lola Montez during her Melbourne season. A month later the hotel cleared out and the Colonial Bank took over the building, converting it into chambers that were intended as makeshift but would serve for nearly twenty-five years. In the boardroom, lately Lola's boudoir, the gaps between floor-planks twinkled with sequins and fly-speck glass beads.

Prior to the hotel, the site had been shared by an auctioneer's rooms (at the corner) and a bookseller's. And before that, it was occupied by the store of Campbell and Woolley, merchants. Here it was, in May 1839, with the store yet unroofed, that Father Patrick Geoghegan presided over the first Mass in the Port Phillip District. Some said the fig tree was planted that day; others, that it was meant to mark the centre of the township. For all we know, both claims – or neither – may be true.

In any case, the ancient fig was years-gone by the time the wreckers were given charge of the old Colonial Bank in April 1932. As demolition began, so did the regretful accolades. Whelan's practice of leaving a building's outer walls standing until last turned out to be a lucky thing. While workmen were still knocking out the innards, the Royal Victorian Institute of Architects (RVIA) called for the building's ornate doorway to be spared. The figures of Britannia and Neptune reclined above the arched lintel, supported by a pair of muscular lackeys whose torsos dwindled to vague, leafy scrollwork. The National Bank agreed to the architects' proposal that the doorway be presented to the University of Melbourne, whereupon Whelan's had to dismantle instead of wreck it, numbering each part for reassembly. Britannia

... and two changes-of-address later.

and Neptune evidently missed the cart, but the rest was fitted to the
front of the University's School of Physiology, then under construction. Nestled between hedges and twined about with ivy, the Colonial
Bank porch's new setting was almost rustic compared with its first.
Thirty-five years later, however, came the School of Physiology's turn

for demolition and the historic doorway was again jemmied off, to be re-mounted in 1973 as foot-entrance to the University's new carpark. And there, in its third life, it still stands, hulking and incongruous, giving admittance to a kind of underworld: the eerie concrete vault under the South Lawn.*

The original relocation of the Colonial Bank porch had been the brainchild of J.S. Gawler, a leading member of the RVIA and lecturer in architecture at the University. Inspired by something similar at the École de Beaux Arts in Paris, Gawler envisaged a mortuary for Melbourne buildings, displaying specimens of different styles of architecture, all salvaged from demolition sites. 'When a famous old building in Melbourne was to be done away with,' Gawler explained, 'rather than let its beauty and worth go to the scrap heap, we could rescue it.' Such specimens would inspire and educate future genera-tions of architects, at the same time preserving historical traces of the old city. Gawler's scheme having so much in common with an anatomical museum – all those cadavers and pickled organs – it was wholly apt that the first stray should be grafted onto the School of Physiology.

The next architectural relic to be delivered in numbered pieces to the University was the entire two-storey facade of the Bank of New South Wales, which had fronted Collins Street, near Queen, since 1858. Its architect, Joseph Reed, when he submitted his design for the bank, hadn't long finished putting shape to the Melbourne Public Library (now the State Library of Victoria). Indeed, he must have had libraries on the brain, since the facade he gave to the Bank of New South Wales was inspired by the Library of St Mark's in Venice.

In the lead-up to the bank's demolition by Whelan's in 1933, much was made of the facade: with its intricately carved friezes, columns, and balustrading, it was 'probably the finest piece of stone

---

* Look for it a short distance south-east of the entrance to the Baillieu Library.

work in Melbourne'. This time the 'rescue' was agreed upon well ahead of demolition, though the University had no immediate use for an old bank facade. But it found one. A couple of years later, when the Commerce building – a boxy, pale brick structure – went up, the Italianate sandstone bank facade was stuck on its front. It must have been, if not the first, one of Melbourne's earliest (and clumsiest) ventures into what would later be called 'façadism'. Ill-fitting it was, both in style and dimension, and something like a controversy ensued. Architects – the very profession, if not the very people, whom the Bank and University had been striving to please – condemned the Commerce building as a travesty. And that's pretty much where J.S. Gawler's rescue plan met its end.

A new Bank of New South Wales had risen in Collins Street meanwhile, and was being lauded as 'a far cry from the ornate and rather typical facade of its predecessor'. The sheer marble front soaring above

Only fitting – the bank front on the Commerce Building, University of Melbourne, c.1940.

a mausoleum-like entrance was compared favourably to its neighbour, the neo-Gothic ES&A (now ANZ) Bank at the Queen Street corner, and won for its designers the 1936 street architecture medal. Thirty-eight years later, Whelan's would wreck it in its turn.

'No move has been made to save the columns from the wrecker's pit.' It was 1939 and Whelan's had started on the old Royal Bank. For more than fifty years it had reigned at the Collins and Elizabeth Street corner, with looks and position befitting its name. Curved round two broad street frontages, it seized the eye in every view or postcard. Fourteen heavy columns reached up two storeys from the street, with two more floors above, all crowned by a double-domed turreted turret. In a street full of well-dressed banks, it was the Royal Bank that held pride of place: directly opposite was The Block.

Regal though it was, the building hadn't always been the Royal Bank. It was built in 1885 by the City of Melbourne Bank, then at its most flush and optimistic. It crashed – the bank, not the building – in the early '90s, and the banking chamber went unused until 1903, when the Royal Bank bought the place for a song. As these things go, the Royal Bank itself was eventually acquired by the ES&A which, liking the name, continued to call the building its Royal Bank branch. It kept the name even after Whelan's finished with it and a new bank – plain-faced and tall – went up on the site.

But while the old bank was still under Whelan's blows, the *Herald* lamented that nothing was being done to rescue the facade, or at least some of its columns –

> *Facade after facade is being tossed into the wrecking pit. This is a new phase in the re-building of our city. Until recently facades which had special merit for design, or stonework, were salvaged … [But] it seems that ideas are changing as fast in Melbourne as the appearance of buildings, and there is now less interest in the retention of old architecture. Some architects would not*

retain even a flawless stone example of a past architectural style.
They claim that construction in stone has been ended by the
march of steel and concrete ...

Sure enough, the architects of the new building on the Royal Bank
site had received 'no instructions' about the old columns. And the

The Royal Bank forms a backdrop (and grandstand) to a street procession, c.1900.

University didn't want them. So they were felled and carted off in pieces to the wrecker's pit – or whatever hole needed filling just then.

The original building on the Royal Bank site had been the Port Phillip Bank, built there in 1841. The offices of Melbourne's first locally financed bank were as substantial as any building in the town at that time, being two storeys in stuccoed stone and fenced around with wrought iron. If only the Port Phillip Bank itself had been as sound as its premises; but it collapsed at the end of 1842, leaving shareholders deep out of pocket. The building was auctioned and the following August reopened as the Clarence Family Hotel. The hotel grew over the years to fill out its allotment and never failed to present a welcoming demeanour, with wide verandahs along both its street frontages and six doors opening off the footpath.

There was a story concerning the Clarence Hotel's demolition in 1884, to clear the way for the City of Melbourne Bank, that Jim Whelan – old Jim – told many times over the years. As related to a reporter in 1932, it went like this: 'Once, when demolishing an old hotel where the Royal Bank is now, thirteen sovereigns were found in the first load of material taken away, and every day after that crowds used to follow the carts in the hope of finding gold.' More than that we do not know, but the building's history as a bank-turned-hotel presents plenty of scope for speculation as to the sovereigns' provenance.

Now, 1884 – that was well previous to Jim Whelan's first job as a wrecker, and yet it sounded almost as if he'd been there. When the Clarence Hotel came down, Jim would have been twenty years old and newly arrived in Melbourne. Was he already employed by a timber merchant and making a delivery near by the Clarence? Or had his first job of work in Melbourne – *before* the timber merchant's – been to cart rubble from the demolition site? Or was it just a tale he'd heard round the traps? Whatever the case, you've got to wonder whether Jim Whelan's future career in wrecking might not have taken root, way back then, in the romance of the Clarence Hotel sovereigns.

In 1937, building activity in Melbourne had surpassed the old record of 1929 and, as a corollary, the demand for wrecking was at an all-time high. 'If the speed of present rebuilding does not approach that of New York – now claimed to be reconstructed once every twenty-five years – the wave of replacement here is flooding at a new peak,' said the *Herald*. The days of a wrecker having to pay for the privilege of 'removing' a building were over; but so – for now – were the days when he could take time over the sorting and salvaging of demolition materials.

Whelan the Wrecker's New York counterpart during that period was the Volk family wrecking firm. When the Volk patriarch, old Jake, was profiled by James Thurber for the *New Yorker*, his great regret was having failed to win the demolition contract for the Waldorf Astoria Hotel, future site of the Empire State Building. Like Jim Whelan, Jake Volk was accustomed to paying for salvage rights; the contractor on the Waldorf job, though, was paid nearly a million dollars. In return, he had to remove every trace of the sprawling hotel in less than five months, requiring a crew of more than seven hundred men. Within the allotted time, the famous Waldorf was successfully reduced to 24,321 loads of wreckage, nearly all of which was thrown aboard garbage scows and dumped out at sea. Millions of bricks which, cleaned, would have fetched $60 a load, and hundreds of bathtubs worth $25 apiece at re-sale – all were sacrificed for the sake of speed. At the same time, a technique called 'breaking through' was further cutting the time of New York demolitions. Wrecking crews worked from scaffolding and sent building rubble flying down chutes direct to the basement, where it was loaded by steam-shovel into trucks and thence to the barges. Obviously, it no longer mattered whether a brick hit the ground in one piece or a thousand.

As in New York, Melbourne builders of the '30s were racing to complete projects at record pace, and wreckers had to work ever faster to win and fulfil demolition contracts. 'When you're wrecking you've got to be quick,' said Walter de Leyland, a rival of Whelan's, when he undertook to pull down a four-storey building in Bourke

Street in just seven days. 'If I had quoted three weeks on this job I'd never have got it.'

Salvage may have taken second place to speed, but wrecking methods in Melbourne hadn't come very far. Scaffolding still wasn't in use, nor steam-shovels – not while men were still game to stand on walls while they wrecked them and barrow-hands came so cheap. Whelan's had a couple of trucks by now, but continued to rely on horse and dray for much of their carting.* And old Jim still maintained that the machine had yet to be made that could outdo brute strength. In 1937, his three sons – now aged from thirty to forty, but collectively known as 'the boys' – mounted a challenge to their Pa's philosophy. While he used a gang of forty men to demolish the Advocate Press building, behind St Francis' Church, the boys took a crew less than half that size to bring down Anzac House in Collins Street, for the extension of the T&G Building.† The Advocate Press stood four storeys tall, Anzac House was five, and both buildings had reinforced concrete floors, the first that Whelan's had tackled. Old Jim's forty wreckers relied on the traditional tools of the trade: pick, sledgehammer, and muscle. The boys – young Jim, Tom, and Joe – hired an air-compressor and concrete-drills. This was one race the tortoise didn't win. It took six slogging weeks to wreck the Advocate Press, while Anzac House came down in just four – and at a fraction of the cost.

The first-time listing of 'Whelan the Wrecker', instead of 'J.P. Whelan, timber merchant', in the Melbourne directory for 1938 was the sign of a new order. Old Jim was seventy-four years old and had been outmatched by a jackhammer. And he was dying. Whelan the Wrecker Pty Ltd was registered as a company on 23 February 1938, and the first meeting of directors – Pa and the boys – was held next

---

*   'Horse maintenance' appeared as an expense on Whelan's books until 1948.

†   Back in 1927, Whelan's had wrecked Burke and Wills Chambers for the first stage of the T&G (Temperance & General – a.k.a. the Touch & Go) Building, at the Russell and Collins Street corner.

day at Mount St Evin's Hospital in East Melbourne.* Six days later Whelan the Wrecker lost its founder and chairman, a tumour having proved deadlier than a falling brick.

> ... anticipating that in the near future concrete buildings of Union House would be demolished, we purchased two new concrete breakers (1 diesel, 1 electric). It is only with the aid of these machines that we will be able to demolish Union House in the quick time of 8 weeks.

This is 'young' Jim Whelan, the new head of Whelan the Wrecker, writing to Harry A. Norris in July 1939. As architect for the extension of the G.J. Coles store in Bourke Street, Norris was seeking tenders for the demolition of Union House, at the rear (Little Collins Street end) of the site. Union House, as the *Herald* reported, 'sets new problems as a wrecking job' –

> It is the first large modern steel reinforced concrete building listed for demolition in Melbourne, and neither the architects nor wrecking firms are quite certain how the wrecking will be carried out. Their comment is that the work will be 'tough going'.

But Whelan the Wrecker was ready.

Contemporary wrecks
Royal Insurance Building (414 Collins Street), 1938
Just as Whelan's were pulling down the Royal Insurance Building, Justus Jorgensen was building the Great Hall out at Monsalvat. Jorgensen and

---

*   Whelan's wrecked Mount St Evin's in 1967.

The Gothic windows of the Royal Insurance Building during demolition ...

the Whelans had first had dealings a few years earlier, when he used materials from the wrecker's yard to build the original cottage on his land at Eltham. Now, in tackling the Royal Insurance Building's renowned Domestic Tudor facade ('the most perfect Gothic stonework in Melbourne, excepting St Paul's Cathedral'), the Whelans thought of Jorgensen and offered him the limestone-carved windows, today the showpiece of his Great Hall. Jorgensen and his Monsalvat collaborator, Matcham Skipper, continued their fruitful relationship with Whelan's – and other Melbourne salvage

... and gracing the Great Hall at Monsalvat.

merchants – over the years. And it wasn't only building materials that were superannuated to Monsalvat. More than once, when wrecking a suburban house, Whelan's offered Jorgensen his pick of plants from the garden.

Tatler Theatre, Harrington's and Hotel Australia (262–274 Collins Street), 1938

This great slab of The Block, just east of Block Arcade, was pulled down for the new Hotel Australia (incorporating the Australia Arcade and Government Tourist Bureau). The buildings, dating from the 1870s, had originally housed Mullen's bookshop and circulating library, Fletcher's art gallery, the Café Gunsler, and Glen's music warehouse.

In time, the ultra-elegant Gunsler's became the Vienna Café, and expanded into the first floor of Glen's, next door. In 1916, the café took over the entire five floors of Glen's building and was reborn as the Café Australia. Designed by Walter Burley Griffin, the new interior bristled with fountains, statuary and murals – the artworks, for once, depicting Australian as well as classical subjects. In the Fern Room were landscapes of wind-blown tea-trees and Port Jackson figs carved by Charles Costerman, while the main dining room featured a mural of tall mountain ash. The café became the Hotel Australia in the '20s and, in 1938, was the last of the four frontages demolished.

On the ground floor, the wreckers exposed earlier murals that had been hidden by the decorations of the Burley Griffin era. The walls of the old 'Glen Gallery', originally a piano showroom, had been painted with portraits of 'musical giants of the past'. They saw light again for a few days in May 1938 and then, with the walls, were gone. But behind the main counter of the Government Tourist Bureau, soon to occupy the site, would stretch a new mural – a photo mural – charting the history of Australian transport.

Almost thirty years later, Tom Whelan and his wife Dorothy celebrated their ruby wedding anniversary with a family dinner at the Hotel Australia. Owen, their eldest, booked the Cantala Room for

'Money Miller's billiard room' – the Cantala Room at the Hotel Australia.

the occasion and recalls Tom exclaiming, as he walked through the door, 'Good heavens above! This is old Money Miller's billiard room.' Henry 'Money' Miller, one of the men who made a packet in the boom of the 1880s, had built a mansion out at Caulfield, calling it 'Cantala'. When Whelan's pulled the place down, fifty-odd years later, they'd had instructions to take great care in dismantling the billiard room. The fine timber panelling and fixtures were to be incorporated in the new Hotel Australia, then being built on the site of Whelan's previous demolition. Hence, the Cantala Room.

CHAPTER 7

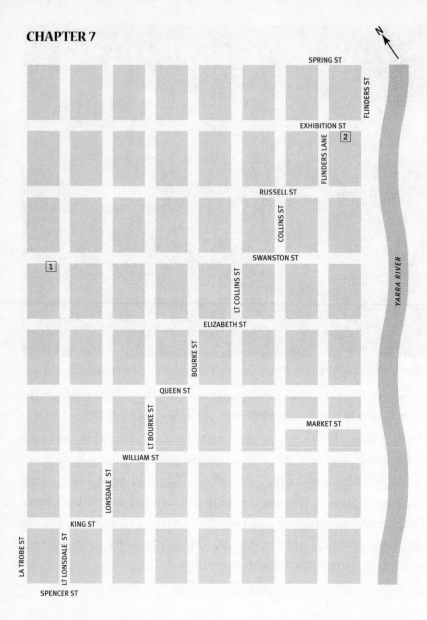

SPRING ST

FLINDERS ST

EXHIBITION ST

FLINDERS LANE

2

RUSSELL ST

COLLINS ST

SWANSTON ST

LT COLLINS ST

YARRA RIVER

1

ELIZABETH ST

BOURKE ST

QUEEN ST

LT BOURKE ST

MARKET ST

WILLIAM ST

LONSDALE ST

KING ST

LA TROBE ST

LT LONSDALE ST

SPENCER ST

1. *Manchester Unity Hall*
2. *Smith's Collins Place cottages*

CHAPTER 7

As if Lives Are Being Lost

Mt Noorat station ~ Manchester Unity Hall ~
Smith's Collins Place cottages ~ SS Orungal

September 1939, the month that war broke out, found a Whelan's gang house-breaking a long way from the city, near Terang in the Western District. The house in question was the magnificent, stone-built homestead on Mt Noorat station. Its widowed owner, living in a cottage on the property, wanted the main house pulled down as she believed it to be cursed. Whelan's obliged, in fact gave £100 for the removal rights. Mt Noorat must have been a trove of salvageable and saleable stuff to have made the job worthwhile when there was no end of lucrative wrecking work to be had in Melbourne. Either that, or the Whelans took the job out of curiosity. Old Jim had said he'd never dug up a ghost – would they?

With the Second World War came an intermission in the making-over of Melbourne. Demolition was at odds with the exigencies of the war effort. With buildings, as with everything, it was a case of making use of what you had.

Tutter Ryan (foreground) demolishing King's Hotel, Russell Street, 1950s (Syd Clarkson in background).

Ten years after the war began and four after it ended, a journalist could write: 'Passing a partially demolished building recently I noticed a sign which reminded me of the dear past: WHELAN THE WRECKER IS HERE.' *The dear past.* It was Whelan's turn for a taste of redundancy. (But it was *just* a taste. Their brassy slogan was lodged in the Melburnian cerebrum too deep for forgetting. While the real thing may have been practically unseen in its native place during the war years, the victorious WHELAN THE WRECKER WAS HERE found utterance a world away, scratched into the rubble of Bardia and Tobruk and emblazoning walls in bombed-out German cities – the conqueror's cry of the Melbourne-bred soldier.)

Before the war, with city wrecking at its peak, Whelan's payroll had run to nearly a hundred men. By 1941, only a handful of employees remained, besides the three company directors: the Whelan 'boys', whose inheritance the business had been. (Their father's property holdings had gone to his three daughters; back in 1938, it had looked like a fair split of assets.) The directors' salaries charted the course of Whelan the Wrecker's sagging fortunes during the '40s. From £15 in 1939, each brother's weekly stipend sank in 1942 to less than half that – £7 5s.– at which meagre level it stayed until well after the war.

Some of Whelan's men joined up. Jack 'Tutter' Ryan was one. A neighbour and friend of the Whelans all his life (he was the same age as Tom), Tutter had joined the firm in the upswing of the depression. He was an expert rigger and came to Whelan's direct from working on the Shrine of Remembrance. Now nearly forty, Tutter joined up because, he said, a soldier's pay was better and more regular than what he could make with Whelan's. Besides, should he meet with misfortune on active service, the government would look after his family; the wrecking trade offered no such security. Jim and Tom Whelan's boys – all aged ten or under – were allowed up on the scaffolding of the half-built (new) Royal Bank, to watch Tutter march up Collins Street with the first contingent of the 2nd AIF.

Within a year of the war's commencement, building activity and its corollary, demolition, dwindled to almost nothing. In the early months of 1940, though, before manpower and materials ran thin, there was still a number of building projects underway in Melbourne. Most had been well-advanced before war came along, but one, at least, was just getting off the ground. That wealthy friendly society, the Manchester Unity Order of Oddfellows, had plans for a second tall building in Swanston Street. Since 1863 the Order had owned land opposite the Museum and Public Library. Now the old hall and shops thereon were to be replaced by a thirteen-storey building, designed by Marcus Barlow on creamy, curved and modern lines. It would be called the MU Oddfellows Building, to distinguish it from the Manchester Unity Building, Barlow's organ-piped masterpiece on the old Stewart Dawson's corner.

Before the Oddfellows built their rambling rooms for pool and billiards, eating and meeting, the site just north of Little Lonsdale Street had housed the John Knox School, adjacent to its namesake church, for the children of dissenting Presbyterians. The school gave way in 1863 to the MU Hall; the church's congregation dissolved in 1879. Only Knox Lane and Knox Place, two of the laneways that varisected the block behind, kept the old name afloat – and still do, insofar as the developers of Melbourne Central have suffered them to remain.

After the three solid-brick storeys of the MU Hall came down in February–March of 1940, it would be more than ten years before Whelan's next city job of any consequence.

A rare sight during wartime – Whelan's sign (and truck) at the Manchester Unity Hall, Swanston Street.

Of course, there's consequence … and consequence. James Alexander Smith's three-roomed cottage in Collins Place would, by modern reckoning, have been a building of too much consequence for pulling down. But in 1941 things were different.

James Smith's was one of a pair of cottages at 23–25 Collins Place. For about eighty years, until the 1960s, the lower end of Exhibition Street – between Flinders and Collins – went by the name Collins Place. It looks as if the intention, at the latter end of the nineteenth century, had been to distance the neighbourhood from the taint of a Stephen Street* address, imbuing it instead with some Collins Street

---

*   Though Stephen Street was officially renamed Exhibition in the 1880s, in an attempt to shake off the street's whorish reputation, it took decades for the new name to catch on.

prestige. James Smith had lived there long before it was Collins Place. His home from infancy to late middle age was a large, free-standing house at 15 Stephen Street, set around with a garden. In 1920 the bachelor Smith moved next-door-but-one, to the tiny conjoined cottage at 25 Collins Place.

Replacing his old home, and hulking over his new one, was a four-storey underwear factory. If he felt a pang at the disappearance of his childhood home, there'd have been a sense of satisfaction too as he watched the new building's steel frame go up and the floors of reinforced concrete dropped in by crane. For James Smith, an engineer and son of an engineer, had been one of the four experts who'd framed the Melbourne Building Act of 1916, giving the green-light to the new ways of building. In 1912, he'd been a member of the three-man panel that selected Walter Burley Griffin's as the prize-winning design for Canberra. Though he lacked a university training, Smith's research and innovations in the field of steam turbines had earned him international regard, and he was council president of the Working Men's College (later Royal Melbourne Institute of Technology). His working life had begun on Melbourne's railways and, in the '20s, he became the first to call for the roofing-over of the Jolimont railyards, with whose insalubrity, as a lifelong resident of Collins Place, he'd have been well acquainted.

Smith was fifty-eight years old when he moved house. As his busy life wound down, 'the picturesque, bearded old figure' leaning in his cottage doorway became a familiar part of the Collins Place streetscape. Yet few passers-by knew of his achievements – a career in engineering, however luminous, was no passport to celebrity. James Smith died in April 1940. Eighteen months later his cottage and its pair were in thrall to the wreckers.

But if Smith hadn't been much recognised in his later years, his cottage had in its. Leading up to Melbourne's centenary celebrations of 1934–35, history buffs had mounted a hunt for the city's oldest building. It was a quest that, though much squabbled over in

Nobody home – Whelan's wreck
Smith's cottages.

the newspaper letters pages and elsewhere, was never satisfactorily concluded.* However, the Collins Place cottages ranked high among contenders, it being generally agreed that there was 'a possibility – even a strong probability' that they were the oldest remaining structures in Melbourne. That the occupant of one of them should have helped shape the city's steel-and-concrete building code and embraced Griffin's modernity seemed only to heighten the cottages' antiquity.

Built in 1844 by a man called Leach (or Leage), in their early days they were used as commercial premises. One was a draper's shop, the other an umbrella maker's. Each cottage originally comprised two brick rooms with detached kitchen at the rear. The space between house and kitchen was eventually closed in; otherwise nothing much changed in ninety-seven years. Then everything changed.

Whelan's first unpicked the slate roof and verandah, then let themselves in through the ceilings. It's a pretty safe bet that, in those days of war-time efficiencies, every brick and board and worn stone step would have gone back to the yard for recycling. In fact, the Collins Place cottages would have been knocked down with something close to tenderness – and not just because of the scarcity of salvage and (in all probability) a desire to string the job out. Over the years, each of the Whelans would confess to feeling sad at wrecking an old house. It was the one misgiving to which Owen Whelan would own up. 'You feel as if lives are being lost.'

---

* La Trobe's Cottage, then still situated on its original site at Jolimont, must surely have been the strongest candidate.

Not only were 23–25 Collins Place perhaps the oldest buildings in Melbourne in 1941, they were also among the city's last remaining houses. While the surviving grand doctors' residences at the upper end of Collins Street had been converted into medical rooms and offices, the cottages of early Melbourne had all but disappeared.

It rather looks as if the owner of the Collins Place cottages, a life assurance company, had just been waiting for James Smith to die. City land values – and taxes – were too high to support cottage dwellings, that was the problem. And so they were demolished, even though the owner couldn't hope to rebuild on the allotment until after the war. In fact, twenty years later the site was still empty. Like a rebuke.

As the war lengthened, demolition work became so scant that Whelan's were forced to look off-shore, securing salvage rights to the burnt-out wreck of the *SS Orungal* that had come to grief on a reef off Barwon Heads late in 1940. One Sunday, when Tom Whelan and his crew were below-deck unfitting a boiler, the *Orungal* was comprehensively strafed by a RAAF fighter-pilot on a practice flight. Even without the hazard of friendly fire, salvaging the *Orungal* was a tricky job, reliant on tides and weather. Whelan's retrieved what they could during the lean years of the '40s and left the rest as a low-tide landmark.

War-time machinery shortages led to another, more lasting diversification in Whelan the Wrecker's business. Though Whelan's had little use themselves for those air compressors they'd bought back in the burly days of the late '30s, there emerged a steady sideline in hiring them out. Soon Whelan's set up a separate plant-hire section, which bought up more and more equipment to meet the demand and branched off, in 1950, as Wreckair.

When, after the war, wrecking work started to come Whelan's way again, it mainly called for knocking down the blast-walls that had been built around factories and fuel stores as an air-raid precaution. Then the new decade flicked over: shortages and restrictions eased, the building industry began to thaw and demolition to gather momentum.

Sensing that he and his brothers might at last see their inheritance turned to account, Jim Whelan felt emboldened to gloat: 'Melbourne's skyline is on its way to becoming a memory.'

I CAN SEE NOTHING BEAUTIFUL …

What's Melbourne going to look like in the post-war years? A lot better, we hope. Take a look around our principal streets today … and you see a curious mixture ranging (almost) from the wattle-and-daub of the pioneers to Hollywood gone mad.

~ CLIVE TURNBULL IN THE *HERALD*, AUGUST 1945

With the constrictions of the war effort still biting, the late '40s and early '50s were a time for civic dreaming and pent-up scheming. The Herald's commentator on architecture, Robin Boyd, denounced 'the great wasteland of the heart of Melbourne', causing the City Development Association – newly formed – to yelp that architects' offices were bulging with plans for new city projects, none of which could yet be built.

Melbourne was in the doldrums and civic pride 'wilting', the Lord Mayor conceded. As one ameliorating measure, his council mooted a new town hall and began preliminary investigations for a site big enough for a public square as well. One candidate was the ten acres bounded by Swanston, La Trobe, Elizabeth and Lonsdale streets. True, the whole area was built-over and largely in private hands, but, with the exception of two churches, there was potential for acquisition. And demolition. At the city council's request, Jim Whelan paced out the site one day, putting a price on every structure's head: 'M. Unity [the MU Oddfellows building, less

*then ten years old] £75,000', 'Empire Hotel £1500', 'Shot Tower £2500',
and so on. By Jim's figuring, Whelan's could wreck the lot for £275,000.
It never happened.*

*The report of the Melbourne Metropolitan Planning Scheme, in 1954,
envisaged a modern town hall and civic square at the top end of Bourke
Street, facing Parliament House. A symmetrical array of flat-faced tower
blocks would complete the proposed government precinct. The historic
Princess Theatre and Windsor Hotel, adjacent, were given grudging space
in the concept plan, with the proviso that, 'when rebuilt, as some day they
must be, [they] can be brought into architectural harmony with the surroundings'. None of that ever happened either.*

*But the Lord Mayor had a hand in one initiative that did come off. While
Jim Whelan wrecked the shot tower in his mind's eye, the city fathers were
mounting their bid for the 1956 Olympics. Preparations for the Games
further delayed post-war development of the inner city, as materials
and manpower were diverted to the construction of venues and athletes'
accommodation. The Olympics themselves, though, gave Melbourne a jolt
of ambition, whetted by self-consciousness, as it felt the world's gaze more
keenly than at any time since the 1880s.*

*Before the Olympics there was the Royal Tour of 1954. Australia had
invited Princess Elizabeth but, thanks to luck and parental mortality,
scored its first-ever visit by a reigning monarch. Preparations for the
Queen's visit, in Melbourne as elsewhere, mostly amounted to a drive
for civic neatness and displayed more the complacence of an amplified
Empire Day than a striving for worldliness. This was nowhere better seen
than in the case of Melbourne's verandahs. Now, to be fair to the young
Queen, the verandahs' doom was not directly attributable to her visit;
rather, it was characteristic of ongoing efforts to render Australian cities
tidy and uncolonial.*

*The municipal campaign against pillar verandahs in Melbourne streets
dated back more than thirty years. It had originated in the early '20s,
when a government minister in a roadster had a run-in with a Collins
Street verandah post and vowed to legislate the elimination of the species.*

This proving impossible, the minister handed the baton to the city council which passed a by-law stipulating that new verandahs must be of the self-supporting, cantilever type. In fact, the council went so far as to insist that any new building in the city's main streets must be furnished with

One long verandah – Elizabeth Street, looking north, in 1916. You could walk the length of the city during a downpour and hardly get wet.

a cantilever verandah, a ruling opposed by the Institute of Architects. Compared with other main streets, Collins was relatively 'unmarred' by projecting verandahs, and the architects were keen that it should stay that way. They wanted a ban on any new verandahs in Collins Street, with the ultimate aim that 'this picturesque street should be kept free in its entirety from any superfluous obstructions beyond the building line'.

But the city council persevered with its cantilever crusade and in 1935 framed a by-law requiring the abolition of pillar verandahs from the main city streets within ten years. The war got in the way of progress, however, so that when the deadline arrived there was hardly any reduction in the thicket of 'anachronistic' verandah posts nudging city kerb-lines. The council granted three years' grace, then three more. Still no one took it very seriously. Then, with the Olympics in the offing, came one last stay of execution: all pillar verandahs were to be gone by the end of June 1954.

There'd always been verandahs on Melbourne's streets, even when the footpaths they'd straddled were non-existent. In a climate tending to extremes of blinding heat and mizzle, pioneer storekeepers had been quick to erect rough, canvas-draped shelters at their shopfronts. An 1859 by-law regulated verandahs for the first time and, from about 1870 onwards, decorative cast-iron pillars roofed with curved corrugated iron were the Melbourne shop-verandah standard. If there were complaints about verandahs in those days, it was usually because their posts afforded lounging-props for larrikins and other low-life.

By the mid-twentieth century, the pillar verandahs edging the main city streets were either 'picturesque' or 'unsightly', depending on your perspective. Following the city council's 1951 edict, a trickle – no more – of verandah-wrecking jobs came Whelan's way. In the final months of grace, though, the council made it plain that this time there would be no extensions, no reprieve: 'They must come down – all of them – by June 30.' A small group of preservation-minded citizens raised their voices in opposition as the fatal date drew near. Many of them were architects, some of whom, years before, had campaigned to have Collins Street cleared of verandahs. This time round, Robin Boyd argued that the verandahs 'gave

Melbourne something that most other cities in the world lacked'. A fellow architect, Sir Harold Gengault Smith, was also a city councillor (of thirty years' standing), but condemned his colleagues as 'pig-headed … vandals' who were 'ignorant of aesthetic values' – 'Why, they've just built a lavatory right in front of Government House.'

> The whole argument [said the *Herald*] upsets a popular
> impression that in conflicts of this sort society is cleanly divided
> into two groups: practical, solid citizens on the one hand, and
> irresponsible dreamers of beauty on the other. This time it is all
> mixed up.

The 'long-haired people' (the Herald's *term) advocating the retention of city verandahs were concerned not just with aesthetics, but also with practical matters of shade and shelter. With their verandahs gone, north-facing shops and restaurants would swelter in summer. And who would stop to window-shop on a wet day? To the contention that existing pillar verandahs could simply be replaced by the cantilever type, braced onto building fronts, the council's opponents argued that the masonry of many older buildings was too weak for that.*

'This week is the City Council's Roman Holiday, as the street verandahs go tumbling all over town.' Whelan's and their rivals were flat-out as the deadline approached. Even so, come the end of June 1954, a few pillar verandahs still stood. Chief among them were those fronting the Oriental Hotel and Ogg's chemist shop, both at the leafy end of Collins Street. Their owners and defenders appealed to the council's Building Regulations Committee to make an exception of these two beautiful cast-iron verandahs. But the Committee was unmoved. 'I can see nothing beautiful about these pillar verandahs,' said Councillor W.P. Barry. 'Ogg's and all the rest of them are dangerous. People have been killed because of these pillars.' When pressed for details of any such fatality, Councillor Barry pointed to an incident twenty-nine years earlier.

A search of the Herald's files for 1925 found that, sure enough, several people had been injured (not killed) outside the Hoyts de Luxe Theatre in Bourke Street by the fall of … a cantilever verandah! In those days, crowds watching a street parade didn't only cram upper-storey windows, but spilled out onto verandah roofs. When the Hoyts cantilever gave way under their weight, the jazz-age verandah surfers had leapt onto the adjacent Theatre Royal pillar verandah, which stood the strain and saved them.

But in 1954 the city council did not blink and, after a few more months of argy-bargy, Ogg's and the Oriental Hotel verandahs were pulled down, robbing pedestrians and tram-travellers of their only shelter between Russell and Spring streets. Ogg's verandah was reassembled at the University of Melbourne, over the entrance to University House, but the Oriental's came down for good. The hotel's manager considered the whole business 'too stupid for words'. It was true, he said, that cars sometimes hit the verandah posts, but the vehicle always came off second-best. The verandah was as sturdy as the day it was built. And he had more reason than most to be aggrieved at the loss of his verandah: as the trademark of the Oriental, its image was embossed on every sheet of hotel stationery and every cup and plate in the dining room.

When the slaughter was over and the cast-iron corpses cold, the Herald reported an item of interest from a recent number of the Illustrated London News. To coincide with the Queen's visit to Melbourne, the popular English weekly had run a photo-spread depicting the city's architectural beauties. And which beauty had featured at the head of the page? None other than Ogg's verandah, with a caption extolling the 'sophisticated urban air enhanced by the approach'.

1955 was the year that Melbourne architects brought their plans out of drawers, the first year since the war not dominated by house-building. 'In all our history,' said the Herald in review, 'it was probably the year of greatest construction and greatest destruction.' It was the year that the city burst its ceiling and that Whelan the Wrecker started felling its oats.

Just down the road from the naked front of Ogg's, at 100 Collins Street, arose Gilbert Court, Melbourne's first new city office building in fifteen years. Its soaring curtain walls of glass and aluminium, modelled on those of the UN Building in New York, were a first for Australia. People called it a 'glass house' and understood that this was what the future looked like. Many, though, were far from impressed with the outlook. Plans for a second glass house in Collins Street were denounced by the artist Norman Lindsay as 'a final triumph to modernistic art, with its slogan of death to all beauty'. Robin Boyd countered that, 'believe it or not', some people found 'this new sterile simplicity ... as refreshing as a glass of iced water' – and, 'Those who argue that iced water is a dull drink, at least must admit that it is a suitable one for office hours.'

It was Boyd, too, who wrote in July 1955 that 'the red tape which restricted Melbourne to 132-foot building-height is broken'. The red-tape buster was another glass house, the 20-storey ICI House, which was commenced the following year at the city's eastern edge. Submitting their plans to the city council early in 1955, the architects had sought approval for a building of 203 feet (62 m) – 71 feet taller than the long-standing height limit. What the council eventually approved was a building of 230 feet (70 m) – 98 feet (30 m) above the limit. The discrepancy in the figures was blamed on an error by a town hall typist; but, whatever the process, the deed was done. ICI's architects simply added two storeys to their plans and the height limit for Melbourne buildings was broken for good.

Of course, before the 'cloud-kisser' went up at the corner of Nicholson and Albert streets, something else had to go. Whelan's wrecked a stand of three boarding houses there: a two-storey pair in bluestone, built before the gold rushes, and a three-storey job dating from the early days of reinforced concrete, which took some pulling down. Folklore relates that the assemblage had been inhabited largely by prostitutes, besides being the favoured digs of performers from the nearby Princess Theatre.

For all its radical verticality, ICI House contained no more floor space than the old maximum-height buildings of ten and twelve storeys. What it did have that they lacked, though, were lawn and gardens, carparking, and floods of natural light ... as well as windows that leaked and cracked *and popped out for no good reason. From 1958, the 'grey grid tower' of ICI House dominated the Melbourne skyline, taking over from the 25-year-old Manchester Unity Building the role of 'city capital'.*

CHAPTER 8

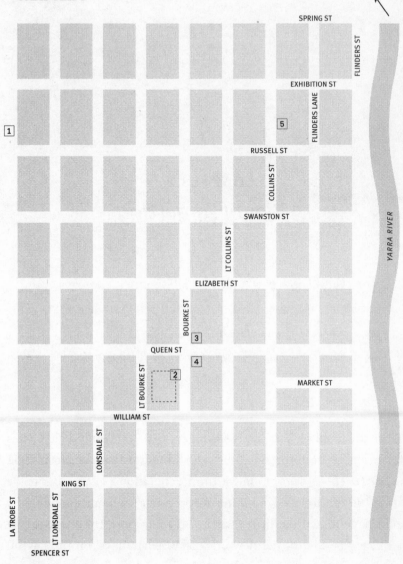

1. 64 La Trobe Street
2. St Patrick's Hall–Goldsbrough Mort
3. Salisbury Building
4. Britannia Hotel
5. Melbourne Mansions

CHAPTER 8
A Way of Forgetting

*64 La Trobe Street ~ St Patrick's Hall ~ insurance company
brigade's fire tower ~ Melbourne's first synagogue ~ Redmond
Barry's cottage ~ Thompson's 'Cottage by the Sea' ~
Goldsbrough Mort ~ Salisbury Building, Britannia Hotel,
Melbourne Mansions*

The dividend on Whelan the Wrecker's 10,000 family-held shares increased from three to fourteen shillings a share between 1952 and 1956. Those years found a third generation of Whelans ready to ride the upturn in demolition work. Some of them undoubtedly would have joined the firm earlier, had there been the work to pay for them. The first of the new crop of Whelan 'boys' on the payroll was Tom's third son, Myles, who enlisted as a desk-bound wrecker in 1953, at the age of twenty-one – 'desk-bound' under doctor's orders, as he was recovering from TB. He wasn't confined to a desk for long, though, but soon was out and about, observing how his Uncle Jim priced a job, supervising on-site, directing scrap and salvage, and gen- erally learning the trade. And Myles always carried a camera with him, to record the stages in a building's Whelanisation. His eldest brother Owen, when he signed on three years later, did the same – only Owen's snaps were all lost when Tom over-tidied his son's shed one day in the late '60s.

By 1957, the business was robust enough to employ Myles, Owen, and Jim's son, Tony, as junior management on the wrecking side, while Tom's youngest, Des, went to Wreckair, the plant-hire division. Their fathers and Uncle Joe – none of them yet sixty – were still running the show, though poor health prevented Joe from taking a very active role. Then there was *their* cousin, Tom Whelan – or Long Tom, as he was called to avoid confusion.

Since old Jim (his uncle's) time, Long Tom had been in charge of Whelan's yard in Sydney Road, Brunswick. Him it was who, at a glance, could assess to within inches the linear yardage of a tangled heap of floorboards or roofing iron. Long Tom never could refuse a priest or nun a favour: whole truckloads of building stuffs went off to this parish or that convent, with never a bill to follow. And it wasn't just with the ordained that he was a soft-touch; he'd extend credit to just about anyone. A week might go by with hardly a tenner in the till, only a crowded slate to show for Long Tom's many transactions at the yard.

As business picked up, Whelan's workforce grew. Jim Parker, who started with them in 1950, was one of the first new hands to be taken on. His father George, an ace block-and-tackle man, had worked for old Jim Whelan during the '20s and '30s. For pocket-money, as a boy, Jim Parker used to ride his bike to a demolition site on a Friday afternoon and collect the gang's tools, returning with them, sharpened, early on Monday. It had been a wobbly old ride to and from the blacksmith's, with the picks tied across his handlebars. Another to join Whelan's in the '50s was Trevor Turner. He first worked with them on a job in Launceston (an early interstate contract), but he and the Wrecker suited one another so well that he moved across to Victoria. His brother Kevin followed soon after, and the pair of them remained with Whelan's until Whelan's was no more.

Many of the Wrecker's regular workers from the mid-'50s onwards were migrants, mainly Italians who at that time were settling in the Brunswick–Carlton area. Tutter Ryan had made it home from the war and was back with Whelan's. And despite his reputation as a hard man – a drinker and brawler – Tutter had a big heart and deep-grained sense of fairness that made him readier than some to accept their new Australian workmates. Out on a job, one of the gang complained to him, 'Now that they're here, the least they can do is speak our bloody language.'

Tutter, who, as a prisoner of war, had been put to work on a German farm, retorted, 'Well, I was in Germany for two-and-a-half effin' years, and the only thing I learned to say was "*Ja*".'

The noise of wrecking is also the sound of progress.
~ *HERALD*, 1958

In December 1955, while their 'panzer division'– armed with diesel compressors, jackhammers, front-end loaders, mobile cranes, and something really new: an oxygen-powered industrial 'lance' – was bombarding the buildings on the ICI site, Whelan's also had their

shingle out a couple of blocks away, at 64 La Trobe Street. Another example of that threatened species, the city house, it was singled out in its last days as the 'loveliest' of all the small buildings in Melbourne. But it had outlived its aesthetic and now was bovvered by the Russell Street police headquarters on the one hand and an undistinguished concrete box on the other. 'It stood in

'*A small god among everyday mortals*' –
64 La Trobe Street, with the wreckers in.

hideous surroundings,' wrote Dorian Le Gallienne, the *Argus*'s arbiter of good taste, 'like a small god among everyday mortals.' Others paid tribute, as it fell, to the house's 'fine balustrade', 'beautifully proportioned windows', and 'generous hospitable entrance' – all of which 'charming' features could be had for a song from the wreckers.

> ... *bits of joinery, ironwork and trimmings are going almost for*
> *the taking. You can pick them up for shillings: Melbourne's past*
> *a bargain; the nation's heritage selling out cheap!*

Robin Boyd called it a 'mad destructive spree'. Before the war, Sydney had been in the throes of its own 'architectural massacre', out of which, by way of reaction, the New South Wales National Trust had emerged. Now support was growing for the creation of a National Trust to 'guard' historic buildings in Victoria. 'Without getting dewy-eyed ... [and] with every wish to encourage normal progress,' explained Robin Boyd, 'many people and several organisations are intent on stopping thoughtless and irresponsible destruction.'

Not that Boyd or anyone else was really talking up Victoria's historic architecture. Comparing it with its stately Georgian counterparts in New South Wales and Tasmania, the best that Boyd could muster in support of Melbourne's 'violent' architectural heritage was that 'Really the only thing to recommend it is that it happens to be ours.' But, like others, he feared that the uniqueness of the city's 'vivid Victorianism' – 'our heirlooms of Victoria's fabulously gilded youth' – might be valued only after it was all gone. A branch of the National Trust was duly formed in Melbourne in 1956, with the aim of preserving historic buildings, relics and sites of national importance in Victoria.

Aims are one thing; the means are another. Victoria's National Trust, in its early years, lacked the backing of planning legislation and by-laws, making it powerless to halt, or even stumble, the relentless push of progress. The Trust began by compiling an inventory of historic buildings, identifying the most precious and alerting government, developers, and the general public to their significance. Beyond community education and offering (usually) unsought advice, however, it was helpless to affect what was kept and what lost. Often, faced with the destruction of one of its listed buildings, the Trust's most forceful suggestion was that the void be marked by a commemorative plaque: *'On this site formerly stood ...'*, that kind of thing.

❧

Memorials are a way of forgetting ...

~ IAIN SINCLAIR*

A call for a plaque was the National Trust's response to the announcement, early in 1957, that St Patrick's Hall, at 470 Bourke Street, was soon to be demolished. Architectural merit was, in those days, practically the sole decider of an old building's significance. Supposedly lacking that quality and having only 'historical associations' to recommend it, St Patrick's Hall was deemed 'not worth preserving'.

Taking up space on the brow of the Bourke Street West hill, between Queen and William, just two years earlier St Patrick's Hall had been named among Melbourne's historic buildings 'too useful or picturesque' to be endangered. It wasn't really picturesque; 'gloomy' was how most people described it. Nor was the old hall so useful – it housed a ballet school – that its owners, the National Bank, would hesitate to sell it as the site for a nine-storey glass house.

'Another Melbourne land-mark is about to fall to the wrecker's axe,' reported the *Herald*, 'and Melbourne just couldn't care less.' Or could it? Owen Whelan remembers a phone call from the site architects – it must have been in June 1957: 'They've started their stirrings, so for God's sake get inside and do as much damage as you can before anyone wakes up.' 'And,' says Owen, 'that's about what

---

* *Lights Out for the Territory*, Granta, London, 1997 – Sinclair is a chronicler of the contemporary and passing London scene.

'They've started their stirrings ...'
– Whelan's began work at the rear
of St Patrick's Hall, only putting their
sign up when it was too late to halt
the demolition.

happened.' Whelan's started work at the rear of the building so that, by the time demolition was apparent from the street, it was too late.

The cause of the cut-short stirrings would've been the building's plaque-worthy 'historical associations'. Gloomy old St Patrick's Hall, you see, had housed Victoria's first parliament – or, to be exact, its first Legislative Council. When the Port Phillip District separated from New South Wales in 1851, the new colony of Victoria had only limited self-government: an upper house, precariously supported. St Patrick's Hall was leased for use as the legislative chamber.

Built for the St Patrick's Society of Australia Felix between 1847–49, the hall had been used as the society's meeting place and as a school for Irish children. It had also been the venue, in January 1851, of the Victorian Industrial Society's inaugural exhibition – the first of those pageants of produce and manufacturing which, thirty years on, gave the Royal Exhibition Building its reason to exist.

St Patrick's Hall was set well back from the street in those days, with an unfenced square of garden, beloved of stray goats, on either side of the entrance. Being nearly new and the most capacious hall in Melbourne, it was an obvious choice for the colonial government's first home. Apart from its size, though, and 'some slight effort at ornamentation over the doorway', the two-storey hall had been built to a fairly utilitarian standard and so required a good deal of titivation before it was fit to serve the legislature.

A CITY LOST AND FOUND

The colony of Victoria was proclaimed on 1 July 1851 – with a Grand Separation Ball held at St Patrick's Hall – but it was November before the Legislative Council was elected and ready to sit. By then, the hall's ground floor had been converted into offices and the first floor fitted out as the government chamber. The only windows upstairs were four small fanlights with panes coloured red, blue and white, but – in a first for Australia – a section of the roof had been replaced with glass. High up on the two end walls were galleries, hardly bigger than window boxes, for members of the public and press. At least one existing fixture of the hall was retained: a splendid chair of mahogany and velvet, formerly used by the president of the St Patrick's Society, became the Speaker's chair.*

As well as £300 a year in rent (rising to £1,500 in 1854) and the improvements to its premises, the St Patrick's Society gained the satisfaction of having the government meet in a building inscribed with the words: 'Dedicated to the memory of Ireland'. A bitter satisfaction, it must have been, leading up to and following the clash at Eureka stockade between government forces and (predominantly Irish) gold diggers. Most of the honourable members who sat upstairs in St Patrick's Hall during the fiery, riven months of 1854 into 1855 supported the subjugation of the diggers. John O'Shanassy, a committee-man of the St Patrick's Society, was one of only two legislative councillors – John Pascoe Fawkner was the other – who (fairly) consistently took the diggers' side.

Victoria was granted self-government in 1855 and the following year elected its first full parliament. Construction of a purpose-designed Parliament House at the head of Bourke Street began early in 1856 and the main sections were ready just in time for the first sitting of both houses in November. When their hall was handed back the following March, members of the St Patrick's Society found it 'an

---

* Presented to Parliament by the St Patrick's Society in 1951, the chair now stands in Queen's Hall, Parliament House.

122

edifice so altered' – that is, improved – 'as to be unknown, except by the outer brick shell'. Moreover, with the money paid by the government in rent, the Society added a colonnaded three-storey stone frontage, bringing the building out to the streetline.

By the end of the nineteenth century, the St Patrick's Society was past its prime and its hall in decline. Melbourne had halls aplenty then, and St Patrick's was little in demand. After renovations in the '20s, it stood unaltered until it stood no more.

But there was nothing there [Owen Whelan recalls] to suggest that it was the site of the first Legislative Council. [...] It was an old, tizzy, sort of a half-baked dance hall arrangement. And very cheap construction. So you wouldn't really ... the association was important, but not the building. I didn't feel any pangs about it.

As St Patrick's Hall came down, Melburnians 'rediscovered' the fire watchtower that stood behind it. A ubiquitous 132 feet tall, it had been not so much hidden as forgotten.

Before the formation of the government-run Metropolitan Fire Brigade in 1891, responsibility for firefighting in Melbourne had been shared – sometimes brawled over – by volunteer brigades and one funded by the insurance companies. The tower behind St Patrick's Hall was part of the insurance brigade's fire station, built in 1883. Back then, the glassed-in lookout on top had commanded the highest vantage-point in Melbourne, encompassing the whole of the city and suburbs – all but a blind-spot to the west, where the dome of the new law courts on William Street blocked the view.

The watchtower was at the rear of the fire station, a long, two-storey brick building that fronted Little Bourke Street at the corner of St Patrick's Alley. The fire engines were kept in the main building, while the horses that pulled them were stabled at the foot of the alley. The city's only paid firefighters (volunteers were recompensed in beer) had their lodgings above the stables.

The whole complex was still intact when Whelan's exposed it to Bourke Street view in 1957, though it had long been occupied by a printing works. After 1891 the station had come under the control of the Metropolitan Fire Brigade, but had been decommissioned in 1919 when the Brigade became motorised. Even before that, the view from the tower had begun to be cut off by tall buildings. With the replacement of St Patrick's Hall by a glass house, the watchtower not only lost most of its remaining prospect but was itself lost from view. Five years later, the old landmark 'found' by Whelan's was lost to the wreckers for good.

The neighbourhood in which St Patrick's Hall and the fire tower stood and fell was much disturbed by Whelan's over the course of sixty years.

An early casualty was Melbourne's first synagogue, pulled down in 1929 right alongside St Patrick's Hall at 472–474 Bourke Street. With a synagogue in East Melbourne and another just completed in Toorak Road, this one was surplus to requirements.

St Patrick's Hall (right) and the synagogue (left), with the fire tower visible behind.

The Bourke Street synagogue in the course of demolition, 1924.

The original synagogue – its foundation stone, like its neighbour's, laid in 1847 – was set towards the rear of the block and had, for years, been in use as a Hebrew school. Also like St Patrick's, the synagogue had improved on its beginnings, building forwards on the block to better present itself to the street. Now its Parthenonic front – 'a quiet but agreeable feature of the ecclesiastic architecture of the city' – rose at just a short remove from the Bourke Street footway.

Before there was a synagogue, Melbourne's Jewish community had met for worship every Saturday at Cheapside House, the Collins Street draper's store of David and Solomon Benjamin. In 1844, the congregation applied for a land grant and was given its choice of unsold town allotments. Officials at the Colonial Office in London, when they learnt of the grant, opposed it as unlawful: under the Church Act, they pointed out, only Christian faiths were eligible for government aid. But slow ships and the quill meant that the objection came too late: the land was granted, the synagogue already built.

The original was small, brick and stuccoed, and was intended from the start to serve as a school once a larger synagogue was built. That came about sooner than expected. With the gold rushes a cash tsunami for Melbourne's Jewish – and gentile – merchants, work could begin in 1853 on a grand new synagogue. Labour being scarce and costly, construction took several years and £14,000; but when finished, the synagogue on the Bourke Street hill was hailed as a masterpiece.

When Whelan's reduced it to a 'substantial pile of bluestone' in 1929, they had orders to save some of the synagogue's fixtures for presentation as memorial pieces to its former congregation. The school building – the original synagogue – was pulled down too, and in place of the lot was built a sandstone-clad office block of five storeys for the Equity Trustees Company. The lane on its west side, which fed the building daylight, was signposted Little Queen Street. For twenty-odd years from the 1880s it had been Bourke Lane; before that it was Synagogue Place. Now only the small print on the street sign – LITTLE QUEEN STREET FORMERLY SYNAGOGUE PLACE – hints at what went before.

The time was up, in 1924, for a low-slung brick cottage that stood way back from the footpath at 494 Bourke Street. For about ten years it had been hidden by an advertising hoarding, a high fence having done the same job for years before that. The cottage had last popped into public view for a short time in 1912 when an old iron building was pulled down on the block adjoining. Soon after, the cottage was branded unfit for human habitation and looked a sure candidate for demolition. But it was left upright, behind the hoarding, and used for storing a secondhand dealer's surplus. Hard against its west side pressed the three-storey bulk of a hardware merchant's – originally a tobacco works and latterly the Church of England's mission house. The approach to the cottage was via a dirt lane off Little Bourke Street, straggling through factory and warehouse yards to end at the cottage door. The old backyard was crowded in by industrial outbuildings, but spreading over a foundry shed was an aged mulberry tree, the last vestige of a garden.

There were panes missing from the cottage's paint-box windows and slates gone from the roof. Inside, the plastered ceilings hung in shreds and the walls were blackened and blistered. Only from the timberwork – fine cedar, though warped by age and weather – might you have guessed that this had once been a better-class dwelling. And you'd have been right. The cottage was built in 1843 for barrister Redmond

Redmond Barry's old cottage was a minor city landmark when John Mather captured it in watercolour in 1915.

(later Sir Redmond) Barry, and one of its five modest rooms once housed the nucleus of the Melbourne Public Library (now the State Library of Victoria). A tall cupboard with double doors and six shelves for books was still fixed to one wall when the wreckers moved in.

Arriving in Melbourne at the end of 1839 – one of 'a small army' of lawyers aboard the *Parkfield* from Sydney – Barry had first made his home in a single-roomed cottage on the future Synagogue Place. The town's courthouse was in those days a block-and-a-half distant, at the corner of Bourke and King streets, the edge of the government precinct. Melbourne's official and professional classes had not yet migrated eastwards, but were living – most of them – close to the hub, at the western end of town. Barry bought an allotment in Bourke Street in 1843 and had his five-roomed cottage built at some distance back from the street. There'd have been a garden in front as well as the sapling mulberry behind and, instead of a hoarding, a fence with a gate. And up the path leading from Bourke Street to the front door would've come visiting, not just the town's worthies and fledgling intelligentsia, but lesser men of the respectable sort whom Barry encouraged to read and borrow from his collection of standard works and periodicals.

In Garryowen's words 'a splendid specimen of masculine organisation', Barry was Commissioner of the Court of Requests from 1840 until 1851 when he became a Supreme Court judge. The following year, in the flush of the gold rush, he sold the Bourke Street property for a sweet profit and his cottage became a doctor's residence. Thereafter, Barry was instrumental in the founding of the University of Melbourne, the Museum and the Library (in whose collection still are some of the books from his cupboard), besides pegging his wig on history by presiding over the trials of the Eureka rebels and the man in the iron helmet.

Somewhere in the vicinity of Redmond Barry's cottage – perhaps even in the old cottage itself – one of Whelan's gang found a bag of twenty-one gold sovereigns inside a boarded-up chimney. 'He'd been having a rough time with sickness,' said old Jim Whelan in 1933, 'so I let him keep them.'

Over the years many buildings, small and large, were pulled down in the neighbourhood for the expansion of Goldsbrough Mort's sprawling bond stores. Goldsbrough Mort's stake in Bourke Street began in the 1850s, with a bluestone woolstore at the north-east corner of William Street. Stores for grain, hides and tallow later went up west of William, and in the '80s the original building almost doubled in size when a bluestone companion was built alongside, the pair being linked by an 'overway' bridging Little William Street. One building that went to make way for the expansion was a contemporary of Barry's cottage, formerly the home of Robert Russell, Melbourne's pioneer surveyor.

Tucked away at the rear of Goldsbrough Mort's, in Little William Street, was a tiny house of four rooms – two up and two down. A 'queer mixture' of bluestone, brick and sandstone, it was built in the 1850s by F.J. Thomson and had been occupied variously as residence, artist's studio and confectioner's shop. Though long overshadowed, the little house stood its ground until 1935 when the pullulating Goldsbrough Mort acquired it from the Thomsons. Their ancestral home may have been lost, but the family's link with the neighbourhood endured in the shape of Thomson Street, the newly named and straightened laneway whose dead-end marked Redmond Barry's threshold. And on the shrunken front door of the Thomson house, when the wreckers came knocking, was a waggish inscription in chalk: *The Cottage by the Sea.*

Goldsbrough Mort vacated Bourke Street in the 1960s, leaving Whelan's to sweep away most of the traces. The bluestone stores west of William Street came down in 1963, with the 1880s addition tumbling ten years later, its site (and that of Thomson's 'Cottage by the Sea') overbuilt by one of the National Bank's 1970s monstrosities. Of Goldsbrough Mort's Bourke Street empire, only the original store at the William Street corner was left standing.

If a plaque was ever mounted on the building that replaced St Patrick's Hall, there's none to be seen there today. The memorials to the neighbourhood's past lives are in its street names: St Patrick's Alley, the former Synagogue Place, Thomson Street, and Goldsbrough Lane west of William Street. Street names, unlike memorial plaques, are a living part of a city – a way of remembering, not forgetting.

Contemporary wrecks

Close by the St Patrick's neighbourhood, all four corners at the intersection of Bourke and Queen streets were redeveloped during 1958–59. Whelan's wrecked at least two of them.

Salisbury Building (south-east corner of Bourke and Queen), 1958

This was the reputed site of Melbourne's first brick structures – a store on the Bourke Street frontage with a two-roomed, shingle-roofed cottage well to the rear – built in 1837 or '38. During the 1850s, Bourke Street between Elizabeth and Queen was largely devoted to the sale of (living) horseflesh. This corner of Queen Street was occupied in those years by the yard and stabling of Bear's Horse Bazaar. The old brick cottage was still standing in 1884, when it was hailed as 'the oldest building remaining in Melbourne' before being pulled down. In its place and cramming the whole corner block was built the great squarish mass of the Salisbury Building, four storeys in solid brick and as impressive in its day as a skyscraper.

Britannia Hotel (south-west corner Bourke and Queen), 1959

The licence from the Eagle Inn (on the site of the Bull and Mouth Hotel) in Bourke Street was transferred to a new hotel, two blocks west, in 1849. A classic city-corner pub, the Britannia survived a gas explosion in the front bar in 1891 ('the building quivered' and a barmaid's hair was singed) and renovations in 1925 (a third storey was added), but succumbed to Whelan the Wrecker. Two old shop-residences next door in Queen Street came down at the same time, to make way for an eleven-storey insurance office which itself has since been demolished.

Melbourne Mansions (91–101 Collins Street), 1958

Completed in 1906, Melbourne Mansions was said to have been the first block of residential flats built in the city. Its site was one of the CBD's last virgin building allotments – actually two allotments, with a forty-metre frontage to Collins Street's Paris end. Though it wasn't called the Paris end in those days, the eastern end of Melbourne's premier street already bore the character that the name denotes. Exclusive,

The brand-new Conzinc Riotinto building towered over its neighbourhood.

stylish, it had long been the preserve of medical men and the moneyed classes.

Melbourne Mansions' ground floor and basement housed medical rooms and shops of the right kind, while on the four floors above were thirty apartments, many of them kept as a city address by Western District squatting families. The building's appearance was in keeping with the elegant tone of the street, featuring arches and balconies and oriel windows, and an amount of restrained wedding-cake detail about the upper storeys. Melbourne's first apartment house operated rather like a private club, with meals laid on in a common dining room or delivered from serveries on each residential floor; only the larger apartments had their own kitchenettes.

Fifty years later, that mode of living was close to defunct, and thirty apartments, however elegant, were a waste of prime Collins Street real estate. Melbourne Mansions had been sold in 1949 to a 'big metals group' – the future Conzinc Riotinto Australia (CRA) – and from that date the building's days were numbered. In 1958, Whelan's got the job of knocking Melbourne Mansions down. It had, recalls Owen Whelan, a 'very high salvage content', the timberwork – panelling, bookshelves, doors, those oriel windows – being especially fine and sought-after.

Replacing the bijou Melbourne Mansions was the decidedly

*un*bijou CRA Building, twenty-six storeys of skyscraper and usurper of the tallest-building title. As *the* Melbourne chronicler of the eventful decade-and-more that lay ahead, journalist Keith Dunstan flagged this as the building that first broke 'the rhythm of Collins Street' and shattered forever the 'charming myth' of that street's Paris end. Years later, he recalled standing at the foot of the CRA Building soon after its completion, in company with Jim Whelan. 'Could you wreck that?' asked Dunstan.

'Oh, absolutely,' Jim replied. And his eyes lit up.

CHAPTER 9

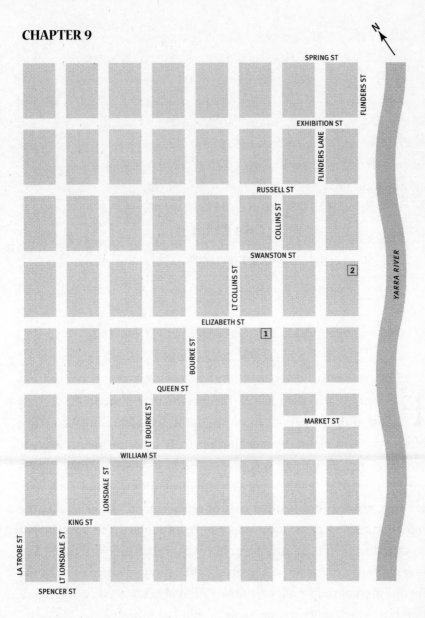

1. CML Building
2. Port Phillip Club Hotel

CHAPTER 9

Forever

Colonial Mutual Life (formerly Equitable) Building ~
Port Phillip Club Hotel

From the early decades of the twentieth century, US tax law allowed the owners of an income-producing building – an office block, say – to claim depreciation on their investment. An average building's useful lifespan was held to be forty years, so that owners were permitted to set aside one-fortieth of a building's value each year, tax free, against the eventual cost of replacement.* In Australia, the building and property industries for years lobbied the government to introduce a similar rule here, but were rebuffed every time. And invariably the ministerial comeback that scuttled their case would invoke Melbourne's 'undepreciable' Colonial Mutual Life Building – a building which, as everyone knew, would last forever.

Well, forever arrived in 1960.

---

* The obsolescence period was reduced – and the annual depreciation deduction increased – in 1954, accelerating the cycle of rebuilding and demolition in US cities.

The announcement came in 1957 that the Colonial Mutual Life Assurance Society was planning to replace its landmark Melbourne headquarters with a building 'worthy of this great Society'. The old building had been conceived with precisely the same ambition; but whereas now 'worthy' was corporate shorthand for 'cost-effective', sixty-odd years earlier it had meant just the opposite.

'The building speaks for itself,' declared its architect, Edward E. Raht, at the opening in 1896 –

> *Nothing is concealed about it, and the construction and*
> *materials are the most solid that could be devised and selected*
> *… The whole reflects the character of the institution that owns*
> *it – there are no dark corners, no weaknesses in certain parts, no*
> *clumsy or misleading embellishments.*

'The institution that owns it' was, in the first place, the Equitable Life Assurance Society of the USA, which had bought the allotment at the north-west corner of Collins and Elizabeth streets in 1890 and commissioned Raht to design for it 'the grandest building in the Southern Hemisphere'. The company was undeterred by the collapse soon after of Melbourne's land boom; in fact, the downturn only stiffened the Equitable's determination to build a structure embodying permanence and stability. The result – the Equitable Building – was epic in scale and form, rising in the lean years of the early '90s as the stricken city's beacon of hope* and, in the words of Edward Raht, 'a monument to commercial enterprise of the present age'.

The Equitable was Melbourne's original two-chain-high building. It never contrived to be the city's tallest; that distinction was left to the 153-foot Australian Building. But, as the 'best proportioned building in the city', the Equitable formed the basis for the height-limit

---

* The *Age* called it 'almost a solitary example of life in the building trade in the city since the community plunged itself into its penitential sackcloth and ashes'.

'The best proportioned building in the city' – the Equitable Building, c.1906.

enshrined in the Building Act of 1916. Most buildings 132 feet in height would run to at least ten storeys – some to as many as thirteen. Not the Equitable: it had just seven lofty storeys. And therein lay its downfall.

The Equitable Life Assurance Society, whose Melbourne offices were built to reflect their permanent commitment to Australia, pulled out of the country in 1923, selling the property to Colonial Mutual Life (CML). Almost immediately, the new owners built a modern block of offices next door and began buying up adjacent properties with a view to future expansion. By the mid-'50s the old building on the corner constituted an obstacle to that expansion. For one thing, its image was out of step with commercial enterprise of the new age, solidity now being suggestive of stagnation. Moreover, it lacked modern comforts and was unyielding to new technologies. But what sealed the building's fate were its proportions: once considered noble, they were now condemned as 'a terrible waste of space'. In 1959, the CML Building's first floor was on a level with the third floor of one of its modern neighbours. With high ceilings, thick-set walls, and cavernous lobbies and hallways, it squandered a prime city block for less floorspace than would fill a building a fraction its size. Architects' plans for a new CML flagship on the site envisaged a building offering *seven times* the floorspace of the old. 'It just had to come down,' said Jim Whelan II.

Recognising that the uprooting of a Melbourne landmark might meet with opposition, the building's owners sought sanction from the fledgling National Trust. The CML Building did not feature on the Trust's list of treasures. Not only wasn't it old enough, but it belonged to a grandiose and uncherished style of architecture dubbed (and the name fairly rings with disdain) 'Americanised Renaissance'. *'Interesting, but not worthy of preservation'* was the verdict. In July 1959, tenders were called for the building's demolition.

Jim Whelan did the costing for Whelan the Wrecker. He'd have gone through the architects' specifications, which included plans showing the lay-out of the building to be demolished. (Ideally, a wrecker liked to get hold of original construction plans, which laid bare the building's entire anatomy; but in this case, as in most, no such plans were available.) Primarily though, Jim sized up the building in person, his only tools a geological hammer, a small magnet – both handy for checking the composition of building materials – and a wrecker's brain.

According to Whelan's lore, the twenty minutes it took Jim to arrive at an estimate for the CML job was a record: the longest he'd ever taken. And his price? He first put down £82,500, then undercut himself to arrive at an all-up figure – including contingency fee and extra insurance – of £80,500. That did it. Whelan's won the tender and agreed to empty the site of the CML Building by 1 August 1960, exactly one year hence.

In his lightning tour of the building, Jim had assessed not just the likely cost of demolition, but the value of the 'dismantled commodity'. The latter represented an invisible column of figures in any demolition estimate: the amount Whelan's stood to gain from the sale of scrap and salvage. Factored into the demolition fee itself were costs, wages, and the hefty insurance premiums that applied to the wrecking trade, plus a slender margin of profit – *if* Jim got it right. But though they no longer had to pay for the privilege of wrecking, most of Whelan's profits still came from 'selling the junk'.

The contract for the CML demolition specified certain components of the building that would *not* become Whelan's property. Sample sections of wrought iron and timberwork, a couple of commemorative plaques, and a small quantity of building stone were to be kept and incorporated, for sentiment's sake, into the new building. Furthermore –

> *Should the Contractor discover materials or items of historic interest or value, demolition in the area shall cease and the Contractor shall immediately inform the Architects and await instructions. Items of historical interest and value remain the property of the Proprietor.*

Most items, however, which the building's owners wished to keep were of a mundane nature: telephone system, wall safe, security gates, electric clocks.

Also spelt out in the contract was the donation to the University of Melbourne of the building's least prosaic feature, an allegorical group of statuary that topped the entrance portico. More than four metres high and cast in bronze, it depicted a sandal-shod Amazon – emblematic of 'the Equitable'* – giving succour to a widow with two children. The group had been modelled and cast in Vienna in 1893 and shipped south in a mighty big crate. Now the Equitable spirit and her charges were destined for the University's new Architecture school at Mt Martha.

> *I went down to see her there one year [Owen Whelan tells] and she looked pretty ordinary because she had an old hat on her head and a cigarette hanging out of her mouth and … you know, various parts of her anatomy were very highly polished.*

The foursome in bronze was relocated in 1981 to the University proper, where they nestle now, in comparative dignity, close to the

---

* A similar sculpture had crowned the Equitable's New York office (long since demolished).

The Equitable goddess and her charges today.

Baillieu Library. But the spirit of the Equitable was designed to be viewed from a supplicant fifteen metres' distance. Brought to earth, she is freakishly huge, each foot Pythonesque, every toe a mega-toe. The folds of her gown, the crease of her ear are woolly with spider webs never meant to be seen. From an eyrie above Collins Street to eye-level – what a come-down.

Whelan's took possession of the CML Building on 1 September 1959. To mark the occasion, a pair of Y-fronts hung at half-mast from the building's flagpole above Elizabeth Street. As usual, the wreckers began inside, gutting the building floor by floor, stripping out joinery, fixtures and, in the case of the CML, a large amount of marble. The walls and floors of the showpiece storeys were lined with imported marble – white, black, grey, pink, veined. Elaborately carved and polished, it featured in skirtings, dadoes and architraves, and skirled into pilasters and columns in the ground-floor vestibule. And hardly a room in the building was without a marble mantelpiece over its poky gas fire.

Above the dadoes rose plasterwork, exquisitely and dramatically detailed in mailroom and boardroom alike. And the joinery ... well, it *was* joinery – there wasn't a nail used in the place. Window frames and sashes, doors and panelling all were of cedar, and the doors were of a size to admit the Equitable goddess herself should she care to step inside. The floors, where not tiled in marble, were of polished Victorian hardwood fixed by a thin coat of bitumen to a layer of cement spread over terracotta blocks – costly, complicated, but fireproof. The

'You'd swear they were designed by Ronald Searle' – the CML Building liftwells.

building's two electric passenger lifts, once the swiftest in the city, were enclosed by an elegant grille of steel and bronze bent work. (An *Age* journalist of 1896 had rhapsodised at the grille's 'exquisite beauty'; in 1959, the same feature would put his *Sun* counterpart in mind of a Ronald Searle drawing.) Indeed, not a single element of the building – none that showed, anyway – seems to have been considered too functional to be decorative also.

At ground-level, Whelan's made one of the street-front shops a sales outlet for the 'dismantled commodity'. The phone there was left connected and Myles Whelan played at shopkeeper.

The phone ran hot. One caller wanted two mantelpieces from the sixth floor, others were after lamps, rubber flooring, lockers, a boiler. A Mr Ekberg rang to inquire what it would cost to buy the building's entire facade; Myles quoted him £10,000. It wasn't long before all the marblework was spoken for. Slabs were bought at six shillings a square foot by monumental masons and coffee lounges. A flight of marble stairs went to replace worn ones at the museum, while a pillared archway in Belgian marble from the vestibule was sold (at a special ecclesiastical price, no doubt) to frame the entrance of a new Roman Catholic church at Braybrook. The more ornate of the marble fireplaces sold for £35; most went for just £10 apiece. Soon, Myles was left with not much more than trinkets to unload: brass doorknobs, locks, hinges, letterboxes ... oh, and 30,000 tonnes of granite.

The demolition of most buildings took a tiny fraction of the time that they'd taken to construct. So far, the CML had run to form: its interior – representing two-and-a-half years' painstaking work by nineteenth-century artisans and tradesmen – was gutted in just four months. Back in 1893, construction of the building's framework and outer shell had taken less than a year. When Whelan's started on the structural demolition, at the end of December 1959, they still had seven months' wrecking time left. Ordinarily that would have been plenty, but, 'Whelan the Wrecker is having a worrying time,' reported the *Age*.

Soon after wrecking began, a Whelan's directors' meeting had sounded a note of concern 'that unknown factors quite apart from bad management could well cause the Company to lose some thousands of pounds in this venture'. The imposition of a time-limit for the demolition, with penalties for late completion, was a new hazard for the wrecker and a most unwelcome one on a job of this size and complexity. Already Jim's figuring was looking woefully underdone. 'We thought we had a magnificent price to pull down the CML,' Owen said later, 'but halfway through we thought, "Shut the gate. How much are we going to lose?"' Not that any of the Whelans blamed Jim: none of them had ever encountered a building like the CML before.

'I think it was built to last fifteen wars and ten centuries,' Myles told the *Age* in January 1960. 'The trouble is there isn't a single wooden joint in the building – all are concrete, steel and stone.' The CML super-structure was granite, backed with brick and terracotta fire-proofing, around an iron frame. In the 1890s such a frame had been a new thing and building regulations had still insisted on load-bearing walls of masonry, with the result that the basement and ground floors were needlessly crowded by walls and piers a metre thick and more. But the bearing walls were the least of Whelan's concerns at New Year, 1960.

The building's Austrian-born, New York-based architect, Edward Raht, had made a determined effort to source building materials from within the colony of Victoria. For the base storeys and entrance portico he'd chosen an unusual reddish granite quarried at Cape Woolamai on Phillip Island, while the vast bulk of the building was clad in grey granite from Harcourt, near Bendigo.* Seventeen hundred tonnes (736 cubic metres) of stone came from Cape Woolamai alone – shipped across to Little Dock, at the foot of Spencer Street – in the form of five- to ten-tonne blocks and huge pillars. Two men were killed while quarrying and dressing stone for the Equitable Building, and three more died when a granite-filled ketch ran aground en route from Phillip Island.

---

* Harcourt being close to the Castlemaine goldfield, bystanders sometimes used to scratch at the surface of the granite blocks piled up at the Equitable Building site, looking for specks of gold.

A mountain-load of granite was only part of Raht's scheme for conveying that theme of here-to-eternity solidity that was central to his brief. So that the building should in no way appear to taper off into insubstantiality, Raht terminated it with a four-metre-wide cornice, the effect being somewhat like a mortarboard. The blocks of Harcourt granite that made up the cornice weighed four tonnes each, on average, with the massive cornerstones nearly four times that. The cornerstones as Raht had envisaged them would have weighed as much as a hundred tonnes each; but as no lifting-gear was capable of hoisting such a burden, the stones were hauled up in sections – the largest weighing 'just' fifteen tonnes – and assembled on the spot to form Raht's monoliths. As this ledge loomed two metres over the street fronts, each stone had to be secured with iron pins to its neighbour and the supporting brickwork.

Picture then the predicament facing Whelan the Wrecker as they started on the process of 'building in reverse'. Fifteen tonnes had been the greatest load that a steam gantry of 1893 was able to bear; sixty-seven years later Whelan's had to rely on a crane with just a *third* of that lifting capacity. How then to get those biggest sections of the cornerstones to the ground? Whelan's called on the expertise of Lodge Brothers, stonemasons, who devised a means of removing the stones using the traditional technique of plug-and-feather – the same method by which the stones had been prepared for the building in the first place. A small hole was drilled and a pin hammered in, causing the stone to split. In this way, forty metres above the street, the stones of the CML cornice were reduced to a manageable size for grappling to the ground. Once each stone section was loosened (and that took some doing) two holes were drilled diagonally in its top face, into which were driven steel pins, fixed by chains to the hook of a crane. By the inward pull of the sling, the stone was secured for its passage to street level.

Council regulations and common sense ruled that it was unsafe to break up and hoist huge lumps of stone over a street full of traffic and

Demolishing the cornice of the CML Building – looking east up Collins Street.

pedestrians. The street below had to be closed during the removal of the overhanging cornice. But the Tramways Board, running services on both Collins and Elizabeth streets, consented to street closures only on weekends and after eleven on weeknights. From January 1960, Whelan's had gangs working round the clock on the CML site, with night shifts the busiest – and noisiest.

This was night-wrecking in more ways than one. Imagine nights made hideous by the batter-and-yowl of jackhammers and diesel compressors and the sleep-splitting shrill of the dogman's whistle. Now imagine living across the street from it. Myles Whelan's own slumber was broken, on several occasions, by phone calls from neighbours of the CML, complaining of the 'night noise'. Myles' site-diary records that a Mr Jago, live-in caretaker of a building opposite, rang one midnight to ask, 'Would you like to visit my wife in Mont Park?'*

In the sorriest situation of all, though, were staff and guests at the London Hotel, which adjoined the CML Building in Elizabeth Street. For months on end in 1960, it must've been the hotel from hell. The London's proprietors sought a court order in February to halt night demolition on the CML site. That was impossible, of course, but Colonial Mutual Life agreed to compensate the London Hotel for loss of occupancy until the demolition was over. For their part, Whelan's replaced the dogman's whistle, at night, with a walkie-talkie, and diesel compressors with electric ones.

Day-to-day relations between the wreckers and hotel management continued testy, though, with complaints ongoing, not just of the noise but of dust and even plagues of mosquitoes. (The cause of the latter, Whelan's discovered, was that the CML basement had filled with water, the result of constantly hosing down the rubble to reduce dust.) One day in May, word reached Myles – the on-site Whelan – that an iron girder had just crashed into the front bar of the London Hotel. 'I don't know anything about this,' Myles told his foreman, recollecting that he was urgently required on another city wrecking site. He had no wish to face the further wrath of the London's manager, Norman Carlyon. Returning a couple of hours later, Myles was surprised to find Carlyon in a 'genial mood'. Not only was he 'not worried' by the incident, but was heard to castigate the chemist next door for ringing the *Herald*. It appeared that the girder had been accidentally dislodged by a crane and, on hitting the ground, had somersaulted down the

---

*   A psychiatric hospital.

laneway beside the hotel, spearing through protective scaffolding to strike the door of the saloon bar, end-on. The door was smashed to splinters and a metre of the girder poked into the bar, but, amazingly, no one was hurt.

It wouldn't be the only near-miss in the course of the CML demolition. In mid-June, a pin snapped as a seven-tonne block of granite was being lowered by crane and the stone dropped ten metres, flattening a new compressor and narrowly missing the dogman, Roger Aldridge. Sam Canali broke both wrists in a fall from the top of a wall and Ted Napier fractured his spine when he stepped backwards into a liftwell. Mostly though, and miraculously, accidents on the CML site resulted in no worse than bruised toes and fingers, besides the replacement of a pair of suede shoes after their wearer, H. Smith of Oakleigh, tripped on the protective decking in Collins Street. Only when the demolition was complete did one of the council's building surveyors tell Myles that he and his colleagues had predicted at least three fatalities on the site, and that (as Myles would recall it) 'if we'd killed only three, we'd have done a damn good job'.

Only three. That wasn't just callous talk. The blokes at the town hall knew that there'd been seven men killed during the building's construction – twelve, if you counted quarrymen and sailors. The contractor had called it 'a most unfortunate building'; around town, it had been known as 'the slaughterhouse'.

> *Almost every step in the progress of the colossal structure …*
> *has been marked by accidents and disasters as appalling as they*
> *have been extraordinary.*
> ~ *Age*, July 1893

Even before construction began on the site, a workman died when a crane hoisting scaffolding timbers collapsed. As the iron columns of the frame were being raised into place, a suspension chain broke, knocking a worker off a wall and to his death. Next a donkey-engine exploded, killing two men and showering the central city with metal fragments and body parts. ('Here and there in Elizabeth-street pieces of a human skull and brains were picked up,' reported the *Argus*.) The engine, when it burst, had been lifting a seven-tonne block of granite to the second-floor level. The walls had reached their penultimate storey when the final fatalities occurred. 'As each upward move has been made measurable by accident,' observed the *Age*, 'so each succeeding accident has been more terrible than its predecessor.' This time there were three dead and more brains scattered in Elizabeth Street, after the shattering of a crane-jib threw the winchmen from their platform, thirty-five metres up.

Workers engaged on the site weren't the only casualties. Passers-by were also at risk. When that crane dropped its load of scaffolding timbers, a young woman was knocked down and her skirt pinned to the Collins Street footpath by a heavy spar. Unluckiest though was William Ellis. On a Saturday in April 1893 he had just collected his week's wages in Flinders Lane and was heading towards Elizabeth Street, hand-in-hand with his four-year-old daughter, Daisy, when a fragment of cog-wheel dropped out of the sky, rupturing his liver and almost severing one of his arms. The three kilograms of iron had been thrown nearly 200 metres from the exploding engine on the Equitable site. The farthest-flung fragments fell on the roof of a building next to the post office in Bourke Street, though no one but Ellis was struck. He died in hospital the next morning, leaving a wife and four children 'entirely without means'. Mrs Ellis was sent £5 by the Governor and the *Age* ran a subscription for the family's relief. But, being unconnected with the building site except by dint of his death, William Ellis wasn't covered by the contractor's insurance. Nor, apparently, did his family qualify for the Equitable's benevolence. So much for 'Charity being kind to the poor', the title in full of the bronze tableau hoisted into place over the building's doorway not long after Ellis's death.

All seven deaths occurred in the space of hardly more than a year. AN UNLUCKY WORK was the *Age*'s headline on the morning after the triple-fatality in July 1893. The contractor was David Mitchell, surely the most experienced building man in Melbourne. He'd been responsible for the construction of such landmarks as the Royal Exhibition Buildings and had a reputation for thoroughness and sound building practice. The run of fatalities connected with the Equitable site left him feeling 'quite unnerved' –

> *The accidents have been more numerous than I can honestly*
> *say I deserve to have had, seeing the care that I have taken to*
> *safeguard the men. Usually I have few accidents, very few, but,*
> *as I have said, this is an unfortunate building.*

'He will not rest easy in his mind,' said the *Argus*, 'till the huge blocks of granite are in position and the whole building is out of his hands.' But with the structure still one storey shy of the cornice, the most monstrous lumps of stone and riskiest stage of construction lay ahead.

Myles Whelan was a hoarder, and in 2003 he still had in his possession a creased and tatty, mildew-spotted scrap of paper found in the course of the CML demolition. He couldn't recall exactly where or how it was discovered; in fact, he wasn't even certain that it came from the CML site. But it must have done, for it bore these words, scrawled in pencil –

> *This Shirt was laid*
> *hear [sic] in Memory of William*
> *Ellis Plasterer who*
> *Departed this life 8/8/92*
> *Rest in Peace*
> *Amen*

The date is wrong (it ought to read 9 April 1893), as is the occupation (he was a house-painter), but here, surely, is a memorial to the unlucky William Ellis, struck down in Flinders Lane. The shirt, when unearthed, was entirely rotten, but the paper wrapped around it had somehow survived.

What could the story be? Well, just suppose that workmen on the site decided, after losing three mates on one day, to take some preventative measures of their own. Mightn't they, like superstitious builders of old, have secreted some amulet-like object within the structure to ward off bad luck? It hadn't been so long ago that a shirt or a shoe was commonly built into floor or ceiling to act as a household charm. Mightn't there originally have been seven shirts laid down in the Equitable Building, only one of them found – or, at any rate, kept – by the wreckers? There might've been, for all we know.* Something, anyway, changed the building's luck after July 1893. Even the hoisting and placement of the massive cornice stones brought no further mishap. There was no one else killed, no more grey matter in the gutters. But you can see why the folk at the town hall would've feared the worst when it came time to pull the 'unfortunate' building down.

The autumn of 1960 was the wettest for twenty years and much wrecking time was lost to rain. And everything, every single aspect of the demolition, took longer than Jim could ever have guessed at a glance. Apart from the stonework, there was the brickwork that backed it up, that encased the pillars of the iron frame and made up those hefty load-bearing walls. The building's architect, back in 1896, had paid tribute to Melbourne's bricklayers, declaring that 'in none of his buildings (and he has built many in different parts of the world) has he had the opportunity of procuring such good brick work as

---

* This is not a theory that comes Whelan-endorsed. Owen Whelan laughed uproariously when I ventured it to him.

here'.* So strong and sound was it that, come 1960 and the wreckers, no pick or jackhammer could prise it apart. Explosives were tried. 'But we couldn't even crack it,' says Owen; 'we had to *chew* that stuff out. It was so hard!' The brickwork's fixative wasn't the usual soft, sandy mortar, but rock-hard Portland cement made with lime from David Mitchell's own quarries at Lilydale. But what would you expect? Impervious, stubborn, immovable: those were the criteria for materials when building to last for ever.

At 7 a.m. on a Sunday late in May 1960, the group in bronze was lowered onto a tray-truck and Whelan's began dismantling the portico. The platform on which the statuary had stood weighed seventeen tonnes, the Ionic pillars supporting it were forty tonnes apiece. And spanning the portico was the wreckers' next big challenge: a majestic red-granite arch, reaching four storeys high. Back in March, Whelan's had received from the project architects an old quantity surveyor's report, detailing the exact dimensions of the task they faced. (A pity Jim hadn't seen it when putting a price on the job.) The keystone alone weighed fifteen tonnes, and 'The Arch is notable from the fact that the stones which compose it are set not in cement but the joints are filled up with metal.' In fact the arch had been fitted together to such perfection that its demolition, in the words of a Whelan's foreman, was 'almost impossible'.

It took nine days just to dislodge the keystone, twenty metres above the street. The first day, Myles recorded in his site diary –

Stone broken into 1 section about 2 ton. Although work on this stone for 2½ hrs with gads, plugs and fethers etc., stone moved only about 3 inches. Will discuss matter further with Lodge Bros.

<hr>

* In fact, said the *Age*, 'he speaks in eulogistic terms of that much abused individual, the Australian working man – the carnivorous ruffian who demands eight hours' work a day, and who has consequently fallen under the disfavour of eminent English economists.'

The CML Building's main entrance, in Collins Street, with its statuary and red-granite arch, including that stubborn keystone.

At the stonemasons' suggestion, a jack was placed under the keystone and heavy pressure applied from below, in an attempt to push it out of place. But 'Still no great movement,' Myles observed and, 'After about 1 hr this given up.' The keystone would have to be 'chewed' away by jackhammer and, 'It will be most tedious,' wrote Myles. Even when the keystone finally came unplugged, the rest of the arch settled only two inches. It turned out that the huge stones had been fixed into position with steel ties, then a 'mortar' of lead and antimony poured between them. This mortar, when removed, weighed thirteen tonnes and constituted a valuable and welcome item of scrap.

August arrived and walls were still standing on the CML site. But, 'Whelan's estimate the building will be down to ground level by September 1.' Come September, 'We'll be out of here in early October,' Myles told the *Herald*. The builders were champing to get hold of the site, and every day past their August deadline was costing Whelan's a penalty. It was 22 October when they finally cleared the site. Surveying the cavity, Jim Whelan mused, 'It was the toughest we ever pulled down.'

The CML demolition had taken 73,385 man-hours, or more than nine thousand man-days, over fourteen months. It had cost Whelan's £118,304 – nearly £40,000 (or half again) more than they were paid for the job. The sale of salvage reduced the Wrecker's net loss to around £30,000. Even so … it looked like a disaster. And yet it wasn't.

Elsewhere in the city Whelan's were wrecking buildings in record numbers, in record time, for record profits. Melbourne was entering an era of unparalleled change and expansion, and for the next twenty years Whelan's rode a wave of activity and prosperity like nothing the company had experienced before. More than ever, they were 'the dominant people' in demolition – 'And I always think it sprang from the CML,' says Owen, 'because there were so many problems associated with that job that we had to alter our thinking.' They were known now as the wreckers who could handle anything.

The chairman of Colonial Mutual Life emptied a ceremonial bucket of crushed granite from the old building into the first batch of concrete for the new. Thin slices of the grey Harcourt granite featured as decorative panels in the cladding of the new CML

Remnants of the CML Building in Colonial Square today, Melbourne Museum in the background.

building,* and facings of polished black marble at shopfront level were another reminder of what had gone. The copper cylinder found beneath the old building's foundation stone – containing the usual relics of pomp and coinage – was returned to the Equitable Life Assurance Society in New York.

Among the new homes found for CML salvage was Whelan the Wrecker's own office, built in 1964 to replace the tin shed that had served for fifty years. The stylish new offices attached to the Sydney Road yard featured a pair of solid cedar doors with brass hinges and a table made from a two-tonne granite window lintel. Most of the granite from the CML Building, though, was sold either to stone-masons or to the Country Roads Board, to be ignobly crushed for road-surfacing. Forty years later, blocks of that granite still lay strewn among thistles in a Cyclone-fenced paddock on the city outskirts. In

---

* These granite panels are still a feature, having been retained, in modified form, when the building underwent extensive remodelling in 2003–04.

2000, Museum Victoria acquired twenty-five of the remaining blocks – examples of both red and grey granites and a range of ornamentation (including the chiselled letters 'CIETY of the') – and installed them on Colonial Square, adjacent to the Melbourne Museum. Tumbled about with seeming haphazardness, they resemble ancient ruins, unearthed. Which, in a way, they are.

Postscript – Almost a year to the day after Whelan's scraped away the last of the old CML building, a crane collapsed on the site of its replacement. Three riggers were killed.

Contemporary wrecks
Port Phillip Club Hotel (232 Flinders Street), 1960

Incorporated within this old and rambling hotel was one of Melbourne's earliest brick buildings. In 1838 merchant John Hodgson built what was then the town's most substantial dwelling, on his half-acre block in Flinders Street. An energetic speculator, he lost all in the depression of 1841 and his grandiose home was dubbed 'Hodgson's Folly'. In the settlement of Hodgson's affairs, the 'Folly' fell to John Pascoe Fawkner who named it 'Yarra House' and leased it as a meeting-house to the Port Phillip Club. A visitor to the Club in the '40s described its members as 'impersonators of the tradition of old English gentlemen, … drinking their decanter of port on the hottest days with abnormal dignity'. Evidently there weren't enough such impersonators in the colony to make the Club pay, as it soon wound up and its old clubhouse went on to be licensed, in 1850, as the Port Phillip Club Hotel. And so it remained, though substantially altered and expanded, until 1960 when Whelan's pulled it down for construction of the Port Phillip Arcade. (This was the city job to which Myles Whelan made himself scarce on the day that a CML girder dropped into the London Hotel bar.)

CHAPTER 10

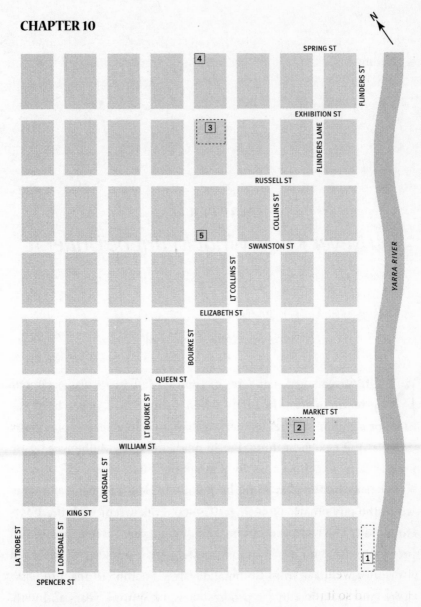

1. Fish Market
2. Western Market
3. Eastern Market
4. Old White Hart Hotel
5. Royal Mail Hotel

CHAPTER 10

You Never Know What Might be Under It

Fish Market ~ Western Market ~ Eastern Market ~
Old White Hart Hotel ~ Royal Mail Hotel

Not fifty years ago, ten acres of central Melbourne was occupied by marketplaces. In a city where ground had never been set aside for a public square, its markets had, over the years, sometimes served as the next-best thing. But in post-Olympics Melbourne, their day was done – had been, really, a long time since.

Whelan the Wrecker hung its signs – *Is Here* and *Was Here* – on two of the city's markets during 1959–60, concurrent with the CML demolition. The third they'd knocked down a year earlier. Two of the three had existed for nearly as long as Melbourne, ranking them either as 'priceless heritage from Colonial days' or 'a complete anachronism' – take your pick. But in the progress-hungry Sputnik years and with the markets inarguably redundant, the city council's refashioning of its market reserves created 'an opportunity possessed by few other of the world's large cities for large-scale down-town development'.

The Fish Market was the last-built and the first to fall. In truth, it had been sinking and cracking for years, owing to the silty ground in which its foundations were sunk. The eccentric pile of buildings collectively known as the Fish Market was constructed in Flinders Street in 1891–92 – the last gasp of the land boom. It stretched all the way from King to Spencer Street and back towards the river, on ground that had formed the apron of the old Cole's and Raleigh's wharves and was now (and is still) bisected by the rail viaduct connecting Flinders and Spencer street stations.

The Fish Market was an oddity for Melbourne: a building out of square. In cities like Sydney, which took shape according to their own geometries, buildings were commonly given curved facades to fit the streets on which they stood. Not so in central Melbourne, where buildings conformed to the dead-straight lines of Hoddle's grid. What made the Fish Market odder was that it wasn't its front that curved, but its back – the rear of its main building mimicked the bend of the viaduct.

The Fish Market's front might have been as flat as that of any Melbourne building, but *straight* it was not. This was a municipal market, remember, selling and storing for export such commonplaces

Outside of the square – aerial view of the Fish Market (top of picture), c.1927.

as poultry, rabbits and butter, besides fish. Yet, to a modern eye, its Flinders Street frontage would suggest a far more glamorous, and certainly less noisome, civic function. Two hundred metres long and three red-brick storeys high, the Fish Market was sprigged with basilisk-spired turrets and a Westminsterish clock-tower over its arched main entrance, and was as grand and garish a public building as could be wished for.

The city's former fish market had stood on the site of Flinders Street station. Its replacement was properly named the City (or Corporation) Markets, but seems rarely to have been called anything other than Fish Market. Behind the showy facade it extended riverwards as a series of long market halls and cool stores, all bowing to the railway curve. It cost a quarter of a million pounds sterling to build and was regarded, in its early years, as a showpiece of the city.

Fish arrived at market well before dawn, trolleyed down (along with butter and rabbits) from the country trains and from boats moored at Little Dock on the other side of Spencer Street. Between four-thirty and eight in the morning, the place was raucous with haggling fishmongers and hawkers – a byword for lusty lungs. A guidebook published in the mid-1890s commended the 'magnificent' new market to the visitor bent on thrill-seeking –

> *On application to Mr D. Wilson, he will be shown the cool*
> *storage rooms, and have a chance of freezing himself in the*
> *midst of summer.*

By the 1930s, the Fish Market seems to have sunk to an object of civic shame. The whole set-up was considered out-of-date and unsanitary. Fish, poultry and rabbits were dressed and sold in the same building, poultry being killed to order in the main market hall. There was no running water in the fish-cleaning area, and the tiled walls were cracked and gappy owing to the building's unsteady foundations. And the reeky Fish Market's situation within the city – albeit at the very edge – compounded its unsavouriness. Already there was talk of relocating.

Another twenty years passed, though, before the city council settled on a new fish market site, on Footscray Road, West Melbourne. The Flinders Street site belonged to the State government and now a portion of it was required for an approach to the planned King Street bridge.* The rest of the land between Flinders Street and river was to be used as carparking – as urged by the RACV since the '20s – except for a strip reserved for a 'riverside beautification scheme'. The *Herald* applauded the plan.

> It [is] a rare chance to restore more than 5 acres of land in the
> Golden Mile, to use it in a new way nearly everyone approves,
> and to boost the morale of a dingy area.

Besides, this was 1957 and, to a TV-savvy eye, 'all the florid, pseudo-Gothic touches' of the Fish Market looked 'comically dated'.

Not for long. Whelan's started work there in December 1957. On such a vast, unneighboured site, gentle handling and containment were not paramount. Brick wall after brick wall could be pulled down by trucks ballasted with rubble from yet other brick walls. A major consideration on the Fish Market site, though, was vibration. Drop too large a section of wall at one time and the concussion could crack the pylons of the rail viaduct, or even derail a train. The most substantial walls to be demolished were those of the building's facade, and they had to be pulled backwards, away from busy Flinders Street in the direction of the viaduct. It was a hectic time for Whelan's, so they contracted out the task of wall-dropping.

Felling the front wall of the Fish Market – three storeys high and more than half-a-metre thick – was the kind of job Whelan's would

---

* Within a year of its opening, a section of the bridge collapsed. Called in to demolish the unsteady section, Whelan's were forbidden to hang their sign on the nearly new structure.

The skeletal spires of the Fish Market – Whelan's in residence.

normally do on a Sunday, when traffic on Flinders Street and the rail-
line was subdued. Their sub-contractor, however, decided to pull
down a huge section of it on a Friday afternoon. He'd undermined the
base of the wall on the lee side, then cut a 'chase' – knocked out several
courses of brickwork – low down on the same side. That ought to have
done the trick, made sure it fell in the direction he wanted, away from
Flinders Street. Mid-afternoon, he put two loaded trucks to the task
of pulling down this mighty slab of wall. They pulled and pulled, and
the wall rocked back and forth, swaying out into Flinders Street but
refusing to fall. It wasn't until a grader from nearby roadworks was
drafted to the offensive that at last the wall came down, with a seismic
CHOONK! Flinders Street, crammed with peak-hour traffic, couldn't be
seen for dust. No harm was done; but the dust, the vibration, the
public risk and disruption … Whelan's expected an official reprimand
at the very least. Miraculously, 'we never got a complaint'.

Soon after, though, with the job nearly done, Whelan's hit some
strife. As per their contract, they invited town hall officials down to
the Fish Market to witness the lifting of the foundation stone. In the

niche underneath was a lead box – a time capsule – laid there in 1891 by the then-mayor of Melbourne. And inside the box were found, besides some papers, just four coins adding up to tenpence ha'penny. According to a council inventory, the box's original contents had included a shilling, half-crown, and sovereign – all, by tradition, from the mayor's own pocket. Now, recalled Myles Whelan, 'there were very loud voices over the phone'. Jim, especially, was incensed by a suggestion that Whelan's had lifted the stone early and 'pinched the sov', the valuable gold sovereign. 'They didn't really have to ring,' said Myles; 'they just had to put their head out of the town hall and listen, because he was raging.'

But if the wreckers hadn't pocketed it, where *had* the sovereign gone? Jim found a likely answer a short time later, when Whelan's came to wreck the old RACV building at the Queen–Little Collins Street corner. Jim personally supervised work in the vicinity of the building's foundation stone, and got to talking one day with an old bloke who'd been hanging around the site, watching the wreckers' progress. (His type was known in the business as a 'sidewalk super-intendent'.) Well, he *must*'ve been old, as he claimed to have worked on the site when the building went up, some sixty-five years earlier. Jim told him about the ruckus at the Fish Market and the old guy, indicating the foundation stone that Jim had been carefully exposing, said, 'Well, you won't find any money under that.' The stone had been laid with all the usual ceremony, he told Jim, and then was raised again, 'just for a second', as soon as the official party left. The coins were snatched and it was 'Drinks for everybody!' at the Temple Court Hotel, on the corner opposite. So, what *did* Whelan's find under the foundation stone at the RACV building? A ceremonial parchment and some newspapers – but not a single coin. As the old labourer said to Jim: 'Who was going to find us out?' It used to happen all the time, he said.

The last vestige of the Fish Market to come down was the ornate archway over which the clocktower had stood. Its wrought-iron gates were relocated to the entrance of Fawkner Cemetery, while two more pairs of Fish Market gates made their way further north to Seymour, to fortify that town's swimming pool and football ground.*

Almost fifty years later, the south-western end of Flinders Street is still known as 'the former Fish Market site' – and not just to the Whelans, but in *Melway*. Unlike most demolition sites, this one has taken its time to forge a new identity – has 'continued to defy progress', as the *Age* said recently. Once the Fish Market was gone, most of the site was tarmacked and marked out for carparking, with Batman Park formed along the riverbank and a traffic overpass built to carry Flinders Street above the entrance to Kings Way. The result was far from the morale-boost hoped for by the *Herald*: the area became *more* dingy and cut-off, the kind of place you'd hesitate even to park your car. Now, with plans to demolish the overpass and build a five-star hotel on the Fish Market site, morale-boost Mark II is in the offing.† The Fish Market's days are numbered – again.

From any of its four street-fronts, you'd never have taken it for a marketplace. It looked like a mercantile fortress: a quadrangle of two-storey terraces, breasting the streets in a uniform facade. Owing to the nearness of the customs house, there was a seafaring flavour to the tenantry – a preponderance of shipping agents, customs agents, tug and steamship owners. Their premises were the Market Buildings, the revenue-producing exoskeleton of Melbourne's Western Market.

The market square (really a rectangle) occupied just two-fifths of the Western Market reserve, dwelling within the block like a soft-shelled crustacean. Access was via arched entrances that pierced the ground-floor level of the Market Buildings at four points: one each in Market and William Streets, two in Flinders Lane. The fourth frontage, Collins Street, offered no hint of the block's inner life. Not that,

* The gates from the Seymour swimming pool went missing a few years ago.
† Possibly in restitution for the site's former use, the development will include an expanded aquarium, promoting the conservation, rather than filleting, of fish.

162

by the late 1950s, there was much inner life to hint at. It was twenty-five years since the Western Market had been a market except in name alone.

The Market Buildings dated from 1868, but the market itself reached back to Melbourne's infancy. The site had been set aside for public purposes when the town was surveyed in 1837. At that time, it was as central a location as could be had. Ships docked at the end of Market Street, and the pre-survey settlement had clustered a safe distance back from the river, roughly in a line with what turned out to be Flinders Lane West – Melbourne's original high street.

From 1838, the reserve housed the town's lock-up – two brick cells and a watchhouse – alongside the police office. The latter had been a storekeeper's premises until the survey made him an illegal occupant of a public reserve. It was then acquired by the government, and doubled, for a few years, as a court house. From the carcass of an immense river-gum near by, a bell was hung as a fire-siren and to ring convict road-gangs to and from their labour. The same tree was the intended home of Melbourne's first public clock; instead, the clock went unmounted until a post office was built in Elizabeth Street.* Also on the market reserve were fixed the stocks, where miscreants were secured by the legs (one leg, in the case of women) to suffer cramp and public humiliation.

In 1841, the town's residents petitioned for a public market to be established on the reserve. Lacking a local authority to run such a venture (Melbourne was still governed from Sydney), a public vote was held to appoint market commissioners, the birth of the Western Market thus representing the first act of self-government by the settlers of Port Phillip District. A year later, a town council took on responsibility for the market.

Melbourne's first market-day – Wednesday, 15 December 1841

---

* Rowdies from the Melbourne Club on one occasion abducted the bell and buried it near the cemetery. Authorities may well have feared a repeat performance with the clock.

– was held in the open air. An assortment of 'rude wooden sheds' was put up soon after. The police office continued in occupation of the south-west corner of the reserve for some years. Rabbits, escaped from market stalls, dug their burrows under the building and there commenced their dynasty of pestilence. The stocks stayed too, even after the gaol relocated to Russell Street, the requisite taunts and persecution being in readier supply on the market square than away on the outskirts of town. Later in the '40s, the first buildings to signal permanency were put up on the market square: an arcade of eight stalls, forming the hub of the marketplace.

The Western Market reserve, however, no longer approximated the hub of Melbourne. The town had expanded north- and eastwards, and residents agitated for a market more conveniently situated. The Eastern Market was duly established at the upper end of Bourke Street in 1847, and found immediate favour. Already the Western Market had a has-been feel about it and, when a fire ripped through its arcade in 1853, it looked as if the contest was over: the Eastern Market had won. With the gold rushes in full roar, the Western Market reserve was put to use as a campground and staging-post for newly arrived gold seekers. It also, for a time, was the venue of an improvised bazaar known as Rag Fair, where overburdened and underfunded new arrivals offered their excess baggage for sale.

But the Western Market wasn't done with, not by a long shot. Melbourne's town council had control of the reserve only on condition that it was used for market purposes; otherwise it would revert to the Crown. Not wishing to forfeit the site, the council in 1855 held a design competition for a new Western Market, combining a traditional marketplace with more lucrative commercial premises. The winning design envisaged the market operating at the level of Flinders Lane, requiring the rest of the block (which rose nearly five metres to Collins Street) to be excavated to that level. At the same time, a portion was shaved off the south end of the market reserve, widening Flinders Lane to enable two-way traffic and, later, the introduction of a tramline to that section of the Lane. All round the market perimeter, bluestone foundations were built, from the base of the excavation up to street level, to support the planned commercial buildings. And then the money ran out.

Six brick stores stood on the levelled market square, and it was in and around these that trading recommenced in 1856. The new (albeit makeshift) Western Market found its niche as a wholesale operation, specialising in fruit, poultry and dairy produce. New legislation in 1863, permitting the council to lease out the Western Market site to a private operator for up to twenty-one years, offered a way to complete the market's development. A revised design divided the market perimeter into twenty-nine parts. On these leased allotments, developers built the uniform complex that came to be known as the Market Buildings. Interested parties were in short supply, however, and eventually all twenty-nine leases were knocked down to one man, the financier, Henry 'Money' Miller. Miller built the Market Buildings in 1867–68 and profited from them handsomely until the leases expired in 1889, when they became council property.

The catacombs formed by the bluestone foundations of the Market Buildings were used for storage by the market traders and as cellars by Matthew Lang, a wine and spirit merchant* whose premises fronted Collins Street. To begin with, there was a fifth entrance to the market: a stairway and passage leading down from Collins Street. But the Market Buildings, and the market itself, proved so popular that the Collins Street entrance was closed and reclaimed as lettable space. Fourteen brick stalls now lined the market square, with many more traders selling direct from their carts. The market ran six days a week, with Mondays and Fridays the busiest. Butter and poultry dealers predominated until 1892 when they moved to the new Fish Market and the trade in fruit expanded to fill their places. Suburban fruiterers

---

* As mayor of Melbourne, 1889–92, it was Lang who'd put the coins under the Fish Market foundation stone.

stocked up twice a week at the Western Market, while street hawkers replenished their handcarts daily with 'peaches from Mildura, … pineapples and bananas from Queensland, golden plantains from Fiji, tomatoes as large as your two fists from Bendigo, raspberries from Lilydale, and giant figs from all parts of the State'.

In 1929, the wholesaling of fruit at the Western Market was still going strong – too strong, in fact. The market had grown so congested that buyers, and even sellers, had to leave their carts and lorries some distance away, where formerly there'd been space enough to park within the market square. The council's solution was to enlarge Queen Victoria Market to accommodate the wholesale fruit traders and, at the end of October 1930, the Western Market lapsed into disuse.

> *Yesterday the market quadrangle was bathed in sunlight. Only*
> *a vague sound of traffic and the noise of construction works*
> *on neighbouring buildings intruded upon the meditations of a*
> *solitary dog which drowsed in the warmth.*

The desolate market square thus described by the *Argus* in January 1931 represented 'an oasis of ineptitude in the commercial heart of the city'.

The city council had hoped it might lease out the defunct Western Market as a carparking station; but the State Government objected, reminding the council that it was bound to use the site for market purposes, or lose it. An attempt to develop it as a general market failed within a fortnight, after local businesses objected and shoppers stayed away. A market was neither needed nor wanted in the commercial heart of the city. It took two years' negotiation, but in 1932 the Government relinquished the site to the Melbourne City Council, and the market-use proviso was dropped.

Now the municipal imagination ranged wide. Should the old Western Market reserve become a civic square, with lawns and gardens above a basement carpark? Might it be the site for a new town hall?

One councillor argued for the inclusion of a rooftop cabaret, another that the old market should be memorialised with a centre for primary and rural industries. Not surprisingly, the council favoured proposals that promised to maximise revenue from the site. There was talk of a seven-storey carpark, with cars conveyed to the upper levels by express elevator. Eventually it was agreed that a tall building, fronted by an open square and with carparking below (but no cabaret), would satisfy nearly everybody. But the scheme went no further before the war broke out.

Since 1934, the market square had been run as a carpark by a Mr Bauld, who charged drivers a shilling a day. The Department of the Interior took over the square during the war, and a portion of the Market Buildings was used as an Air Force hostel. But the city council hadn't forgotten its pre-war deliberations and in July 1946 launched a competition for the design of a building on the Western Market site. They got their design – for an 'imposing and massive' ten storeys, with parking for 500 cars – but post-war building controls prevented a start being made. Moreover, the council hoped to attract private investment, as it had in the nineteenth century, to build the prize-winning design in return for a 21-year lease. This time, though, there were no takers. Building restrictions ended, the Royal visitors and the Olympic Games came and went, and all the change to the Western Market site was a lick of paint on the shabby Collins Street frontage. Only when legislation extended the lease to ninety-nine years did things start moving. Council again called for development proposals and in 1959 announced the imminent construction of a 25-storey office block with a garden plaza on the site of the Western Market.

At the end of January 1960, a Whelan's gang commenced 'to drive away the last ghosts of one of Melbourne's oldest landmarks'. A report from the *Herald*, a few years earlier, conveys an idea of what the wreckers found in the Western Market underworld –

Cellars and underground passages run gloomily and desolately
in all directions and even the caretaker has not explored some of
the underground cellars, which sprawl like catacombs beneath
Collins Street. Flights of stairs and mysterious barred gratings
abound, and strange heaps of debris lie decaying in dust in
hidden cupboards cut into the bluestone.

One of the cellars had been used to the last by the old wine firm of
Matthew Lang –

Barrels of wine still stand in rows along the walls, and the
liquor is still drawn off into ancient bronze flagons. Gas, in
part, illuminates the cellar, and an incandescent lamp burns
continually, for the experts prefer to test the color of the wines
by its white glare.

Talk of driving away ghosts makes the process of demolition sound
almost reverent. But don't be misled. Whelan's tackled the Western
Market with a heft and ferocity, and an *ease*, that surprised even themselves. At a Whelan the Wrecker directors' meeting three months
earlier, the question had been raised: 'Would it be possible to buy
machines to reduce our wages bill?' They had gangs working a regular
seventy to ninety hours a week. The answer, in the form of a traxcavator, arrived just in time for the Western Market job.

Whelan's were becoming more businesslike all round. In 1958,
following the lead of the building industry, they began asking for
progress payments rather than a lump sum on completion of a job.
Deals were no longer sealed on a handshake, but with contracts in
triplicate, covering (almost) every contingency. As the refashioning
of the city gathered pace, contracts commonly imposed a penalty for
every week a demolition ran past its deadline. Only rarely, though,
when speed was critical, was an inducement offered to finish a job
ahead of time. The Western Market was one such instance.

Try this with a traxcavator – wrecking the old way at the Western Market.

The conjunction of traxcavator and bonus clause was a happy one for Whelan's. As with the Fish Market, they had little need to be neighbourly, and their new toy gave them the grunt to pull down vast expanses of wall at will and to clear away rubble in record time. In the hurry, there were mishaps. Flinders Lane was buried under a hail of bricks one Sunday, stopping the tram from running. Another time, a wall fell backwards into Market Street and Whelan's 'beast' swallowed half-a-dozen parking meters in the scramble to clean up. And while the market's foundation stone turned up amongst the rubble of a humbled wall, its accompanying box of keepsakes was nowhere to be found.

By the middle of March 1960, Melbourne's oldest market had been reduced to: 3,161 loads of rubble; 28½ loads (plus ten trailer-loads) of scrap; ten loads of rubbish; 76½ loads of firewood; 128,600 yards of good timber (including thousands of yards of jarrah flooring); 9½ loads of joinery; twelve loads of lead; 4½ loads of iron; and half a load of copper and brass. Given twelve weeks to wreck the Western Market, Whelan's and their traxcavator had done it in just seven, netting a bonus of £2,500 for their early finish. It was a success that went some way towards offsetting the Wrecker's losses on the intractable CML job, and spurred them on for the third leg of their market-wrecking trifecta.

Gone since 1960 and now twice-removed from its site, the Eastern Market lives on under the skin of the city. Its afterlife owes something to Peter Carey's* novel, *Illywhacker* (whose conman protagonist served his apprenticeship at the Eastern Market, learning about vegetables and the art of invisibility), but the market's immortality was mostly earned for itself, a hundred years ago and more.

Its development as a market ran along familial lines with that of the Western Market. But, of the cross-town sisters, the Eastern Market was the pretty one, the party girl, the one that'd do anything for a laugh. For decades either side of 1900, it epitomised the gaslight-and-shadows racketiness of Bourke Street East, home to theatres, wax-works and late-night bars; haunt of street gangs; and shopfront to the red-light hinterland. The glory of the Eastern Market had faded by the 1930s, when the *Herald* summed up its history thus: 'It was intended for the sale of vegetables and fruit, but Destiny had marked it out for a more romantic life.'

Reserved for public purposes in 1837, it was mooted first as the site for a church, only to be knocked back by the Methodists as being too far out of town. That isolation suited it for a female penitentiary, which was set down in 1840 near the corner of Stephen (Exhibition) and Little Collins streets. Another portion of the block was used, from 1842, as an unofficial market for hay and corn. The market site was made official in 1847, and the hay and corn dealers were joined by market gardeners, fruit growers, and sellers of every kind. The council, which controlled the market, built just eight stalls along the western boundary; the rest of the reserve would be covered, on market days, with carts and trestles set up in the open air. A line of 'miserable shanties' that grew up along Bourke Street lowered the market's tone until an outbreak of fire in 1855 supplied an excuse to pull them down.

Throughout the '50s, stallholders petitioned the council, without success, for permanent buildings to be erected at the Eastern Market. Despite its lack of shelter, though, the market proved far more popular

---

* Speaking of Peter Carey, the Whelan the Wrecker sign made its first Bacchus Marsh appearance in 1965, on the premises of P.S. Carey Motors, owned by the dual Booker prize-winner's father.

than its west-end counterpart. It was open every day, with Wednesdays and Saturdays the chief days for fruit and veg, and Saturday nights a gaslit bazaar.

> *Cheap John, in a cart ornamented with Chinese lanterns and hung around with saddles and bridles and bundles of clothes pegs, is busy selling a packet of envelopes, letterpaper and sealing wax by Dutch auction. The great competition is in apples. We hear a man roaring at the top of his voice, 'Heating happles, three pounds a shilling.' Another not less noisily announces 'Bakers and boilers, four pounds a shilling.' Next we come to a miniature drapery shop, where a man in a white beaver with a blue paper of pins fastened round it is inviting attention to his wares: 'Now's your time, ladies, a Paisley shawl for three and sixpence,' and then he wraps it round him to show its beauties. Looking over the shoulders of the crowd, we see a man selling soap, to which he ascribes miraculous cleansing powers … But the feature of the Market is the confectioners' stalls, blazing with light and glittering with wonderful feats in the art of making sugar candy.*
>
> ~ LEADER, JULY 1858

A grant from the government in 1859 afforded shelter at last for the Eastern marketeers, in the form of four long, open-sided sheds ranged parallel with Stephen Street. They were called 'arcades' rather than plain 'sheds', the corrugated iron roof of each one forming a double-arch 'of quite the railway station style'. At the same time, the market reserve was enlarged to take in the former site of the female prison (latterly a prison hospital), making it nearly half as big again as the Western Market. There was terrific competition for the 224 stalls at the new Eastern Market. All were quickly filled and yet more traders spilled over to line the roadways. On Saturday mornings, growers' carts extended up Bourke Street almost as far as Parliament House,

'Cheap John' stall at the Eastern Market, 1877.

while Stephen Street was the venue for a Saturday-night pigeon exchange, conducted by 'a moving mass of boys'.

The Saturday night bazaar went from strength to strength once the market was roofed in. The variously cheap, shoddy and secondhand character of the wares on sale gave rise to the name Paddy's Market (which in time attached itself to the market in its workaday aspect as well). Chief among the fast-food stalls and barrows were those selling oysters, a cheap snack and a messy one. Sunday mornings would find the Bourke Street footpath in a 'filthy' state, 'caused by oyster shells and stinking oysters being thrown over the surface'. In the packed and dazzling Saturday-night marketplace, oyster-vendors' cries merged with those of sideshow spruikers, making it hard to tell seller from showman –

> ... *every kind of marketable and unmarketable commodity*
> *seem suddenly mixed in one monster incantation, in which*
> *brass bands and nigger melodists, nasal prophets and itinerant*
> *wizards, gongs and drums, make up one terrific din and*
> *grotesque pandemonium.*
>
> ~ *ILLUSTRATED MELBOURNE POST*, 1860

Clearly the Eastern Market was as much meeting place as marketplace, on occasion acting the part of a public square – 'which Melbourne so strangely lacks'. Actually, there was nothing very strange about the omission, since, at the time Melbourne was laid out, colonial authorities frowned on public squares on the grounds that they 'encouraged the spirit of democracy'. Just such a spirit was manifest at the Eastern Market, where a 'people's forum' grew up in the late '50s, with stump-speakers expounding on the hot topics of the day. Things got too hot in August 1860, when the market – just a stone's throw, remember, from Parliament House – was the scene of a political meeting that erupted into riot. Hundreds of protesters chanting 'A Vote, a Rifle, and a Farm!'* mobbed the House, where Parliament was in session. Rocks were lobbed, every window broken, police rough-handled, the Riot Act read, and the odd parliamentarian jostled. A bill rushed through the very next day forbade gatherings of fifty or more people within a half-mile of Parliament House, and gun-slots were cut into the House's facade, giving a clean line of fire down Bourke Street. Which measures seem to have worked. 'The trade of the agitator is gone,' declared the *Argus* in 1864, 'the voice of the Eastern Market is hushed – the oracles of the stump are dumb.'

There were still the open-air preachers, though – 'turbulent as politicians and provocative as demagogues'. As many as four rival pulpiteers took to the field some Sundays, straining to howl one another down and inciting scuffles and slugfests between their several congregations. There was something about the Eastern Market, it seemed, that stoked excitement to a pitch and put a match to tempers.

There was friction too between the market gardeners and hay farmers. The former had the run of the market for the first shift of the day, and were meant to make way for the latter at 10 a.m. But the fruit and veg men dragged their heels and pretty soon were calling for a marketplace to themselves, where they could keep on selling till their carts were bare. The hay market† was relocated in 1874, but the

---

* They were urging land reform, to 'unlock' the vast holdings of the squatters for settlement by small farmers.

† The last remnants of the hay market, at the head of Elizabeth Street, were wrecked by Whelan's in 1963, to make way for the dental hospital.

Eastern Market remained overcrowded, with as many as six hundred stallholders vying for space each Wednesday and Saturday.

In 1878, the city council sought designs for a new Eastern Market, built on two levels. The Queen Victoria Market, already operating in a small way, was enlarged to accommodate fruit-and-vegetable sellers from the Eastern Market during rebuilding. For years, stallholders had resisted such a move, but now they found the Victoria Market so much to their liking that, two years later, when the Eastern Market reopened, few chose to return.

Unlike its predecessor, the new Eastern Market was entirely enclosed. Imposing two-storey shops faced Bourke and Stephen streets, with 'dwarf towers' over the market gateways, while a row of butchers' shambles faced Little Collins. Behind the frontages, the market's upper level was laid out in three long galleries with arched, sky-lit roofs. Along the sides of each gallery ran a series of decorative iron archways into which were set the permanent stalls of the general market. These were filled, in time, by sellers of flowers, pets, ironmongery, tobacco, books, and fancy goods, to name just a few. It was the lower level, lit (insufficiently) by lightwells, that was meant to replace the old growers' market – or rather, *half* the lower level, the other (eastern) half being taken up by 'a magnificent range of lofty and extensive brick cellarage'. Moreover, there were shops set round the walls of the lower marketplace, leaving less than half an acre clear for the growers and their carts – hardly the 'increased space' they'd been promised. Several fruit-sellers took out permanent stalls at the Eastern Market, but its days as a teeming produce market were over.

The new Eastern Market looked doomed to fail, and might have done so if not for E.W. Cole. Cole had trafficked books at the market – first from a barrow, then from a stall near the Bourke Street entrance – for nine years before founding his Book Arcade in Bourke Street proper. In 1881, the council leased its newest white elephant to Cole for a three-year term and, almost overnight, the Eastern Market sparked into life. Cole offered stalls at reduced rents and invited in the sideshow men, the brass band, and the hucksters – the staples, in other words, of the old Paddy's Market – and the whole of Melbourne seemed to follow.

Now every night was Saturday night at the Eastern Market. The galleries were lit with the 'cold blue splendour' of electricity, supplied by the pioneering Australian Electric Company; but there were still dark corners enough for romance and deception to flourish. Jim Crilly, showman extraordinaire, found no end of ways to simultaneously fleece and amuse the penny-paying public. Those tempted to 'Walk in and see the man-eating shark!' would find, behind the curtain, a man seated at a table eating a fillet of flake. Likewise 'the horse with its tail where its head should be' turned out to be, not a freak of nature, but a nag standing with its tail in a manger. There were shooting galleries, hoop-las and Aunt Sallys (effigies at which to hurl missiles); there was a Yankee doctor who pulled teeth in public, to brass-band accompaniment; there were livestock stalls selling possums, squirrels and monkeys; there was Charlie the tattoo artist and the strong woman who challenged any man to fight her; there were phrenologists and peepshows, fortune-tellers and astrologers. Among the soothsayers was Madame Zinga Lee, who wired herself up to a weak electric current so that clients would get a 'funny feeling' as she read their palm. (Madame's other claim to fame was her 'buxom' arms, which supplied the model for a figure of Queen Victoria at a waxworks down the road.) With just a penny, a schoolboy could treat himself to a plate of boiled peas and drink in the sights for free.

In this fashion, the Eastern Market continued to flourish long after E.W. Cole's three-year lease expired. All through Melbourne's boom years, while their social betters 'did' the Block, the working classes made the Eastern Market their favoured promenade. And its popularity hardly flagged in the '90s, when the gangs, or 'pushes' – the Crutchies, the Flying Angels, the Bouveries, and Squizzy Taylor's Bourke Street Rats – regularly clashed in its crowded arcades. Towards the end of that decade, the market was the scene of 'the Eastern Market Tragedy', a crime that served to frame the lurid seediness of the place. Frank Cartwright was the big-shot of the Eastern Market then. A vaudeville artist and 'ballyhoo man', he ran twenty-odd stalls of the sideshow sort. One was occupied by his fortune-telling wife; next door was the astrologer, 'Professor' Medor. A reputed crackpot, Medor was the butt of practical jokes, one of which – a pair of carrots hung over his door – seems to have unhinged him completely. He burst into his neighbour's stall with a revolver and Cartwright, rushing from the other end of the market, was shot in the head then almost decapitated by the carrot-crazed astrologer. The case was given a long run in the scandal-sheets and left the market with a taint that would prove hard to live down. In 1921, when the body of a twelve-year-old girl was found in Gun Alley, close by, the press was quick to cast the Eastern Market – harbourer of lowlife – as prime suspect.

Often during its long heyday the market was described as 'oriental' or 'almost Eastern' in atmosphere. By the 1930s, its heyday was past, eclipsed by the attractions of St Kilda and the talkies. There were remnants of that atmosphere still, though, in an alleyway of herbalists' stalls, an artist painting to order in a picture-framer's shop, and the chirrup and yap of pet shops and poultry dealers. But the once-hectic lower level of the market was given over now to carparking, the only trace of the old times being a weighing machine in one corner. 'In those days,' a veteran stallholder reminisced in 1933, 'you could try your strength on a punch-ball or feel an electric shock or see your horoscope for a penny. All you can do now is weigh yourself.'

That same year, the Eastern Market was nearly lost to fire. The city council patched it up and then, having recently gained control of the site from the State government, set about considering how it might be redeveloped for a profit. The likeliest scheme was for a Broadcasting House, to be let to the Australian Broadcasting Commission. Then came the war and, as with the Western Market, all schemes were put on hold for the duration.

The post-war city had no taste for sentimentality, and the Eastern

Market was assailed in 1945 as 'This dreary morgue … a vast, rambling monstrosity, half waste and given over to the decayed stalls of forgotten corn-curers and poulterers.' The site was plagued by the same setbacks as the Western Market, visions for its redevelopment going nowhere until the advent of a 99-year lease. Finally, at the start of 1960, came the announcement: Pan American Airways would build a fourteen-storey international hotel, the Southern Cross, to replace the 'anachronism' that was the Eastern Market.

The old place had been steadily emptying since 1953, when a freeze was imposed on new tenancies. There were still a few florists' shops, furniture dealers, a book seller, print shop, milliner, dressmaker, tailor, ironmonger – but not a single fruit stall, no pets for sale, no spiritualists or healers. All the life of the Eastern Market was gone, and now the 'senile' building itself was condemned to the wreckers.

Owen Whelan remembers going round the market with his uncle Jim, to price the job. As they sized it up for demolition, 'You know,' said Jim, 'this place is dead. But I used to come here with your grand-people as a kid, and they'd always shout me something special.'

'Oh, what would that be?' asked Owen.

'A plate of peas for a penny!'

One afternoon a few months later, doing the rounds of Whelan's city wrecking sites, Owen called in at the Eastern Market. 'You should've been here half an hour ago,' said Gordon, the time-keeper. A Rolls Royce had pulled up at the site office and a well-presented, elderly gent had asked if he could take a look around. 'As a kid, I sold papers on this corner,' he'd told Gordon, 'and when I'd finished, I'd nick inside and shout myself a plate of peas for a penny.' Owen had just missed seeing his second old man alight with glee at the memory of boiled peas on a plate.

Demolition began on 2 May 1960. First the stalls were stripped out, then the shops around the market perimeter, then it was on to the roof of the galleries where Whelan's men had the perilous pleasure of smashing the glass 'lantern windows' before dismantling the rest. With their canopies gone, the market galleries were reduced to an Ash Wednesday landscape of cast iron pillars, three metres tall and crowned by spindly iron lace inset with crests bearing the City of Melbourne coat-of-arms. Most of the crests were incorporated as decoration in the Club Grill of the Southern Cross Hotel, with just a few sold or souvenired as garden features.

Demolition continued through June 1960 on two fronts: the brickwork of the Little Collins Street frontage and the Bourke Street verandahs. Flanking an entrance at the Bourke Street corner was a pair of square pillars, faced with mirror-backed display cases. When they removed the mirrors at the end of June, the wreckers found layer upon layer of old advertising placards; and behind the placards on the westernmost pillar lay the foundation stone of the Eastern Market. It was badly cracked, but at least they'd found it. 'They can't touch that stone,' reported the *Sun*, 'until some folk come down from the Town Hall. You never know what might be under it.'

Eastern Market, c.1888, with the site of the foundation stone circled.

Actually, recent experience had given both Whelan's and the folk from the town hall a pretty good idea of what they might find. That crack in the stone had the Whelans worried – had thieving navvies dropped it in their eagerness to spend the Lord Mayor's sovereign? Wary of unpleasant surprises, Whelan's had their foreman raise the stone before the official ceremony, to check that the contents were intact. On the morning of the ceremony, the foundation stone was fitted with a couple of iron pins, slung to a crane, and Whelan's foreman did as instructed. A quick look satisfied him that all was well. But he did more than instructed. Before the stone was settled back into place, he slipped something else underneath: a scrap of cardboard inscribed FOO WAS HERE. Come midday, there were dignitaries gathered round and a TV news camera trained on the foundation stone. Only as the crane began tremblingly to lift the stone did the foreman, in a whisper, let Owen Whelan in on the joke. Owen's response sent the foreman scuttling forward to help guide the stone from its resting place. He managed to dispose of FOO before the stone swung clear to reveal a tarnished copper canister, unmolested, in the niche underneath. Even better, the canister rattled: the coins coughed up by the mayor in 1878 were all still safe inside.

The Bourke and Exhibition street frontages came down during July, leaving only the lower market level and cellars. Whelan's took to them with traxcavator, swinging ball, and dynamite. On 23 September, the Wrecker's site diary records: 'The last walls were pulled today. Nothing remains standing.'

Amongst the inventory of materials to which the Eastern Market had been reduced ('2,813 loads of rubble, 79 tons of cast iron …') was a lucrative thirty tons of lead from the roofs. In all likelihood, Jim would've anticipated that when preparing his demolition estimate. He taught the Whelans-in-training always, when they found themselves in a tall city building, to look down and note, for future reference, which of the neighbours had lead on their roofs.

On the Western Market job, the pursuit of speed had seen Whelan's consign a million-plus bricks to landfill. But at the Eastern Market 1,088,500 bricks were salvaged intact. Taken away for cleaning, nearly all of them were returned to the city soon after and set down just a block from where they'd tumbled. After the Eastern Market, Whelan's next job was to pull down the Old White Hart Hotel, at the corner of Bourke and Spring streets. There'd been a White Hart Inn on the site since 1847, ten years before Parliament House took its place opposite. The Old White Hart that Whelan's felled was the hotel's third incarnation, built around 1900. In its place was to be built an extension to the Hotel Windsor. The plan was that the new wing should blend in with the old and, to that end, the architect stipulated the use of recycled bricks. You might think it wouldn't have mattered, since the extension, like the old Windsor, was to be plaster-rendered. But with new bricks there was a danger that they would expand as they aged, causing the render to crack. The architect insisted on 'a brick without movement' and Whelan's were well-placed to supply it.

One last concurrence was the Royal Mail Hotel, wrecked by Whelan's in October 1960. At the south-east corner of Bourke and Swanston streets, its site was regarded at that time as 'the best left in the city for retail development'. The Royal Mail had stood there, in shifting guise, since the mid-1840s, originating as 'an uncouth-looking, large, rough edifice' built by a road contractor for his private residence. It became a hotel in 1848, taking its name from the principal business of its first owner: he was contractor for the Melbourne–Sydney mail route. Modifications to the Royal Mail (including a 'Continental luncheon-room') in 1934 had called for partial demolition, overseen by the bowler-hatted Jim Whelan the First. One of the building's original walls at that time yielded up bricks bearing thumbprints – thought to be a mark of convict manufacture. A visiting Tasmanian identified the brick-clay as being of Port Arthur origin and, in that year of Melbourne's centenary, the bricks from the Royal Mail were declared to be among the city's oldest.

When, near the end of Whelan's *annus mirabilis*, 1960, the Royal Mail was brought to ground, the rubble of uncouth edifice and luncheon-room was scooped up by machine, holus bolus, so that a thumb-dented brick was bound to go unnoticed.

FINDINGS KEEPINGS

We've never found a bag of gold or that sort of thing – to our knowledge.

~ OWEN WHELAN, 1967

Whelan's used their first diesel excavator – a 10-RB with a half-yard bucket – to clean up on the Melbourne Mansions job in 1958. With less of the rubble passing through their hands, wrecking crews found fewer coins after that.

From the '50s onwards, demolition contracts included a clause to the effect that 'Any antiquities, coins, memorial stones, caskets and objects of value or historic interest other than building materials shall remain the property of the proprietor and be handed over to the Architect.' But Owen Whelan concedes now that –

It was usually 'findings keepings', because if a bloke came along and said, 'Owen, look, I've just found a golden sovereign,' [I'd have to say] 'Thank's Bill, put it in here. I'll give it to some architect, far removed, who'll pass it on to someone further removed …' No, you'd never hear about anything being found on the site.

Bill Whelan (no relation) with coins found under the floor at Hosie's Hotel, 1953.

Old Jim Whelan, as we have seen, had felt free to boast of finding sovereign hoards and the like – though only, you suspect, at some distance from the event. One story carried down since his time relates the discovery of seventy-five or eighty sovereigns in the wreckage of a building in Collins Street. Was it Anzac House, up near Russell Street, pulled down by Jim's sons in 1938? Owen thinks it might've been. And the tin that held the sovereigns – was it under the floorboards or plastered up in a chimney? Whatever the case, the office in which it was found had formerly belonged to a dentist. Had he served time for robbery or planned to melt the sovs down for gold fillings? Theories abound. As to what became of the tinful of sovereigns afterwards ... on that point the record is silent.

A man who might've known something about it was George 'Scratchy' Roberts. He worked with Whelan's from old Jim's time until the late 1960s and owed his nickname to the vigour with which he would pull up floorboards to 'scratch' for coins underneath. 'When we're demolishing a hotel,' Owen told a reporter in 1968, 'the old hands always want to be the first to start on the bar-room floor. They know small change filters through the floorboards.' Wrecking a Bourke Street hotel in the early '60s, a Whelan's gang had struck a minor bonanza in the shape of a rat's nest. 'There was a tremendous scuffle,' Owen recalled, 'and quite a lot of sixpences and threepences rolled onto the floor before a couple of fellows took a day off on the proceeds' – about £5. One curious thing, Owen remarked, 'We've never found a penny in a bank.'

On house demolitions, the most rewarding spots – not just for coins, but for valuables like jewellery – were around hearths and behind mantelpieces. Tom Whelan once found a diamond-studded watch that way. Also popular as a scratching-place was by the back door, where delivery men used to be paid and where, sometimes, small change would be lost – eventually to be found by Whelan's.

CHAPTER 11

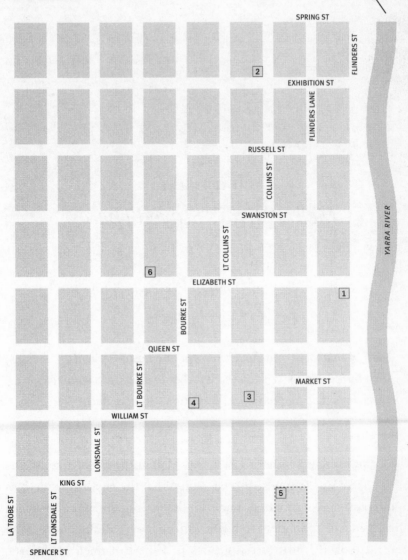

1. Hosie's Hotel
2. Occidental Hotel
3. Scott's Hotel
4. Menzies' Hotel
5. Federal Hotel
6. Tin Shed

CHAPTER 11

Melba Always Stayed There

Hosie's Hotel ~ Occidental Hotel ~ Scott's Hotel ~ Menzies' Hotel ~
Federal Hotel ~ Tin Shed

Most of that city's grand old belle epoque hostelries had
been torn down by Whelan the Wrecker to allay international
suspicions that Australian architecture was out of date.

~ BARRY HUMPHRIES

The Waikiki-blue Southern Cross was Melbourne's first hotel of the
jet age. Here was (supposed to be) a sign that the city had made it as
an international destination. But even the developers of the Southern
Cross weren't as confident to begin with as their building made them
seem. It took the visit of the Beatles in 1964 to launch Melbourne
into the '60s and set the Southern Cross as the new standard for city
hotels.

If you wanted daiquiris and a kidney-shaped swimming pool – as
the Beatles plainly did – the Southern Cross was the *only* place to
stay. Melbourne's conventional top hotels were all eighty years old
or more and geared to an age of rail and steamships and tea-dances.

Gracious and *dignified*, even *homely*, were the modest encomiums on which their reputations and bedrooms were built. They relied for their traditional patronage on the Victorian squatter class, visiting town for their three 'seasons' each year. Behind them came the interstate trade, with international travellers a comparative rarity. At any rate, it was supposed that guests from overseas would appreciate the indigenous qualities – comfort, service, plain food – of Melbourne's better hotels, the way they would, say, the steamy charm of Raffles Hotel in Singapore. As the twentieth century advanced and their staple custom died away, however, the hotels looked yearningly to the international tourist trade. And it became clear that old-world charm alone would not do.

A commentator in the *Sun* observed in 1958 that the big hotel companies 'can't get rid of any Australian atmosphere quickly enough. Personally,' he went on, 'I think this a mistaken attitude' –

> *and that even that glamorous figure, the hypothetical American tourist spilling dollars as he walks, would be glad to stay at a comfortable Australian hotel rather than one that looked as if it had just been run up in Hackensack, N.J.*

The hotels had been aware of their limitations for decades before that, though, and had long sought ways of attracting not just lodgers from abroad but fun-seekers from the suburbs. In 1920, an *Argus* reporter seeking nightlife in the city had found 'singularly little'. Once the theatres emptied, the streets became deserted and 'to the would-be reveller Melbourne is a city of dreadful night'. The man from the *Argus* could find only 'one or two establishments which make some attempt to emulate the night-club of London and the cabaret of New York, and with the aid of a string band and a few coloured balloons attain the atmosphere of a kind of "bowdlerised" Bohemia'.

To blame was Victoria's 'Temporary Restriction Bill' of 1915, which made it illegal to serve alcohol after 6 p.m. The same Act outlawed dancing on licensed premises after that same hour, an absurd restriction that the managers of Melbourne's most reputable hotels sought to overturn in 1930, arguing that 'in these times of depression people should be given some opportunity of enjoying themselves and forgetting their troubles'. Overseas, trends like cocktail parties, dinner-dances, and *dinuit* (dining at midnight) were taking off; in Melbourne, you couldn't take a drink with dinner or shuffle your feet in a hotel after six. 'Moving with the times' was an impossibility.

Visitors from abroad found Victoria's drinking laws ... well, Victorian, and anything but a drawcard. Reports like one in the *Herald* in 1937, headed HOTELS LIKE MORGUES, regularly drew attention to the complaints and disparaging remarks of overseas guests regarding the dullness of the city's hotels. Pearson Tewksbury, owner of the Oriental Hotel at the top end of Collins Street, was perhaps the most vocal advocate for change. A regular overseas traveller himself, he never failed, upon returning, to blast the fustiness imposed on Melbourne's hotels.

Within the trussed-up liquor laws, Tewksbury, more than any other city hotelier, did all he could to keep abreast of international trends. In the '20s the Oriental was remodelled 'on the newest cosmopolitan lines', featuring self-contained suites – in contrast to the usual communal bathrooms – and a restaurant-café. In the '30s the Oriental proposed introducing the 'picturesque Continental innovation' of a boulevard café – a scheme for which approval would take *twenty-five* years, but which would eventually give Collins Street its 'Paris end'. After the war Tewksbury visited the US 'in search of new ideas', then drew up plans for a new, high-rise Oriental, to attract international tourists. Though the Olympic Games were by that time in the offing, Tewksbury declared he 'wouldn't spend tuppence' on upgrading his hotel just for the Olympics ('a momentary phase in our normal life'). Accommodation for overseas visitors was, he insisted, 'both an urgent and permanent necessity'.*

---

* Tewksbury's Oriental Hotel features more fully in Chapter 13.

A referendum in March 1956 offered a chance to overturn the six-o'clock-closing law in time for the Olympics. A majority of Melburnians, however, opted for capital city Dullsville – or to STICK TO SIX, as the slogan went. And it turned out that there was some tourism capital to be had from the antiquated licensing laws. During the Olympics, Melbourne's 'six o'clock swill' came in for almost as much international press coverage as the Games themselves. Accounts of 'the swill' – the thirty minutes each day during which hotel drinkers stampeded to quaff as much beer as possible before closing-time – appeared in newspapers from New York to Moscow. To the local press, though, it was a matter of shame. In all his travels, Reg Leonard of the *Sun* had nowhere experienced anything as 'revolting and disgusting' as 'the daily demonstration of piggery' in the hotels of Melbourne. One result of the six o'clock swill was 'the occupational disease of brewers' architecture': bars tiled wall-to-floor, for easy hosing down after the daily maelstrom.

A 'momentary phase' it may have been, but the 1956 Olympics mightily overtaxed the accommodation capacity of Melbourne's hotels. Back in 1947, Pearson Tewksbury had scorned the temerity of courting the Games when the city had barely enough accommodation to satisfy the interstate trade. In the event, only about 3,200 Olympic visitors would find beds in city and suburban hotels, leaving 15,000 to be billeted in private homes. To boost the number of hotel beds in the lead-up to the Olympics, amended liquor laws had insisted that every hotel must offer accommodation. It was this, in part, that led to a flurry of hotel wreckings in the early '50s.

Hosie's, for example, was among the city's most popular hotels, but hadn't a single bed for hire. Its position opposite the Elizabeth Street entrance to Flinders Street station (it had originated as the Hobson's Bay Railway Terminus Hotel) made it ideally placed for six o'clock swillers, but its popularity rested chiefly on a reputation for good food. Originally, it had accommodation for six guests, but when James

Hosie, whose name still clung to it, ran the hotel for three years in the 1880s, the bedrooms made way for dining rooms. Hosie was the same man who founded the Scotch Pie Shop in Bourke Street, among other successful ventures in the food-and-drink line. He sold out in 1888 to the soon-to-be legendary Melbourne victuallers, Michael Parer and the Barbeta brothers. Hosie's heyday as an eating-house came in the early years of the twentieth century, when its landlord supplied the kitchen from his own farm and a threepenny meal from Hosie's – an inch-thick steak or a mountain of sausages and mash – would keep a railwayman stoked all day. Threepence more bought a pint of beer.

Built of brick and bluestone in 1854, Hosie's was sturdy enough and flourishing enough to outlast its centenary. But the new licensing regulations meant that, in 1953, the hotel had either to add guest accommodation or close for good. The former course meant demolition and rebuilding, and that's the way it went. Whelan's pulled down the old Hosie's in August 1953, starting with the dining room doors. Half an hour after their brass trim received its final daily polish, the doors were on their way to Whelan's yard. There was a splendid staircase as well, and a fanlight painted with a portrait of an auburn-haired 'Olivia'. 'Who is Olivia?' the *Herald* wanted to know, but answer came there none. Dressed in a fashion far older than the hotel, was she modelled on Shakespeare's countess from *Twelfth Night*, or the Vicar of Wakefield's daughter? Whatever her origins, Hosie's landlord declared Olivia 'too nice a piece of work to go' and secured the fanlight from the wreckers.

In place of the old hotel arose a 'super-Hosie's': thirteen storeys tall, with a coloured glass and aluminium facade 'of contemporary American design', and – to satisfy the Licensing Court – a complement of bedrooms. Despite the thirteen floors, though, Hosie's pocket-sized site made it a bijou hotel, accommodation-wise. Allowing space on every floor for three lifts (two passenger, one goods) plus stairs left not a great deal of room for sleeping. But Hosie's had done its bit for Melbourne and the Olympics. And so had Whelan's.

An unprecedented number of city hotels closed in the course of the '50s. On top of the blighting liquor laws, the cost of running a city drinking-hole increasingly outstripped the return, putting pressure on hotel-owners to turn valuable sites to more profitable use. Then there were the flashy motels in the suburbs which, by the end of the decade, were applying competitive heat to the big city hotels.

Seventy-five years earlier, British travel writer Richard Twopeny had ranked the United Service Club Hotel, at the Collins–Stephen Street corner, among Melbourne's best residential hotels. Renamed the Occidental, in 1958 it was under sentence of demolition. The rambling old hotel had suffered quite a decline since the palmy days of the land boom. Back in 1848, the (then) Duke of York Hotel had been the only public-house at the doctorly east end of Collins Street. Its heyday as a lodging-house of repute ran from the 1870s, when it was rebuilt and enlarged, into the early decades of the twentieth century. As proof of the hotel's standing at that period, it was claimed that 'Melba always stayed there when she came to town.' In the end, though, it played scruffy country cousin to the trend-sensitive Oriental, across the street.

A licensing inspector went through the Occidental in 1956 and found it 'old-fashioned in many respects'. Dishwashing was done in a galvanised-iron tub, besides which –

> … the hotel's ventilation was inadequate, the bar room too
> small … the toilet facilities should be improved, the bathrooms
> modernised, and the vestibule used for food-serving should be
> renovated and fly-proofed.

The Occidental satisfied neither Board of Works sewerage standards nor municipal building regulations. The absentee owner, unwilling to spend £10,000 on improvements to a struggling concern, instead 'disposed of' the hotel and land for a price exceeding £100,000. The new owners proposed building a 'bigger and better' Occidental, before deciding that, since 'Melbourne is not a tourist terminal', they couldn't hope to recoup their outlay.

Though the future of the site was uncertain, the future of the Occidental was not. It closed in September 1958. During its final half-hour, the Occidental was so thronged with shouts that the supply of glasses was exhausted; then, 'With perfect timing, the last keg ran dry as the cry of "Time, gents, please" sounded in the tiny, wooden-panelled bar for the last time.' Three days later, the hotel's contents were auctioned – everything from mahogany luggage racks (£1 each) to a lamp that hung outside the door (five shillings). The varnished timber bar was bought by the makers of the movie *On the Beach* for Ava Gardner to lean on as she dosed herself for doomsday.

With its narrow and twisting passageways, 'quaint' upper gallery and potted palms, the old Occidental had looked, said the *Sun*, 'as if it had been there since the gold rush'.

> *It was one of the last links with a more leisurely, easy-going*
> *Melbourne when Australians were content to be themselves and*
> *the customs and decorative schemes of Honolulu and Las Vegas*
> *were not regarded as necessarily the high peak of civilisation.*

The residential side of the Occidental had long been under the benevolent management of a Mrs Baird, who knew all her regulars by name and ancestry, fed them good, plain food, and made sure that, in lieu of central heating, there were stoneware hot-water bottles in their beds. The Occidental was, in other words, a country hotel plonked down in the city and burdened by precisely the sort of 'Australian atmosphere' that the big hotel companies were keen to do away with.

Whelan's were given an eight-week deadline for the Occidental demolition. Two years later, the site was still empty, except for cars. As a charity fundraiser, a display home stood on the corner block for a while – the first house built in Collins Street for ... nobody could say how long

Wrecking the Occidental Hotel.

– then was demolished in turn for the Reserve Bank's Melbourne office. Whelan the Wrecker's own office, built a few years later, would incorporate a relic of the Occidental Hotel: a pair of frosted-glass swing doors misleadingly inscribed 'Residential Lounge'.

'We'll all be sorry to see a hotel like Scott's go. It's a part of Melbourne.' That was the general manager of the Australian National Travel Association, responding to the news, in 1961, that Scott's Hotel would shortly close. 'At the same time,' he went on, 'we welcome the new international-type hotel.' He meant the just-opened Southern Cross, which was certain to 'absorb' most of Scott's trade.

Scott's would be the twenty-third city hotel closure since 1951, and the first of Melbourne's top hotels to go. Until the Southern Cross was built, the top city hotels were five in number and long in tooth. Besides Scott's, there were Menzies', the Oriental, the Windsor, and the Federal, the last-named and youngest being seventy-three years old. Within a decade, Whelan's wrecked all but one of them.

Scott's was the oldest of the top hotels and, by some reckoning, the longest-lived hotel in Melbourne. Its progenitor was the Lamb Inn, licensed in 1837. George Smith bought the allotment at the town's first land sale, in June that year, and built his inn out of timber scavenged from pre-survey buildings that had been displaced by roads and public reserves. The Lamb Inn incorporated fragments of John Pascoe Fawkner's hotel – built in 1835 on what turned out to be the Customs House reserve – and of a house blocking William Street, belonging to John Batman's brother, Henry. The impression this gives of a cobbledy construction is probably misleading, for when the 'fast [i.e., sound] weather-board hostelry' was put on the market in 1840 it boasted thirty-one rooms, with cellars set into its stone foundations. But in the three years intervening, the Lamb Inn had gained a reputation for fastness of another kind. 'Never was a sign more inappropriate,'* wrote a visitor from van Diemen's Land in 1839 –

> *Instead of its affording rest and shelter to the weary traveller,*
> *the orgies that were kept up day after day and night after night*
> *within its walls, converted it into a perfect den of drunkenness*
> *and vice.*

The culprits were not the scum of the town, socially speaking, but rather its cream: the younger sons of good families, set loose far from home. Their larks – furious-riding, vandalism, and high-end thuggery – earned them the label 'Waterfordians'† from the press. On New Year's Day 1839, in a meeting at the Lamb Inn, their society took formal, and lasting, shape as the Melbourne Club. Though the Club shortly removed its headquarters to the other side of Collins Street, it retained a rough shed at the rear of the Lamb Inn, for use as a 'deadhouse' – a refuge for the desperately drunk.

After it changed hands in 1840, the Lamb Inn's new owners added a long brick room to the west side of the building. Ostensibly a billiard-room, it was also used for coroner's inquests, which is why, years later, a Melbourne pioneer recalled having seen his first dead man – a bushranger with a bullet in his brain – stretched out on a billiard table at the Lamb Inn. Blame the loss of the Melbourne Club or blame the cadavers, but the Lamb Inn fell out of favour in the early '40s. It went unlicensed for several years, during which time the billiard-room was

---

* Evidently the writer construed the inn's name as a reference to the lamb of God, 'which taketh away the sin of the world' (John 1:29).

† After the reprobate Marquis of Waterford, then at the height (or depth) of his depravity.

occupied by Redmond Barry's Court of Requests, for the recovery of small debts.

In 1849, the Lamb Inn and its billiard-room were replaced by the all-brick Clarendon Family Hotel which, in turn, was largely rebuilt after Edward Scott became owner in 1860. Described as a man of 'distinguished air ... who imparted a tone of aristocratic superiority', Scott aspired to the same qualities for his hotel. Though he would move on after just eight years, the reputation built under Scott's stewardship was such that the hotel kept his name ever after. Scott sold his hotel in 1868 to William C. Wilson, in whose family's ownership it remained for eighty years without ever taking their name.

William Wilson himself managed the hotel until 1903. His description – 'a most courteous gentleman, of stately mien and carriage' – cuts him of the same cloth as his predecessor and, under his management, Scott's Hotel continued to shine. In the '70s, Anthony Trollope stayed at the rival Menzies' Hotel, but conceded that 'the Scottites declare that to be as good – a thorough Scottite will perhaps say better'. It makes you wonder what set the two hotels, and their customers, apart. A clue might be found in the observations of Richard Twopeny. 'Menzies' and the Oriental are most to be recommended,' he wrote in 1883; 'after these try the United Services Club, or, *if you be a bachelor*, Scott's.' Something of the old Lamb Inn spirit seems to have endured, then, though its manifestations are hard to pin down. Scott's was bachelor-ish – how? Fond retrospectives, such as the Scott's 1937 centenary booklet, depicted a certain clubbishness, it's true. But it was a seemly clubbishness; nothing risque peeped through. Nothing, for instance, about an abortion clinic in the hotel basement, for which, it seems, Scott's was infamous.

After the original Wilson's death in 1903, the hotel underwent a period of modernisation and expansion. To its Collins Street frontage, alongside Temple Court, was added a seven-storey wing of bedrooms fitted with private bathrooms, putting Scott's at the forefront of the ensuite trend. From that period through till the 1950s, Scott's shared

SCOTT'S HOTEL

COLLINS STREET (WEST) MELBOURNE.

SCOTT'S is the Quietest and yet Most Central of all the Leading Hotels.

SCOTT'S is within Walking Distance of the Railway Stations, Wharves, Theatres and Shopping Centres.

SCOTT'S has just been REBUILT and REFURNISHED with all the latest improvements in Sanitation, Heating and Ventilation, Private Telephones and Hot and Cold Water in Bedrooms, Fireproof Floors and Walls, thus making it the most comfortable, safe and up-to-date Hotel in Australia.

Bed and Breakfast, 8/6.   Inclusive Terms, 14/- per day.

Descriptive Tariff Free by Post.

Suites of Rooms—Terms on Application.

C. W. WILSON, Proprietor.

From Melbourne Guide Book, 5th ed., 1911.

top billing as 'the place to stay' in Melbourne with its rearward neighbour Menzies' and Pearson Tewksbury's Oriental. 'Everyone who was anyone stopped with us,' a former Scott's pageboy recalled. 'And that Dame Nellie Melba was *someone*. She was fiery,' he said, 'but when she was there you should have seen the bank notes flying around.' As for the hotel basement, it became the premises of a firm of stock and station agents.

Beginning in 1955, Scott's changed hands three times in six years. The first new owners planned to upgrade the hotel; the second talked of incorporating an improved Scott's with a department store and office block. But the third buyers, the Royal Insurance Co., didn't beat around the bush: Scott's Hotel would be demolished. Near the end of 1961, 'Ellen and the Two-Shilling School' advertised in the *Sun* classifieds for a new watering-hole. Ellen was a barmaid at Scott's back bar, and the Two-Shilling School a group of local businessmen who met there daily. 'Twenty-five thirsty members urgently require elbow-room in similar establishment, equivalent service, same locality. Bring own Barmaid,' ran their advert. The group's guiding principle was to avoid getting into a large drinking 'school' – where shout followed shout, all the way to inebriation – and to that end, 'We just put 2/ on the counter, have what drinks we like, and leave.' On the last Friday of December 1961 they set down their florins, drank their sparing fill, and left Scott's Hotel for good.

A week-long auction stripped the hotel of its contents and fixtures before the wreckers took possession in May 1962. What was left, though, was an eye-opener to the younger Whelans. They found the rear-annexe kitchen, which had served Scott's prestige Buttery restaurant, rat-infested and blackened with grime. Myles was nearly ill when he thought of the times he'd eaten there. Owen had gone with Jim to price the Scott's demolition, and remembers taking out his geological pick to test the mortar between bricks in the seven-storey addition. 'What the heck are you doing?' asked Jim. Owen told him: just checking how hard it would be to pull down. 'Put it away, pal,' said Jim, resignedly. 'It'll be rubbish.' He knew it had been built by Pop Shillabeer, a contemporary of his father's and 'a terrific bloke', but who was 'renowned for waving a cement bag in front of the concrete-mixer'. And Jim was right. The concrete was so light-on that the floors fractured during demolition and the building practically knocked itself down.

'The sad truth of the "Top Hotel" business in Melbourne is there aren't enough "Top People" to go around,' reported the *Sun* in 1963. So the hotels (all but the unbending Windsor) were reduced to wooing the 'Middle People' instead. 'We need ordinary people with ordinary bank accounts,' is how one top-hotel manager put it. The Oriental had its trendy Rib Room, family smorgasbords were on offer at the Chevron on St Kilda Road, and a jazz band serenaded lunching businessmen at the Southern Cross. Increasingly, though, city hotels were losing guests to motels and diners to the new breed of classy licensed restaurants. February 1966 finally saw the end of six o'clock closing, but the extension of drinking hours until 10 p.m. couldn't save the – hitherto – top hotels.

That they fought hard to save themselves is apparent from the extent to which the once-lofty Menzies' let its dignity drop. To counter the hep-cat aesthetic of the Southern Cross, Menzies' transformed its Chandelier Room into a 'Hollywood-style' cocktail lounge studded with 'big name' floorshow attractions like Al Martino, Shirley

Bassey, and the Shadows. The biggest challenge for the top hotels, explained Menzies' long-time manager, Henry Timmermans, was the rise of youth culture. Until the '50s, entertainment trends had been set by the older generation, whose needs Menzies' and its fogie peers felt well-equipped to meet. But, 'Today,' said Timmermans, 'it's the young people who set the tone.' Menzies' pulled out all stops with the introduction in 1967 of 'Menzies Big Beat', a $4.50 buffet meal 'with a semi-discotheque atmosphere'. Try as it might, though, Menzies' atmosphere remained more drawing-room than discotheque. And its west-end locale didn't help. Not even the vintage-camp of bare-breasted bronze lamp-bearers flanking the hotel entrance could pull in the rising, frugging, *spending* generation. Menzies' was doomed.

The hotel had been built in 1867 on Archibald Menzies' share of gold from the phenomenal Balaclava Hill mine, near Rushworth. Menzies had run a hotel in La Trobe Street, popular with gold diggers, and his investment in one of his customer's concerns had paid off magnificently. His new hotel, at the corner of Bourke and William streets,* was claimed to occupy 'the highest ground in Melbourne', close to the business centre 'yet sufficiently retired to ensure almost the quiet of the country'. Its opening was timed to coincide with a visit by the Duke of Edinburgh, whose return custom Menzies successfully wooed. Royalty being thin on the ground, though, the hotel relied most of the time on the patronage of the squatter class. For sixty or seventy years, it was a Melbourne society tradition to lunch at Menzies' on the day the English mail arrived. And at the same period that Scott's was the supposed resort of bachelors, Menzies' hosted some famous bucks' parties, including one in 1887 at which a lone champagne glass, out of a hundred or more, survived the festivities intact.

Archibald Menzies died in 1889, by which time there were bigger hotels than Menzies', but still none classier. It was the only hotel south of the equator entitled to use the Royal Crest on its napery. To the

---

* Formerly the site of Victoria's volunteer militia headquarters.

From Melbourne Guide Book, 5th ed., 1911.

original three storeys, two more were added in 1896. Three squat towers (Menzies' had shared architects with the dwarf-towered Eastern Market) gave way to just one, loftier and with more flounce to it, at the Bourke Street corner. At the same time, the hotel interior was remodelled. One of Menzies' proudest features was its reading-room, on the ground floor facing William Street. Fitted with double-thick carpets, it boasted red velvet divans, tables covered with crimson-and-gold tapestry, walls hand-painted with native flora, and heavy silk curtains against the noise of city traffic. There was a writing-room besides, 'like an elegant school room' with ranks of writing tables beneath a cherub-painted ceiling.

As well as royalty and the squatterage, Menzies' played host, over the years, to the city's most distinguished visitors: musicians, actors, writers and statesmen. Anthony Trollope stayed there in the '70s and felt 'bound to say' that 'I have never put myself up at a better inn at any part of the world' – a commendation on which Menzies' would trade for nearly a century. Mark Twain, in Melbourne on a lecture tour, insisted on stoking the Menzies' boilers as part of his daily fitness regime. Sixty-odd years later, actor–singer Danny Kaye would request a table-tennis table in his suite and spend half the night playing ping-pong. Dame Nellie Melba, needless to say, 'always' stayed at Menzies' (her father, the contractor David Mitchell, had built the place), though she once snapped at a desk clerk, 'I hate this bloody pub.' The pianist Paderewski, a Menzies' guest in 1904, found the food there so bad that he and his wife had to subsist 'almost entirely on pineapples' from the Western Market. H.G. Wells stayed on the fourth floor, as did John Masefield, in Melbourne for the dedication of the Shrine of Remembrance. Returning from the ceremony, the Poet Laureate was conveyed to his floor by Harold, the liftman. 'It was very moving, Harold,' said Masefield. But what Menzies' resident philosopher wanted to know was, 'Did anybody speak the bloody truth?'

A grand, Adam-style dining room extended the William Street frontage in the '20s and the hotel passed out of Menzies family ownership soon after. The new owner's plans for building up to the height limit and giving an ensuite to every room were cut short by the war. In fact, had he but known it, Menzies' day was nearly done. One last glimmer of reflected glory lay ahead when, in 1942, the top floor became for a time General Douglas MacArthur's South-West Pacific headquarters. The Federal Hotels chain acquired Menzies' in 1954 and sought to highlight its 'solid dignity' and 'old-world charm' by reintroducing top-hatted doormen. Here was the first hint of gimmickry and out-and-out pitching to a market identified by Federal Hotels as the 'ultra-conservative European type'. An enormous crystal chandelier – billed as the biggest in the southern hemisphere – was hoisted to the ceiling of the dining room, re-christened the Chandelier Room.

Once words like 'glittering' and 'sophisticated' began attaching themselves to the dining experience, inevitably the word 'penthouse' wasn't far behind. The end of the '50s saw renewed plans to redevelop Menzies'. Its eastern neighbour on Bourke Street, Selborne Chambers – a long arcade-like building, lined with barristers' chambers – was acquired in 1960 as the site for a multi-storey, penthoused Menzies' extension. In the event, a far more modest scheme came off. The ground floor of Selborne Chambers was gutted by Whelan's in 1961, and refitted as a new Menzies' bar. Where the chambers arcade opened onto Little Collins Street, an old arched doorway, formerly fitted with iron gates, was left unwrecked 'as a rustic touch'. The empty upper storey of Selborne Chambers was simply bricked off.

In Menzies' proper, the well-worn leather club chairs were booted out of the lounge as part of a Dundee-meets-Hollywood makeover. With Diana Dors and Frank Ifield warbling in the Chandelier Room and cocktail waiters in tartan jackets, Menzies' was ready for 'jet-borne guests from all over the world'. But the '*semi*-discotheque atmosphere' of its buffet suppers sums up Menzies' dilemma in its dying days. While still too staid for jet-setters, its mod contrivances drove the traditional clientele into the unswerving embrace of the Hotel Windsor. Of Melbourne's grand hotels, only the Windsor refused to acknowledge the '60s, and it alone would survive them. Menzies', like the rest, had a date with a wrecking-ball.

All but the bars closed at the end of January 1969, after which the hotel's contents were sold by 'TV auction'. Rather than traipsing all over the building, buyers bid for items displayed on TV monitors in the Chandelier Room. The auction ran for more than a week, commencing with items on the top floor and working its way down. Fifteen kilometres of carpet were snapped up, as were stair balustrades, a hundred marble slabs (the famed Menzies' bathmats),

Wreckers tearing up the floor of Menzies' Chandelier Room.

rare wines, and a huge, slenderising mirror in a gilt frame crested with cherubs. The bed from General MacArthur's room, 601, was knocked down for $70 to the quiz-king, Barry Jones. Other 'personality' beds on offer included those slept in by Elizabeth Taylor (with her second husband) and Richard Nixon, who'd sagged the springs during his term as vice-president under Eisenhower. Menzies' manager, Henry Timmerman ('Father' to his staff), watched it all go. 'It's terribly sad to see part of your life torn apart,' he said.

The wrecking of Menzies' left Owen Whelan sad, too. Growing up in West Brunswick, he used to catch the No. 55 tram into town, getting off at Bourke Street, opposite Menzies'.

> You'd look across ... and it was always busy with well-to-do
> people, and lovely cars pulled up outside, and the doorman.
> You'd be gawking there for ages. And then – guess what? The
> wheel turns and all of a sudden it's your turn to pull it down.

But the carcass of Menzies' was 'a big disappointment'. With its trappings all gone, the place looked pretty threadbare – was pretty threadbare. The carpets that remained were tatty, the floorboards creaked, the enamel was worn off the bottom of the deep old cast-iron baths. And the kitchens bore the same grimy decrepitude the wreckers had found at Scott's.

One thing they didn't find at Menzies' was fleas. Back before the war, according Jim Whelan, 'You could stand at the doorway,' of a building awaiting demolition, 'and see the fleas jumping around. It is a very strange thing,' he went on, 'but we hardly ever see them about in the buildings we wreck today.' Speaking in 1961, Jim had nearly fifty years of wrecking behind him and only a few ahead. Like his father in his final years, Jim was seeing big changes in the way demolition was done.

By the early '60s, Whelan's had abandoned the original Jim's *modus operandi* of completely gutting a building before knocking the walls in. Building regulations had caught up with them (or vice versa) and now, for safety's sake, they'd leave the floors in and demolish the masonry one storey at a time. Hard-hats met with resistance from older workers in particular. It took only a matter of months, though, before they felt undressed without them. Scaffolding came in about 1965. It had long been compulsory on building sites, but it took a union campaign for the demolition industry – wedded to its daredevil tradition – to follow suit.

In a short space of years from the late '50s, the swinging iron ball became as eloquent a proclamation as Whelan the Wrecker's sign. Expansive city wrecking sites – the markets, the big hotels – and the advent of tower cranes made it possible to swing the ball; the growing number of reinforced concrete demolitions made it necessary. As old Jim Whelan had discovered in 1938, you *could* knock down a reinforced concrete building using sledge-hammers and wrecker's picks, but it was hardly cost-effective to do so. In the '60s, more than ever, Whelan's challenge was to find faster and cheaper ways of wrecking. That meant more machine-power, less men. The iron ball was crude technology with maximal grunt. It came in different shapes and sizes, suitable for different jobs. And, contrary to the popular image, the ball wasn't always swing-

Whelan's iron ball smashes a wall of Cliveden Mansions, East Melbourne, 1968. (See Chapter 12)

ing: it could also be dropped – CRUNCH – to break up a concrete floor.

Joe Whelan, the youngest of old Jim's 'boys', died in November 1965. Struck by arthritis at a young age, Joe had for years been in charge of the till at Whelan's yard. He was a great talker, Joe, never too busy for a yarn with a customer, the postie, whoever. If, as a result, his till-keeping was a trifle approximate, it was nonetheless not open to question, as Tony Whelan was to learn. Tony was new to the firm, a mere office boy of eighteen, when he ventured to point out that the till never balanced. Joe roared, and sacked him on the spot. Tony rode forlornly home, only to be roared at by his father in turn. 'You get back there!' Jim told him, and he did, resuming his career with the Wrecker after less than an hour's lay-off.

A fair amount of roaring and bickering went on between the three Whelan brothers, Jim, Tom and Joe. They squabbled like – they were – brothers who'd worked together all their lives. During their more heated rows, Whelan's yard would clang with verbal wreckers' blows, employees and customers peeping from the sheds, waiting for the air to clear. But if their squabbles were brotherly, so was their staunchness. Take on one of them, and you took on all three.

At Christmas 1965, Whelan's yard was a quieter place. Tom Whelan had lost both brothers in the space of a fortnight, Jim following Joe just short of his sixty-eighth birthday. *Sun* columnist and Melbourne aficionado, Keith Dunstan, remembered Jim Whelan as 'big, bluff and friendly with the best knowledge of this city of anyone I knew'. It was true: Jim made a study of every building he pulled down, could tell you all about its history and the fineness or otherwise of its craftsmanship. As he said himself, 'There's no use doing a job unless you find out something about it, is there?'

Following Jim's death, the job of estimator fell to Owen, and he became the public face of Whelan's in Melbourne. Myles was based in Sydney where he'd established a Whelan's outpost in 1961. Their cousin Tony was Melbourne operations manager. The company had been reorganised not long before Joe and Jim's deaths, concentrating

A bunch of Whelans at the yard, c.1960. From left, Joe, Big Joe (cousin and some-time Whelan's employee), Long Tom (yard manager), Rocky Tom, his eldest son Owen, and Jim. Joe, Rocky Tom and Jim were brothers and directors of Whelan's. 'The boys in all the families were either Tom, Jim or Joe. So we had our Jim, our Joe, Big Joe, Rocky Tom, Long Tom ... and so it went on for ages.' (Tony Whelan) The photographer was one 'Happy Jack', who drove a truck for Whelan's.

the ownership of Wrecker in the hands of Jim, Tom and the three boys. Now Tom, at sixty-three the Whelan elder, became managing director.

The last of Melbourne's grand hotels to fall by Whelan's hand – and their crane and ball and traxcavator – was also the last-built, and the biggest. The fortunes of the Federal Hotel, since the war, had traced the same downward spiral as the others'. It owed its few extra years' grace to the same cause as a good part of its downfall: an unglamorous situation at the bluestone end of the city.

Built in 1887–88 and opening to coincide with the Centennial Exhibition, the Federal carried the wedding-cake flamboyance of Melbourne's boom era to a new peak. Its design, the result of a botched competition, was a queasy combination of 'Corinthian, Ionic,

Doric, early English, late English, Queen Anne, Elizabethan and Australian', making the Federal the epitome of what Keith Dunstan called 'the Victoria-gone-berserk school'. Its two facades featured every decorative motif imaginable. There were griffins, eagles, cornucopia, cherubs, classical nudes, and a vast tableau depicting 'Aurora Australis', complete with Venus surfing in a seahorse-drawn chariot. Over the entrance in Collins Street were the inscriptions RESTEZ ICI (Stay Here) and SOYEZ LE BIEN VENU (Welcome), framed by two filmily clad females, one in a perpetual state of wardrobe-malfunction.

At the close of the nineteenth century, the *Bulletin* dubbed the Federal 'the most humorous of all the Melbourne monuments erected to Land Boom greed and pharisaical snuffle'. For, despite appearances, the Federal Coffee Palace – as it was originally called – had been bankrolled by a group of temperance-minded businessmen. Coffee palaces were on the increase in the late 1880s and '90s, offering teetotal refreshments and affordable accommodation as part of the gathering anti-liquor movement. James Munro, Premier of Victoria from 1890–92, was one of the men behind the Federal, as well as the Grand and Victoria coffee palaces.* The so-called temperance hotels were more the result of wishful thinking, however, than market demand. Attracted by its tariffs, the Federal's guests merely quenched their thirsts at licensed premises near by. The coffee palace reportedly was awash with smuggled liquor from which the Federal itself profited nothing. Unable to survive on tea and principle alone, in 1897 it sought a licence and became the Federal Palace Hotel.

The place really was palatial. Its foundations encompassed half an acre, with 500 rooms, 350 of them bedrooms, contained in its seven floors and basement. Even in early photos, though, it's apparent that the Federal kept the wrong sort of company for a truly grand hotel: a pawn office on the corner opposite, the Melbourne Coal Company to

---

* The Grand would become the Hotel Windsor, while the Victoria Hotel, behind the town hall, is the former Victoria Coffee Palace.

Palace of dreams – the Federal Hotel, c.1915.

the rear, and warehouses and skin stores all around. Over the years, industrial smoke and car exhaust stained the hotel's exterior a black-edged grimy grey. Next door on Collins Street was the bluestone vast-ness of the Australian Estates wool and produce warehouse, which was bought by the Federal in the 1940s, renamed the Federal Buildings, and a portion of it refitted as a 500-seat dining room (Australia's biggest) in time for the Olympics.

The Federal Hotel struggled, like its peers, to survive the '60s, transforming its Regent Room – formerly 'something akin to a Pharaoh's tomb' – into a French provincial square, set indoors and motifed with reclining nudes. But in its dying decade the Federal outdid the rest in capturing – or being captured by – the 'swinging' ethos. Above its seven storeys, at the Collins Street corner, rose a tower with five storeys of its own (nothing dwarf about this one), domed like an emu egg and crowned with a thimble-sized cast-iron balustrade and a flagstaff. Back when the Federal was first built, its bulk had obscured the view from the bay to the old signal beacon on Flagstaff Hill, and an illuminated blue star had been fixed, as a guide to shipping, to the top of the Federal's tower. Norman castle-style windows gave views on all sides, the walls were cedar-lined,

Balustrades galore – The Federal's first-floor vestibule in the dying years of the hotel.

and a glorious rosewood staircase spiralled up the tower's centre. Yet this city gem was never occupied until 1967 when rally driver and socialite, Peter Janson, saw its potential. He fitted it out with sunken bath, smoke-room, four-poster bed, and rooftop garden, making it 'the bachelor's pad to end all bachelor's pads'. Janson lived there for four years, leaving behind playboy detritus – champagne bottles and a strappy sandal – for the wreckers to find.

There were seven kilometres of bell-wire in the Federal Hotel, twenty-five kilometres of skirting boards, eight of gas piping, and roughly five million bricks. The walls were solid brick, a metre-and-a-half thick at their base. The central vestibule, reaching three storeys high, had kept its original French Renaissance design, all branching staircases and colonnades, heavy with decorative flourishes picked out in gilt. Owen Whelan promised that he'd try to save the figurines above the front door. 'But it's terribly hard,' he told Keith Dunstan. 'They're only made of plaster and they're apt to disintegrate as soon as you touch them.' That's exactly what happened.

The bluestone-fronted Federal Buildings were pulled down at the same time. Built in 1883 for the storage and sale of wool, grain and skins, they covered one-and-a-half acres between Collins Street and Flinders Lane. Also included in Whelan's brief were several smaller buildings, some alongside the Federal Hotel in King Street, others tucked behind it off Flinders Lane. 'You should've seen the bluestone building we pulled down at the back of that,' said Myles Whelan. 'It was beautiful – if you like bluestone.' At the architects' direction, Whelan's pulled it down first. Otherwise the demolition of the hotel would have revealed its bluestone neighbour to public view and, 'There would've been an outcry.'

Contemporary wrecks
Tin Shed (south-east corner Elizabeth and Little Bourke streets), 1964

Melbourne's Elizabeth Street post office, as originally designed, was meant to extend all the way from Bourke to Little Bourke Street. Only about three-fifths of the plan was executed in the first stage of building. The remaining two-fifths of the site was occupied by a series of makeshift wooden buildings, half of which were swept away when the post office was later extended. But, despite repeated undertakings

The Tin Shed during its days as a 'temporary' telegraph office.

to budget for its completion in the 'next' public works estimates, the northernmost portion of the post office's intended span was never built. Instead, the Little Bourke Street end of the post office block remained, for more than sixty years, the city's most infamous eyesore.

A 'temporary' wooden building on the site housed the city's telegraph office from 1872 until 1906 when, in a ruinous state, it was replaced by a shed of corrugated iron. Like its predecessor, the shed was built as a temporary measure, pending funds from the Commonwealth for the post office's completion.

At the height of summer 1913, the *Argus* headlined the shed 'A Disgrace to Melbourne' –

> *Besides being used as a telegraph office, this building has another and more important use on hot days. It is then a Turkish bath.*

In 1920, the telegraph department moved to new premises in Spencer Street and the Tin Shed – as it was then widely and unaffectionately known – was leased to Allan W. Taylor, a pioneering dealer in motor accessories.

Every decade thereafter brought predictions of the 'miserable' structure's imminent demolition. AT LAST! 'TIN SHED' TO GO ran a headline in 1938. 'Three cheers,' said the Lord Mayor, 'it's the best news I've heard since I've been in office.' Nothing transpired though but the war. In 1946 it was TIN SHED TO GO again; but a year later, 'the Old Tin Shed continues its serene existence'. Though the city council complained that it was 'no better than a cow shed', it was powerless to condemn a Crown building. 'If we were worried every time someone said the Old Tin Shed was to be pulled down,' said Allan Taylor, the tenant, 'we'd get no work done.'

Almost as regular as its death sentences were claims for ownership of the land on which the Tin Shed stood. From decade to decade the claimants changed but, with minor variations, their story was always the same: an ancestor had bought, or won, the deed to the allotment from a sailor back in Melbourne's founding years. Writing in 1888, Garryowen had scoffed at such claims. At the time of the early land sales, he said, the land in question 'was a species of bog ... no sane man would put a shilling in it'. Hadn't a humorist of the period dubbed that stretch of Elizabeth Street 'the post office coast'? Time and again, though, the Land Titles Office was called on to check Folio 1161714 of Volume 5809 and assure the public that no deed had ever been issued for Crown allotment 1, section 31. Even so, descendants of Private Thomas Nash, who was quartered in Melbourne with the 80th Regiment in 1838–39, maintain to this day that Nash won the Tin Shed site from a sailor in a card game and carried the deed in a waistcoat pocket for the rest of his life. A Nash nephew pressed his claim in the 1930s, until the prospect of back-taxes deterred him.

OLD TIN SHED TO GO – OFFICIAL. It was 1962 when the Postmaster-General announced that the Tin Shed would be replaced ... by another eyesore – a post office information centre and telephone kiosk built of concrete breeze-blocks and skirted by a windswept pedestrian plaza. The Lord Mayor, Cr. Nathan, deplored the PMG's plans as 'disgraceful': 'I would not keep my racehorse there.' Allan Taylor vacated the Shed, but its demolition was postponed until after the Queen's 1963 visit – 'in case,' suggested the *Herald*, 'she is interested in grotesqueries'.

'We've been waiting around for years to have a go at the old shed,' said Jim Whelan as his wreckers set to work there in February 1964. So great was Jim's pleasure at the prospect that he submitted a zero tender – Whelan's did the job for nothing. Once the roof was off, the wreckers were surprised at the Tin Shed's solidity and craftsmanship. 'It seems that the builders in 1906 really knew how to put a shed together,' one of them told the *Age*. The demolition yielded about £350 worth of recyclable timber (including some beautiful oregon joinery) and corrugated iron, the latter being trimmed up and re-rolled at Whelan's yard and sold at a shilling a foot.

Aside from its salvage value, the Tin Shed demolition was a coup for the increasingly PR-savvy Wrecker. Owen Whelan borrowed antique postal uniforms from the GPO and had his men wear them for the press-call on the first day's wrecking. A photo in that afternoon's *Herald* showed Trevor Turner and Syd Clarkson sweltering in worsted jackets and caps as they tore into the Tin Shed roof. The job, lasting only five days, was an all-good news story for Whelan's. By pulling down Melbourne's 'scruffy monument to procrastination' – and for free – they performed what amounted to a public service. For nobody, it seems, was sorry to see the end of the old Tin Shed.

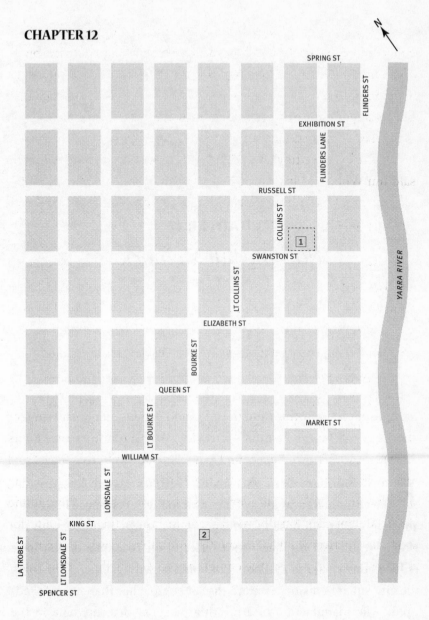

1. *City Square site*
2. *Colonial Storekeeper's*

CHAPTER 12

Nothing But Memories

Victoria Buildings ~ Queen's Walk ~ City Club Hotel ~ Cathedral
Hotel ~ Cathedral House ~ Chandris Lines Building ~ Guy's Building
~ Green's Building ~ Town Hall Chambers ~ Wentworth House ~
Regency House ~ Colonial Storekeeper's ~ Cliveden,
Jolimont cottage, Geological Museum, St Patrick's College

For Melburnians born after about 1960, it's easy to imagine that the city square was always the (nominally) open space it is today. You might even suppose the square originally *was* a square, with the Hotel Westin just the latest in a series of encroachments that have reduced the square to a ribbon. But you'd be wrong. Opened in 1980, the city square's history is more that of encroacher than encroached-upon. The manufacture of a meeting place, at that late date in the city's development, meant the destruction of existing ones. A vibrant expanse of central Melbourne was wiped clean for the sake of a grand gesture that came too late.

Melbourne was denied a public square at its inception, you may recall: partly to deter 'a spirit of democracy' from breaking out, partly to maximise land sale revenue. Surveyor Robert Hoddle has generally been held to blame for the lack of empty spaces in his grid; yet his recommendation, in the 1840s, of a site for 'a very handsome square' went unheeded.* Critics of such official shortsightedness warned then that a remedy at some future date would cost Melburnians dearly.

Proposals for a square lay dormant until the 1920s, when they resurfaced under the influence of the American trend for 'civic beautification'. A site in front of Parliament House or over the railyards near Princes Bridge were the favoured options until the '30s, when the Western and Eastern market sites became frontrunners in the civic square stakes. After the Second World War, the field widened to include the sites of the Queen Victoria Hospital, Exhibition Buildings, Victoria Market, town hall, and (present-day) Melbourne Central.

It was 1961 before the civic square firmed from an idea to an intention and the city council resolved to settle on a site. With the spread of the suburbs and the rise of the car (and the corresponding dearth of parking space), the city's importance as a shopping hub was on the wane. Planning wisdom was that the creation of a central meeting-place would draw people – and their shopping bags – back into town. Melbourne's Lord Mayor at the time was Sir Bernard Evans, a leading architect, and it was his advocacy that pushed to the head of civic square contenders a site opposite the town hall, bounded by Collins Street, Swanston Street, Flinders Lane and Regent Place.

A leap of imagination was needed back then to envisage that site forming a 'harmonious composition' between town hall and cathedral. All the other sites in final contention featured at least a peep of open space and were in public use and ownership. Sir Bernard's favourite, however, was densely built over and held in private hands – ten different pairs of them, at least. The property at the Collins–Swanston corner changed hands in 1963 to a London-based developer with plans

---

* The block bounded by Lonsdale, Russell, La Trobe and Swanston streets was instead filled by the Melbourne Hospital and public library and intersected by Little Lonsdale.

for a sixteen-storey office block. Yet, even as Whelan's were knocking down the buildings thereon, the city council continued its designs on the area and in 1966 acquired the corner block as the ready-flattened first stage for Melbourne's belated city square.

It would take fourteen more years, six times the projected outlay, and truckloads of aggravation to see the square completed. (And even then … but that's another story.) Whelan's involvement there lasted a decade, during which Melbourne's temper for demolition began to undergo a change.

First to be struck from the city square site (before it was so declared) was the pile comprising the Victoria Buildings and City Club Hotel. The large corner block fronting Collins and Swanston streets had been declared 'one of the most desirable business sites in the whole British Commonwealth' when it was offered for sale – for just the third time ever – in 1954. Henry Buck's, gents' outfitters, had long occupied most of the Swanston Street frontage, and for years the government tourist bureau had showcased Victoria from premises right on the corner. Threading elbow-wise through the Victoria Buildings' ground floor was the tone-y Queen's Walk arcade, tenanted by tailors, furriers, jewellers, frock salons, and chocolate shops. Here was Melbourne with its white gloves on.

Above the shops were three storeys of offices and one of attics, and above *them* was Queen Victoria, large as life, juggling orb and sceptre, high on the corner parapet. It was from Her Majesty, of course, that the Victoria Buildings and Queen's Walk took their names in the optimistic year 1886, when the complex was built as head office for the Freehold Investment & Banking Co. The imposing corner entrance opened onto a banking chamber for just a few years, though, before the Freehold Co., like so many of its peers, plunged into liquidation in the early '90s. But even in those pinched times, the shops on Queen's Walk and the Victoria Buildings' street-fronts held their value and good names.

'The place for a square' – the city square site in 1966, with the Victoria Buildings partially demolished.

At the corner of Queen's Walk, on Swanston Street, was the Athenaeum Café of Gregory Matoorekos, one of several Greek-born proprietors of high-class dining establishments in central Melbourne. As new arrivals in the '80s, most had started off as fruiterers or oyster-sellers. Matoorekos had been one of the latter, upgrading to his 'commodious' premises on the Queen's Walk corner in 1893. Like his countryman Antony Lucas's café nearby,* the Athenaeum was an elaborate affair, with ten dining rooms dedicated variously to ladies, gentlemen, ladies *and* gentlemen, 'etc.'.

---

* On the future site of the Capitol Theatre – see Chapter 4.

Upstairs on the Victoria Buildings' Collins Street coast, early in the new century, was the Yorick Club, celebrated salon of artistic and literary types. Unlike its big-name peers, such as the Melbourne Club, the Yorick never put down roots but led a gypsy existence, renting space up and down Collins Street. Scratch the surface of almost any building wrecked by Whelan's along that thoroughfare and you'd find a Yorick Club tenancy.

Witness the City Club Hotel, to the east of the Victoria Buildings in Collins Street, originally licensed in 1870 as the Yorick Club Hotel. After six years, the Yorick having relocated, the hotel changed its name. Starting off as a modest two storeys, it grew to two-and-a-half, then three, before being rebuilt in the 1920s as a four-storey edifice in keeping with its neighbour. Like the Victoria Buildings, the revivified City Club, with its emphasis on high-class dining, cultivated a well-heeled clientele.

Until the half-acre corner block, complete with Victoria Buildings and City Club Hotel, changed hands in 1920, it had belonged for eighty-two years to Dr Thomas Black or his estate. Black (the story goes) had acquired one of the best plots of ground in Melbourne *by accident*. In Sydney back in 1838, a government land sale had been underway when Black, strolling by the auction rooms, popped in to see the cause of the excitement. A well-bred fellow, he gave a nod in reply to an inquiring glance from the auctioneer and so found himself owner of Section 6, allotment 18 in the Town of Melbourne. Black followed his purchase south, then stayed on to become one of the city's leading citizens. Certainly he never had cause to regret his £167 nod; in years to come, the site would earn him £3,000 a year.

In the 1840s, Black built Charlotte Place, a row of five two-storey shops, on his land's Swanston Street frontage. Three of the five were knocked together in 1853 to form premises for the Bank of Victoria, Melbourne's first successful bank, of which Thomas Black was an instigator. He was also active in the Acclimatisation Society (which introduced blackberries to Victoria and founded the Melbourne Zoo) and was instrumental in sending Burke and Wills to their doom. His mansion at Richmond, Pine Lodge, built partly on the proceeds of his city land, was ultimately wrecked by Jim Whelan the first.

Market gardener Matthew Neave gave up his vegetable stall at the Western Market in 1846 to open a hotel, the Prince Albert, on land leased from Black at the Collins Street corner. The hotel was short-lived – outlasted even by the Prince Consort himself – but Neave retained possession of the building, and naming-rights. From 1854, the corner shop of Neave's Buildings was occupied by two Danish brothers, George and Gustav Damman. Formerly farmers, latterly failed gold-diggers, they now set up as tobacconists and made themselves a name. For well over a hundred years, Damman's Corner formed a shifting Melbourne landmark. Although Damman's address never altered from 'corner of Swanston and Collins streets', over the years

This scene of coronation celebrations in 1901 shows the Swanston Street frontage of the later city square. The photo was taken from an upper window of Stewart Dawson's building by Gustav Melbourne Damman, of the tobacconist's firm whose shop long occupied the site of the Victoria Buildings.

they occupied three *different* corners at that intersection. In 1882, they moved to the corner diagonally opposite and, forty-nine years later, as that building (Stewart Dawson's) was readied for demolition by Whelan's, Damman's relocated across Collins Street to the south-west corner. Their original shop in Neave's Buildings was pulled down in 1885, when Thomas Black's holding was cleared to make way for the Victoria Buildings.

'Right in the busy heart of Melbourne a "little street" has died.' While the *Sun* mourned the closure of Queen's Walk in 1965, city traders decried the disreputable hulk of the Victoria Buildings, tenanted only by pigeons for a whole year before demolition began. Owen Whelan, who tendered for the job, was the third in his line to do so. The first had been his grandfather, who'd made a bid to wreck the Victoria Buildings back in the '20s. The then-owner had changed his mind, as had the ANZ Bank which sought a demolition quote from Jim Whelan II after buying the property in 1954. This time, though, there was no change of heart.

The size of the site meant that the occupants of the town hall, opposite, got to watch Whelan's 2½-ton wrecking-ball at full swing. There was still a place, though, for men with picks and steady heads – and that place was atop the walls on the streetfronts, where flying bricks weren't so welcome. They did their best to get Queen Victoria down from the parapet in one piece, there being a plan to incorporate her into the new building on the site. But like others of her sort, she turned out to be cement-rendered plaster, not stone. The crumbling monarch saw out her years propped up in Whelan's yard, armless and aloof.

By 1968, Melbourne City Council had acquired – at no small cost – all the properties it needed to clear an open vista between town hall and cathedral. Next up for the wreckers were the Cathedral Hotel on the Flinders Lane corner and its neighbour, the Chandris Lines Building.

'Where now will Archbishop Woods have coffee and crumpets?'

A forlorn Queen Victoria at Whelan's yard.

wondered the *Sun* upon the closure of the Cathedral Hotel. The hotel
and the house of God would have made awkward neighbours, you'd
have thought. But the little back bar had 'such a quiet and pleasant
atmosphere', said the Archbishop's chaplain, that 'Dr Woods always
found it very relaxing before the 8.15 service.' The hotel's last night
– a Saturday – turned out quieter than usual after the beer ran out two
hours before closing time. Among those to share in the last keg was
Jack Anstee, a regular of twenty years' standing. 'Though I shifted to
Frankston to work,' he told the *Age*, 'I still drive in daily for a nip of
companionship.'

The 85-year-old hotel had an air of comfortable antiquity, particularly in its ecclesiastical back bar, the fixtures of which were sold at
auction to the Swan Hill Folk Museum for outfitting 'a pioneer log-
cabin style pub'. Not much was left for the wreckers but, just like old

times, Whelan's men managed to turn up a forgotten cache of champagne and a gold sovereign as they unpicked the Cathedral Hotel.

Next door, at the corner of Flinders Lane and Quirk Alley, stood
the six-storey Cathedral House. Built about 1930 of concrete and
brick on a steel frame, it had replaced the elegant premises of Joseph
Ellis & Co., galvanised iron merchants. Retiring from the family firm
in 1928, Joseph Ellis's son, John, had reminisced on his sixty years in
Flinders Lane. He'd been born there in 1868 and attended St Paul's
school which used to stand opposite. Before his father set up shop
there in 1856, the 'two-windowed shop with house upstairs' had
been run as the Dublin Boarding House. Joseph Ellis replaced the old
shop in 1877 with a narrow three-storey building whose front was
so filigreed with urns and pediments and the like that it seemed to
belie the inscription SPOUTING MANUFACTORY, above the door. Back then,
there'd been a tobacconist's on the site of the Cathedral Hotel and,
before that, a grocer's – of which John Ellis remembered only the lolly
counter from his boyhood.

Ellis's was sold in 1928 to the owner of Surrey House, which it
abutted at the rear. Surrey House faced Swanston Street and its owner
had plans to join the two buildings and transform Quirk Alley into
an extension of the fashionable Queen's Walk. Ellis's old building was
pulled down and its replacement, Cathedral House, linked in an L-
shape to Surrey House. But Quirk Alley – named after early resident,
James Quirk – was never pushed through and so never went up in the
world.

Surrey–Cathedral House was bought and renamed by the Chandris
shipping line in 1965, just a year before the council announced its plans
for a city square. The chairman of Chandris Lines and the owner of the
neighbouring Guy's Building were among those who condemned the
scheme from the outset as a waste of prime commercial property. But
they sold up and, after the Chandris Lines, Guy's Building was next to
go. A single-fronted three-storeys, it had the most insignificant frontage on the block. Until just a few years earlier, though, it had for half a

There goes the neighbourhood – Green's Building, the last to go in Swanston Street.

century been a Swanston Street landmark as Wise's fish shop and café. Now there were banking offices upstairs, with a fruit shop at street level. When Guy's Building came down in 1969, the two ends of the city square were close to meeting. Only Green's Building stood in the way.

The six-storey Green's Building had been put up early in the century, in place of a two-storey pair that had, since the gold rushes, accommodated a succession of warehousemen, coffin-sellers and ironmongers. In the flashy company of the Victoria Buildings, Green's had never stood out as anything special. So now was its moment: for two years, until 1971, it had the Swanston Street frontage to itself. Then it too was razed, and the town hall had its vista.

But not yet its city square – that was still a long way off. In the meantime, the old Victoria Buildings site, empty now for five years, had been fashioned into a makeshift plaza, paved and planted to offset the demolishers' hoardings. And, later in 1971, the council had Whelan's pull down the perfectly good (or, at least, perfectly gorgeous) Town Hall Chambers, opening out a stunted vista on Little Collins Street, at the town hall's farther end.

Built in 1887 for the Temperance & General (T&G) Assurance Society, the building on that corner had been one of boomtime Melbourne's minor splendours. Its two-street facade – six storeys on Swanston Street, sloping to three up Little Collins – catalogued the decorative niceties of its era. It had replaced the Rainbow Hotel, originally licensed to Louis Michel, one of the discoverers of gold in Victoria.

Melbourne City Council bought the T&G Building in 1928 as an extension of its town hall offices, renaming it Town Hall Chambers. Eventually it too was outgrown by municipal bureaucracy, and in the mid-'60s Whelan's pulled down a cluster of buildings uphill on Little Collins Street as the site for new council offices. When the time came to demolish Town Hall Chambers, the fact of its having recently housed the council's building department – Whelan's sometime-antagonist – must have lent extra heft to the wreckers' backswing. The resultant clearing at the Little Collins Street corner was named Melbourne's temporary city square. But, besides being too small, the little square never ceased to feel like a missing tooth, the pressing bare brick wall of its neighbour – lately a party wall – ever remindful of absence.

Where have all the flowers gone? Town Hall Chambers' upper facade.

Back on the city square mainframe, there was still demolition to be done at the site's eastern end. Wentworth House and Regency House, back-to-back facing Collins Street and Flinders Lane, represented the next stage of clearances. As originally envisaged, the city square was to have been paid for by a multi-storey development on the site of these two buildings. But in 1969, the city council bought the adjacent Regent Theatre, intending that *it* should become the commercial development site, leaving more space for the square. In 1970 came the announcement that a 53-storey skyscraper – the tallest in Melbourne by far – was to be built on the Regent Theatre site. Critics warned that the tower's shadow would cast one-third of the city square into perpetual gloom, and an *Age* headline bluntly voiced what just about everyone else was thinking: IS IT WORTH THE TROUBLE? –

> ... *most of us were led to believe that we were getting a city square. Instead we end up with a mere adjunct to a huge commercial building.*

A protest group was formed to Save Our Square, and union bans imposed in 1973 halted demolition on the city square site. Under intense public pressure both to retain the Regent Theatre and maximise public space, the council abandoned its plan for a large commercial development in conjunction with the city square. From that point on, the square became a liability.

By the time union bans were lifted in 1974, the cost of demolishing Regency House and Wentworth House had risen by almost 50 per cent. The buildings had been empty for more than three years, as had the shops on Regent Place, the arcade alongside the theatre. The Regent Theatre itself was closed and stripped and boarded up. On the corner of Regent Place, Ernest Hillier's popular soda fountain and confectioner's had been closed and gutted since the end of 1970. Through a window and a mist of tears, the *Age's* John Larkin surveyed the wreckage –

> *The floor was covered with old twisted pipes, presumably from the fountain ... The tops of the old tiles on the counter were smashed and the soda taps strewn around like they mattered*

no more ... The high cashier's counter, surely passed on from
Dickens, was gone ... Worst, they had broken the big mirror ...

'Goodbye to another essence of Melbourne,' Larkin wrote: 'an old-fashioned sense of being inside a home inside a city.'

Wentworth House had been built at the end of the '20s as part of the Regent Theatre development. Before that, since the 1840s, its site had been filled by the office and printing works of the *Argus* newspaper. In the early years, the morning after a ship arrived, Collins Street outside the *Argus* office would be packed with readers eager to get their hands on the news from Home. The original Argus Building ('of humble aspect') gave way in the '80s to something finer, which in turn came down for Wentworth House – which now bowed brokenly to the city square.

Next and last to go was the Flinders Lane-facing Regency House.

The Argus Building (right of centre) and its Collins Street neighbours form the back-drop for the laying of the town hall's foundation stone. The size of the crowd hints at a shortage of thrills in 1867 Melbourne.

"... and we erected this statue as a tribute to the man who first uncovered this beautiful spot ..."

Jeff Hook's take on the future city square, from the Sun, 1966. (Can you spot the hook?)

It had been called that only since the '20s, when it was thoroughly remodelled to match its new neighbours. On the ground floor, shops were knocked through its solid brick walls onto the newly created Regent Place. Tim the Toyman and the Peter Piper Bookshop faced Irresistible Frocks and the Old London Tea & Coffee House across the arcade. Overhead were four floors of offices and warehousing. Since 1861 this had been the site of Beath, Schiess & Co.'s clothing factory and these five storeys were their palatial 'new' premises, put up in the '70s. In later years Beath, Schiess had expanded in both directions on Flinders Lane, their three buildings separated by rights-of-way.

One was Argus Alley, running from Flinders Lane to the rear of the Argus Building. Beath, Schiess shared the premises on the alley's west side with a family-run warehousing firm that gave its name to the Andrews Building, pulled down by Whelan's five years earlier, in the pause between Guy's and Green's.

And that was all of it. That was the square, emptied – ALL BUILDINGS REMOVED, as a city map of the period labelled the void. A Melburnian returning after ten years away wouldn't recognise the spot. Dozens of familiar landmarks gone: swept away, just like that. Not pecked out and replaced piecemeal, giving eye and memory a chance to absorb the change. Just gone, all gone – and not just the structures, but other, older markers too. Along with Argus and Quirk alleys went the last moorings for memory. The historical slate was wiped. But Melbourne had its place for a square.

∞

The citizens of Melbourne are being deprived of another part of their heritage by some faceless bureaucrat armed with thoughtlessness and a rubber stamp.
~ KEITH NICHOLLS OF TOORAK, LETTER TO THE *AGE*, APRIL 1970

A lull in the city square demolitions, in 1970, saw a Whelan's gang at work on an insignificant assignment at the west end of Bourke Street. Insignificant to Whelan's – at a single storey, it was a pushover – and to the State Public Works Department which had ordered the demolition. The National Trust considered it significant, up to a point, but Keith Nicholls was unequivocal: 'It must be saved.'

The building in question was the oldest of an antiquated bluestone group west of King Street. Besides St Augustine's Church and the cells of the (former) West Melbourne police station – both of which remain standing – there was this one, at the King Street corner. Owned by the State Government, which planned to build a taller pile of offices in its place, it had, in the course of 113 years, housed various public instrumentalities: most recently the State Relief Committee; before that, the Government Labour Bureau; before that, the Industrial and Reformatory Schools Department. But its defenders harked back to its original designation: the office of the Colonial Storekeeper.

It had been the job of the Storekeeper (or commissariat officer) to procure supplies for all government departments. He let contracts for the supply of everything from convict rations (in the earliest years of the colony) to tools and firearms, kangaroo-leather briefcases, postmen's uniforms, lunatic restraints, washing tubs, drinking water, firewood, and prisoners' petticoats. In 1857 the bluestone building at King and Bourke was purpose-built for the Colonial Storekeeper. Its narrow entrance faced Bourke Street, its long side was on King and both frontages were hemmed by a fenced-in strip of garden. This corner was a vestige of the 'government block' that, until a few years earlier, had encompassed the whole ten acres from Bourke to Collins and Spencer to King.

The bluestone colonial store replaced an earlier brick structure on the site. Built as an office for the Crown Lands Department in 1840, it had served as courthouse, then immigration office, before the Colonial Storekeeper moved in. It was to its brief tenure as Melbourne's first Supreme Court that the old building owed some small renown. In 1841, the Crown Lands officers had been shoved off to a shed on Batman's Hill and their former office fitted out in preparation for the arrival from Sydney of Judge John Walpole Willis. A one-roomed cottage at the rear – also pulled down in 1857 – served as chambers. Back in 1838, that tiny brick building had been lauded as one of the sturdiest on the government block. Its lucky occupant then had been Robert Russell (of Russell Street fame) whose job it was, as Clerk of Works and availability of paper permitting, to draw up plans for more public buildings of the sturdy sort. Judge Willis, who would hang his robes there for two years, turned out to be that dread creature, an irritable eccentric. To appear before him – as accused, witness or counsel – sporting facial hair was to invite a charge of contempt. His outbursts from the bench were reckoned 'as good as a play' in the theatre-less Melbourne of the times. Eventually, though, they led to his removal from office.*

Judge Willis had to share his chambers with the town's small coterie of barristers, among them Redmond Barry. After the Supreme Court moved to Russell Street in 1843, the old building for a few years housed Commissioner Barry's Court of Requests before it too relocated, to the late billiard room of the Lamb Inn. It must have been around 1850 that the Colonial Storekeeper set up shop in the former

---

* By a curious coincidence, cranky Judge Willis was son of the physician who had famously 'cured' George III of insanity.

courthouse, soon to be condemned as a 'tumble-down' and replaced in bluestone.

In 1970, though the low-slung building cast hardly a shadow, trees along its two sides still leant over the footpaths. The interior lay-out had been altered to suit successive tenants and vibration from heavy traffic had caused cracks in the plaster; but still the building was substantially its old self.

The National Trust had classified it 'C' – worthy of preservation. When informed by a journalist, though, that Whelan's had started knocking down the Colonial Storekeeper's, the head of the Trust could only sigh, 'Again.' More than ten years after its establishment in Victoria, the National Trust's classifications still were as good as toothless. Proceeding from a conservative, fine-arts-and-antiquarian base, the Trust's preservation efforts focused more on mansions in leafy suburbs and cathedral-ish banks than on workaday structures at the grimy end of town. Moreover, the Trust's successes tended to result from caste influence, not protest. In the case of the Colonial Storekeeper's, Keith Nicholls, a civil engineer as well as a National Trust member, took it on himself to mount a rescue campaign.

Protester Sue Hunte at the Colonial Storekeeper's.

'Somebody had to do something,' he told reporters as he stuck SAVE OUR HISTORY placards to the building's front verandah. 'I could not just stand by and see yet another piece of history destroyed for so-called progress.' Whelan's kept on gutting the building as he spoke. Next day, about sixty architecture students from Melbourne University picketed the building for half an hour, creating a hubbub for the press. Whelan's site supervisor, Mick Zita, told the *Age* it was the oldest building he'd seen in Melbourne, but solid enough to stand for another hundred years. 'It's only the woodwork that's going.' Literally. Once the picketers left, the wreckers went back to pulling up the floorboards and tossing them out through the de-glazed windows. The Public Works Department called a halt to the demolition of the main building later that day, directing Whelan's to start work instead on the brick and timber outbuildings at the rear.

Dick Hamer, Minister for Local Government and a supporter of the National Trust, was responsible for the reprieve. Keith Nicholls had been joined in his campaign by Peter Kortschak, a young architect, and the pair had asked for time to present an alternative plan for the site. The wrecker's hand was stayed on a Friday and on Monday ('HE WORKED ALL NIGHT TO SAVE CITY RELIC') Peter Kortschak submitted a plan showing how the proposed office block, with no loss of floorspace, could incorporate the verandahed bluestone store as its entrance. But the government was unmoved, insisting that preservation of the Colonial Storekeeper's 'would make it impossible to properly develop this important site'.

Still, all was not lost. The site of the old building, Mr Hamer announced, would be marked by 'a plaque with historic details'. The National Trust agreed that, since the significance of the Colonial Storekeeper's lay in its history rather than its architecture, there was no need to *keep* the building, only to commemorate it. A plaque, said the Trust chairman, would be 'quite appropriate'.

Who remembers the Colonial Storekeeper's building now, or would know that it ever stood at that corner? Whelan's reduced it to rubble inside a week and after that, for close to twenty years, the site stood empty. But when eventually a blackened glass tower did go up, space was left at the corner for a faint echo of the old: a tiny square of shade-tolerant garden, overspread by a gnarly tree, surely a remnant.

In 1990, the long-promised plaque was installed in the thicket. It relates no 'historic details' of the Colonial Storekeeper's, however, commemorating only the State Relief Committee which occupied the building during its last thirty years.

What was it Iain Sinclair wrote? 'Memorials are a way of forgetting'? This time, the forgetting came first.

Contemporary wrecks

The leafy suburbs needed all the protection that the National Trust's influence could secure. During the '60s, countless stately nineteenth-century houses in Toorak, South Yarra and elsewhere were summarily demolished and their gardens gobbled up for cheap and crowdy blocks of flats. While those suburbs fall outside this book's purview, they certainly weren't beyond Whelan's. East Melbourne and Jolimont, on the fringe of the CBD, shaped up during the '60s as National Trust heartland. They still contain some of the city's oldest and best-connected buildings. But there used to be more of them.

Cliveden (Wellington Parade, East Melbourne), 1968

Old? Not especially. But well-connected, yes. This showpiece of the land boom was built in 1887 as the town house of Sir William Clarke, parliamentarian, philanthropist, and Australia's first native-born baronet.

The fabulous Cliveden (modelled on the same-named country seat of the aristocratic Astors, in Buckinghamshire) boasted every decorative conceit that inherited wealth could buy, including more stained glass than a cathedral and elaborate joinery carved to order by an imported squad of Florentine craftsmen. Cliveden was converted, at Sir William's death, into a top-notch apartment house, Cliveden Mansions.

The lightwell at the centre of the rambling structure made

Whelan's job easy when they set about demolishing Cliveden in 1968, to make way for a tan-brick Hilton Hotel. Using a crane with a 40-metre jib, they swung their ball with abandon, knocking the place down from the inside out. Stained glass and joinery – oak staircase, mantelpieces, balustrades – were set aside by the wreckers for embellishing the future grand dining hall of the Hilton Hotel, to be named the Cliveden Room.

Georgian cottage (Jolimont Square, Jolimont), 1968

A scaled-down Whelan's crew tackled this cottage, on the property of the Adult Deaf Society, straight after Cliveden. Keith Dunstan, in the *Sun*, pronounced it 'a very unhappy affair'. The French-windowed brick and timber cottage was 'the last of a glorious nest of houses' built in the early 1840s around 'Jolimont', the modest home of Governor La Trobe.* Georgian-style houses like this one were a rarity in Victoria, in recognition of which the National Trust had classified it 'B': 'Highly significant, to be preserved.' Significant it may have been, but preserved it was not.

Geological Museum (Macarthur Street, East Melbourne), 1965

Built in 1910, this small, classical-styled museum was the Geological Survey of Victoria's reward for discovering brown coal in South Gippsland. The State Electricity

The sign says it all. Vale the Geological Museum.

---

*   La Trobe's Cottage was relocated in the 1960s across the river, to the outskirts of the Botanic Gardens.

Commission had its original office in one of the basement rooms. The museum itself, a showcase and research centre for Victorian geology, was little-known by Melburnians and even less visited. But to worshippers of graptolites and hornsfel it was 'more than a museum – it was a kind of temple'. The Geological Museum was one of several public buildings cleared off the Macarthur Street block in the '60s to make way for a battalion of new State Government offices.

St Patrick's College (Cathedral Place, East Melbourne), 1971

Back in 1955, in the lead-up to the formation of the National Trust, St Patrick's College had been one of a handful of Melbourne buildings reckoned so inarguably notable as to be 'presumably safe' from demolition. Close by St Patrick's Cathedral and built of the same sombre bluestone, the college pre-dated the cathedral. It was built in 1855: two storeys high, with a tower at either end. By 1971, the College was defunct and the Catholic Church proposed building new diocesan offices on its site. Like the Jolimont cottage, St Patrick's College – 'one of the earliest and greatest Roman Catholic buildings in Victoria' – was classified 'B' by the National Trust. But this one the Trust and the East Melbourne community fought hard to save.

The last of St Patrick's College.

Protests and petitions proved fruitless, though. The National Trust called it 'the greatest loss of any historic building' since that body was formed, fifteen years earlier. 'The fight to preserve is being ended by the bulldozers.' There was nothing subtle about Whelan's approach to the job. The cocky, and wholly superfluous, WHELAN THE WRECKER IS HERE signs on the diminishing bluestone shell must have seemed like an 'up-yours' to the building's defenders. As a sop to them and a gesture to posterity, one of the towers was left to stand at the corner of the new structure.

The demolition of the 'presumably safe' St Patrick's College made sparks fly from the beacon fire of Melbourne's threatened heritage. The trouble was, no law existed that could prevent it, or others like it.

IS WRECKING VANDALISM?

> ... the indefatigable Mr Whelan moves on, tearing down this
> city, leaving nothing but memories.
>
> ~ KEITH DUNSTAN IN THE *SUN*, JULY 1968

Something was changing. The old city was disappearing, yes; but so it always had been. What was different was the speed of it and the scale, and that people were beginning to notice.

The inhabitants of most other Western cities had been likewise jolted during the '60s by the demolition of landmarks in their midst. Often a structure's landmark status was recognised only too late. In cities with histories longer than Melbourne's, buildings of recent – Victorian or later – age were especially vulnerable. New Yorkers were shocked in 1963 by the demolition of the massive Beaux Arts railroad temple, Pennsylvania Station (built 1910). That act of 'public vandalism', however, led to the enactment of a Landmark Preservation Law which, in the years since, has withheld more than a thousand New York buildings from the wreckers.

In the heart of London, the monumental Coal Exchange was found to impinge (by just one metre) on the route of a road-widening scheme. Built in 1846–49 as the trades hall and customs house of Britain's coal industry, the Coal Exchange ennobled grit-and-grime motifs – colliery cables,

*shipping ropes, miners' tools, lignitic fossils – both in its architecture and
its lavish scheme of decoration. But in vain was it acclaimed 'the prime
City monument of the early Victorian period'. The Victorian Society
(defender of nineteenth-century architecture in Britain) was granted a
short time to find a new home for the building's centrepiece, a fabulously
ornate cast iron rotunda, twenty metres in diameter and capped by a dome
twenty-five metres high. The strongest show of interest came from the
National Gallery of Victoria for which new premises were then under
consideration. That scheme fell through, however, when the Victorian
Society was unable to raise £20,000 towards the cost of shipping the
rotunda to Melbourne. The Coal Exchange was demolished, rotunda and
all, in November 1962.*

*But the loss of the Coal Exchange provoked nothing like the public
outcry set off that same year by the demolition of London's Euston Station.
As the first railway station built in any of the world's major cities, Euston
was an irreplaceable monument of the Railway Age. And, like the Coal
Exchange – only more so – Euston Station glorified the industry for which
it stood. The station's Great Hall and entrance arch were constructed on a
scale more in keeping with the enthronement of caesars than the passage
of the train-travelling public. Defenders of Euston Station battled hardest
to save the colossal arch. But to no avail.*

*Reflecting on 'The Euston Murder', Hermione Hobhouse concluded that
'The only person who emerges with credit from the affair is the demolition contractor, Frank Valori.' Valori offered to have the stones of the
dismantled Arch numbered, in case the authorities should consent to its
re-erection. (They didn't.) And it was Valori, the demolisher, who, out of
a shared sense of loss, presented the Victorian Society with a cast-silver
model of the Euston Station arch.*

As in the case of Penn Station, wrote Hobhouse –

The fight to save the Arch was not perhaps as totally useless as
it appeared in 1962, for latent public opposition to such acts of

destruction was altered and organised as never before, and has been growing since.*

Much of the swinging in '60s London, wrote Peter Ackroyd in his London: The Biography, *was done by wrecking-balls.*

What it represented was a deliberate act of erasure, an act of forgetting … It was as if time, and London's history, had for all practical purposes ceased to exist.

Ackroyd charted a trend of large-scale redevelopment – and attendant demolition – in that city during the '60s decade of at least three centuries past, hinting at some cyclical schema behind 'these great waves of vandalism', the latest of which went by the name of progress.

A writer in the Melbourne literary journal, Meanjin, *in 1968 called progress 'one 19th century religion which still thrives here'. Regardless that other world cities were at the time heaping sacrifices on the altar of that same religion, the author attributed Australians' 'relentless passion for the demolition of old buidings' to 'the immigrants' natural concentration on the future' and an enduring frontier mentality. His article's title was 'The Whelan Frontier'.*

… in Melbourne the image of one demolition company ('Whelan the Wrecker') has acquired a cosiness reserved in other countries for corner-store tradesmen and street musicians. It is almost as if some folk memory of felling timber on outback selections has persisted in tacit approval of those who in lieu of trees, axe buildings – the new frontiersmen.†

* Hermione Hobhouse, *Lost London: A Century of Demolition and Decay,* Macmillan, London, 1971.
† Noel McLachlan, 'The Whelan Frontier', *Meanjin,* June 1968, pp. 251–56.

The man most responsible for promulgating the Wrecker's folksy image was Keith Dunstan, of the Sun News-Pictorial. *'Progress can swamp a city,' he had written in 1960, vis-à-vis Whelan's 'orgy of destruction' that year; 'but Melbourne is absorbing its progress with dignity.' A decade later his equanimity was slipping. A cartoon accompanying a Dunstan piece titled* WHO NEEDS PROGRESS? *had the writer trailing in Whelan the Wrecker's rubbly wake, feverishly re-assembling the gems they'd demolished. In spite of his growing disquiet at the scale and form of 'progress' in Melbourne and the destruction carried out in its name, Dunstan's affection for Whelan the Wrecker – the chief agents of that destruction – seems never to have faltered.*

Barry Humphries shared Dunstan's ambivalence about Whelan's role in what he considered the desecration of his home town. 'I love Melbourne,' said Humphries in the late '60s –

> Why? Because it needs someone to love it. Everyone else seems
> to be trying to pull it down. I wouldn't be surprised if Whelan
> the Wrecker got a knighthood.

At the same time, you felt that he wouldn't have minded that too much. Humphries had long made fond use of the name and idea of Whelan the Wrecker. Besides being the quintessence of post-war Melbourne, the name – a laugh in itself – doubtless appealed to his ear for suburban euphony. More than once it would surface in Humphries' doggerel, as in '… the shadow of Whelan's lead hammer / Hangs over the old Melbourne Club.' On a visit to New Zealand in 1966, he whiled away 'The happy hours with camera and Baedeker / Observing signs which read WHELAN THE WRECKER'. *(Humphries had happened on the site of Whelan's first trans-Tasman job: the National Bank in Wellington.) 'O land of contrasts, wonderful New Zealand,' he extolled, 'Go there before it's well and truly Whelaned.'**

In Melbourne that same year, Humphries sifted through junk at Whelan's

---

*   *Australian,* April 1966.

yard – exclaiming at a toilet seat, 'A picture frame!' – and left with a bulky parcel under his arm. Not long afterwards he was photographed in Lebanon, amid ruins of the Temple of Jupiter. And draped across a lump of ancient masonry was the cloth sign he'd procured in Brunswick: WHELAN THE WRECKER WAS HERE.

As the '70s dawned, Melbourne buildings were being mown down at an unprecedented rate. For the city's leading demolisher, each year brought 'new peaks' of business. But the breakneck pace of redevelopment, said the chairman of the Victorian branch of the National Trust in 1970, was resulting in 'the destruction of part of our heritage for which succeeding generations may well hold us up to execration'. Or even the present generation. At a public forum entitled 'Is Wrecking Vandalism?', Owen Whelan put his company's by-then standard defence: 'It's no good going crook at us. We're just the tools.'

Both Whelan's and the developers who hired them were at that time

Whelan's retrospective – Barry Humphries at the Temple of Jupiter, Lebanon, in 1966.

still practically unhindered by the issue of heritage preservation. Sure, there'd been an undercurrent of concern as far back as the late '50s, when Whelan's were urged to make a swift and stealthy start on the demolition of St Patrick's Hall as 'they've started their stirrings'. In the decade and more since, public disquiet had been shaken and stirred by the untrammelled pace of the city's redevelopment. Too much was changing too fast, and passive sentimentality at the erasure of landmarks was hardening into active opposition. One of the defenders of the Colonial Storekeeper's building, when it lost its reprieve, said bitterly, 'The Government is way out of line – they don't understand people.'

For more than ten years the National Trust had been listing and ranking Melbourne's historic buildings; yet, without statutory controls, there was nothing to prevent any building's demolition. Only rarely did the National Trust succeed – by working 'quietly and reasonably' – in steering developers away from the jewels on its list. In 1968, for example, a Trust campaign had saved the ultra-Gothic ANZ Bank chambers, at the Collins and Queen corner, from the maw of progress and the wrecker.

Ever since the Labor Party split in 1954, the conservative parties in Victorian parliament had been virtually untroubled by opposition. Even though the National Trust had some support within the government, legislation for the protection of historic buildings was a long time coming. The State's first planning statute, the Town and Country Planning Act, 1944, had required local councils to consider 'the preservation of objects of historical interest'. But 'preservation' was not the same as 'conservation', and 'objects' did not extend to architecture. In any case, merely to 'consider' preservation was a meaningless requirement: it might consist of a vale at the first fall of the wrecker's pick. The Act was amended in 1961 to include the 'consideration' of architectural objects, but still it lacked any means of preventing their demolition.

As a result of sustained pressure from the National Trust, Victorian parliament in 1972 amended the Town and Country Planning Act to include the following requirement –

The conservation and enhancement of buildings, works, objects and sites specified as being of architectural, historical or scientific interest, by prohibiting, restricting or regulating the pulling down, removal, alteration, decoration or defacement of any such building, work or object.

As only 'specified' sites were to be protected, each local council had to compile its own list of significant places and objects. Melbourne City Council was quick to act, in 1973 specifying the entire CBD as an area of significance. It would no longer be enough, in applying for a demolition permit, to satisfy technical and safety requirements. In every case now, a building's significance and its place in the cityscape would not only be considered, but its demolition could be prevented. The blanket protection measure came undone, however, in 1975 when it was found that the city council might be liable to compensate developers if demolition permits were withheld on heritage grounds.

Fortunately, by that time, the city's most important buildings were protected under the higher authority of the Historic Buildings Act. Based on a model prepared by the National Trust, that Act was pushed through State parliament with the backing of the Labor opposition in 1974. It established a register of the best examples of historic buildings in Victoria and gave them protection from demolition. The Act's aegis did not extend to buildings that fell short of State-wide importance, however, and it focused on individual buildings at the expense of significant streetscapes. They were meant to be protected by local government measures, such as that attempted – and abandoned – by Melbourne City Council. Moreover, the Historic Buildings Preservation Council, which administered the Act, included representatives of 'public vandals' such as the real estate and building industries, but not building trade unions which were taking an increasingly militant stance on conservation issues.

Thus, with the city council lacking the means* and the State government

---

*   And complicit, anyway, in the case of the city square.

the will to halt them, developers' (white-)elephantine schemes for central Melbourne proceeded virtually unchecked throughout the '70s. Here and there a building stamped SIGNIFICANT *was made immune from demolition; the Gothic ANZ Bank, so recently under threat, was one. But, increasingly, swathes of the city were clear-felled. Entire quarters of central Melbourne – whole little worlds that people knew by heart – were scratched off the map.* ALL BUILDINGS REMOVED.

Melbourne was losing its familiarity, fast.

It was starting to speed up and people were saying, 'Hey, wait a minute!' You know, when you get change, it's only natural for people to say, 'Oh gee, look at that lovely …, I remember going in there as a girl.' They think, 'Gee, that's some of my life.'

OWEN WHELAN

Significance, like memory, is a slippery thing. While the Historic Buildings Preservation Council attempted to measure buildings' significance on a comparative, State-wide scale, most people used a scale founded on attachment and memory. At the heart of many a heritage skirmish lay the rationale: 'It's significant to me; therefore it's significant.' (Just as Snoopy howled when he found a six-storey carpark on the site of the Daisy Hill Puppy Farm: 'YOU STUPID PEOPLE!! YOU'RE PARKING ON MY MEMORIES!!!'*)*

When Whelan's tearing-down was done, Keith Dunstan wrote, only memories remained –

But isn't it curious? After a few weeks you have to strain to remember what the old building looked like.

CHAPTER 13

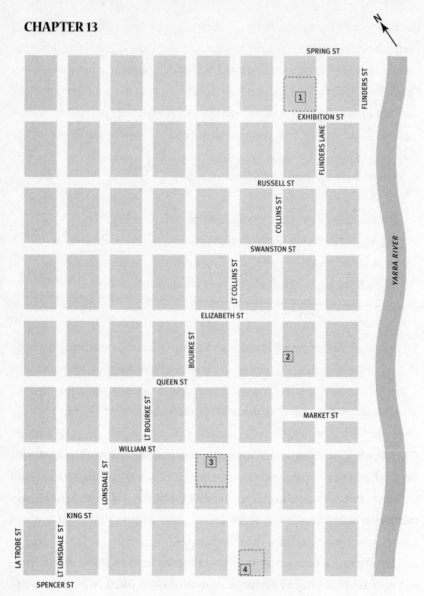

1. Collins Place site
2. Union Bank
3. St James' Buildings
4. Board of Works

CHAPTER 13

All Buildings Removed

Collins Place development ~ 13–15 Collins Street ~ Freemasons' Hall
~ Ryan House ~ Oriental Hotel ~ 59 Collins Street ~ Astoria Hotel ~
Hartnell House ~ Union Bank, St James' Buildings,
Board of Works building

To test Keith Dunstan's formula of forgetting, you'd have needed only to take a tram-ride, once every few weeks during 1972, along Collins Street's Paris end. Two thirds of a block – 3¹⁄₃ acres – of city heartland was clear-felled there in so short a time that Melburnians hardly had time to adjust their memories.

It's fair to call it 'heartland' though it lay at the city's eastern end, since this was the Melbourne commonly evoked when drawing favourable comparisons with Sydney. (And were there any other kind?) For its two blocks east of Russell, Collins Street embodied the leafy and cultured metropolis of the south. And the further east you went, the more rarefied the air. Here, after all, resided – still resides – that epitome of no-name–no-need exclusivity, the Melbourne Club, demesned by medical specialists with middle initials and bespoke clothiers. But for a couple of minor glass-house incursions, the last block of Collins before Spring Street was a hold-out against the dazzle of the new. Notice that use of the past-tense: *was*.

Back when the town was still defined by its docks, this had been virtually Melbourne's first suburb. Collins Street East, in the mid-nineteenth century, was an avenue of doctors' residences, set back from the street-line behind gardens. With the spread of the suburbs and the advent of the telephone, the doctors made their homes elsewhere, and many of their old residences were replaced by medical chambers, two storeys and taller, and shopfronts built right to the footpath. Sometimes the original building remained at the rear, as in the case of 13–15 Collins Street where a two-storey surgery-residence (by 1952 'the only building in Collins-st. with a flower garden in front of it') hid the ruins of an earlier house. The demolition of 13–15 in 1955 shed light and public sentiment on the tumbledown 'old city farm house' behind. In the same dusty courtyard stood coach-house and stables, all overspread by an enormous magnolia tree.*

At the end of the '60s, Collins Street East, the Paris end, still represented Melbourne's fondest image of itself: the city on a human scale. It was a scale that, for more than a decade, city planners had been attempting to replicate in the shadow of skyscrapers, offering incentives (additional storeys) to developers in exchange for an apron of plaza at street-level. The result, too often, was a grim, pebble-dashed wind-pocket where not even pigeons would linger. In 1971 came a proposal for twin towers of forty-seven storeys apiece, set within a vast, compensatory plaza, at the east end of Collins Street. Described as 'the most radical of its kind in Australia', the development would consume all the ground (and most of the daylight) east from Exhibition Street to the erstwhile magnolia. And all the addresses, too: not just numbers 17–65 Collins Street, but 22–70 Flinders Lane and 44–60 Exhibition

---

* The emptied allotment served as carparking for more than a decade before being built over by a root-faced apartment block.

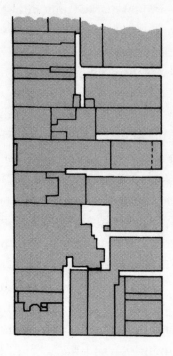
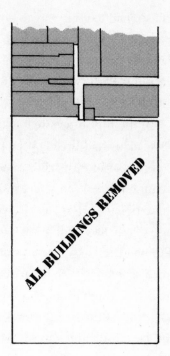

Street. In an echo of that last street's former name, the development would be called Collins Place,* while its fifty-nine addresses would boil down to just two, one for each tower: 35 and 55 Collins Street.

Those who've come to know Melbourne post-Collins Place, or who've forgotten what preceded it, can perhaps best appreciate the development's impact by comparing 'before' and 'after' maps of the site. Detailed plans produced by insurance companies and the Melbourne & Metropolitan Board of Works at thirty(ish)-year intervals from the 1880s traced the evolving outline of every building in the city. It was common, across the decades, to see allotments coalesce as single large buildings replaced multiple smaller ones. The disjunction between the maps of the 1940s and those of the '70s, however, comes as a shock. The patchwork scheme of morphing that the eye is

---

* Until the 1960s Exhibition Street, south of Collins, was called Collins Place – see Chapter 7; before the 1880s, Exhibition Street (Collins Place included) was called Stephen Street.

accustomed to gives way to bomb-blast erasures marked only with the epitaph: ALL BUILDINGS REMOVED. Taking in the scale of annihilation at a glance is enough to make you flinch – nowhere more so than the site of Collins Place. You can see why the newspapers dubbed it 'The Blitz of Collins Street'* and 1972 'the year of the wrecker'.

Of the fifty-nine street addresses rendered down to make Collins Place, many had already been fused with neighbours over the course of a century or more. A case in point was Freemasons' Hall, which alone accounted for seven street numbers: 25–31 Collins Street and 28–34 Flinders Lane. Here, as elsewhere in Melbourne, the street number-ing system had changed around 1890. Originally, a single number, 190, had been assigned to the whole Collins Street frontage filled by Freemasons' Hall. Built in the 1880s, it extended the full depth of the block, the hall itself occupying the rear half, with the front part assigned to offices and rooms for lodge meetings, supper, and cloaks. The facade of Freemasons' Hall was fairly restrained by boomtime standards: the arched windows and entranceways fit the scheme of the neighbourhood, only the cupola'd towers at either end seeming a tad ostentatious for the sedate end of Collins Street.

Around World War Two, the offices of the Masonic Order expanded into the building next door, eastwards. Like *its* neighbour (with the magnolia in the yard) 17–19 Collins Street was a two-storey brick centenarian, originally built as a doctor's residence. When the Freemasons acquired it there was still a garden at the front, over which a row of shops was planted in 1955, altering beyond recognition 'everything that made the house remarkable' and hiding the rest from view. In the course of the building works, a sheaf of age-mottled foolscap papers was found behind a cupboard. They were hand-written duty rosters for the 40th Regiment, detailing the red-coats' posting to Ballarat at the time of the Eureka uprising. For five years in

---

* Wrote Keith Dunstan, 'The stethoscope end of Collins St. now looks like a cross between the London blitz and the ruins of Pompeii'; others substituted 'the Berlin end' as a more apt continental allusion.

Collins Street East, 1921.

the 1850s headquarters of the British military forces in Australia had been housed here.

Freemasons' Hall, the old house, the new shops and two factories at the rear comprised the first parcel of demolitions for Collins Place. The pulling-down of Freemasons' Hall by the Roman Catholic Whelans made for 'a lot of chiacking' at the golf club, says Owen Whelan. They ribbed their Masonic mates: 'Oh, we're doing it all for free.'

At 33–37 Collins Street was Ryan House, a five-storey dormitory of medical chambers, built in 1937 by ophthalmologist Dr Edward Ryan. It had replaced a pair of elegant three-storey terraces dating from the 1860s, in one of which Dr Ryan's surgeon father, Charles, for many years had his practice.

Number 37, the westernmost of the pair, had shared a party-wall with the neighbouring property, an old residence of original Collins Street character. Built in the 1840s, it was for many years the townhouse of squatter-parliamentarian Sir Charles Ebden. For three days in 1863 it had acted as Victoria's Government House when Ebden gave lodging to the new governor, Sir Charles Darling, until the vice-regal residence was vacated by his predecessor. From the 1880s until

1910, it was home to Dr Louis L. Smith, a medical man and sometime member of parliament, of whom a bust in bronze is mounted near the Exhibition Buildings in commemoration of his 28-year tenure as a trustee of that institution. His son, the architect Sir Harold Gengoult Smith, served forty-four years in the same capacity, besides three decades as a Melbourne city councillor. Sir Harold was one of Collins Street's fiercest defenders, particularly during the great verandah blitz of 1954, when he condemned his fellow-councillors as 'vandals'. 'I was born in Collins Street,' he thundered to the council chamber. And so he had been: in the old house at no. 41, with its fluted columns and statues in the garden behind a cast-iron fence.

Sir Harold's birthplace by then was long-gone, having yielded in 1911 to the implacable vision of P.W. (Pearson) Tewksbury. Tewksbury had made his fortune young, from gold dredged out of the Ovens River upstream from his native Yackandandah. When, in 1910, he and his wife moved to Melbourne, they made their home in a suite at the Oriental Hotel, next door to the Smith house in Collins Street. A falling-out with the manager caused them to relocate their household to the nearby Grand Hotel (now the Windsor); but they soon became homesick for their former digs. Tewksbury's solution? He bought the Oriental, sacked the manager, and moved back to Collins Street for good.

The Oriental had stood at 43–53 Collins Street since 1878 when it replaced the Bedford Hotel, built twenty-four years earlier on the former site of a sawmill. Together with Menzies', the Oriental ranked in the 1880s as one of the city's best hotels. Directly opposite the Melbourne Club and a short stroll from Parliament House, it was especially favoured by the squatter class – besides that most peripatetic of lodgers, Dame Nellie Melba.

The energetic Tewksbury gave the old place, and the neighbourhood, an immediate ginger-up. He acquired the old Smith house, pulled it down, and in its place added a new wing to the Oriental at a cost of £60,000. At the same time, he established the City Motor Service, offering chauffeur-driven cars that were quartered at a garage

– one of the first in the city – behind the Oriental in Flinders Lane.*
In measuring up for the hotel's new wing, it was discovered that the
western wall of 37 Collins Street, adjoining, encroached one brick's
width onto Tewksbury's property. The owner of no. 37 refused to pay
for the purloined eleven centimetres. It wasn't until 1936 that Dr
Edward Ryan would agree to cough up £135 for the one-brick Collins
Street frontage and an end to Tewksbury's badgering.

After further renovations ('on the newest cosmopolitan lines')
in the years following World War One, the 'sumptous' Oriental was
extolled in a 1925 guidebook to Melbourne: 'The lofty dining rooms,
the luxurious self-contained suites, and the restaurant-café downstairs
are reminiscent of the finest hotels abroad.' This was no accident.
Pearson Tewksbury, a voracious world-traveller, never returned home
without a fresh idea for the Oriental. In 1933, he proposed introducing
the 'picturesque Continental innovation' of a sidewalk café. He told
the *Herald* that Melbourne's climate, 'with sunshine eight months of
the year' (he himself usually wintered abroad), lent itself perfectly
to such a scheme. And no, he did not believe that Australians were
too self-conscious to eat in the street. At least, said Tewksbury, 'The
younger generation would not care if people looked. As for the others,
they could stay inside.' But the city council – including Cr. Smith,
whose childhood home Tewksbury had torn down – withheld its
consent.

The ground floor of the Oriental underwent a complete transformation just before World War Two. When the hotel entrance was
moved eastwards (congruent with Smith's former garden) so too was
the ornate cast-iron verandah that formed the insignia of the Oriental
Hotel. No sooner was the war over than the irrepressible Tewksbury
announced plans for an all-new Oriental, thirteen storeys high, with
500 rooms, picture theatre, underground carpark – and open-air café.

---

*   In 1923, Tewksbury introduced Yellow Cabs, the first metered taxi service, to
    Australia.

'I am an old man now, and I want to see the new hotel built before I die.' Having said which, Tewksbury sailed for America 'in search of new ideas'.

Just five months later, in April 1947, Tewksbury was gripped by an idea for the Oriental that, while certainly new, was likewise rooted in his sense of (im)mortality. He now proposed to sell the hotel, at the bargain price of £200,000, for use as a War Nurses' Memorial Centre. His mother, Tewksbury explained, had been a personal friend of Florence Nightingale and had wanted to go with her to the Crimea. A fundraising appeal for a nurses' cultural centre had already raised £100,000, and it was expected that the State Government would cough up the rest. Within a fortnight, however, Tewksbury withdrew the offer, citing consideration of his large staff and the scarcity of hotel accommodation in Melbourne. He owed it to the city, he said, to proceed with his plans for rebuilding the Oriental. Members of the War Nurses' Memorial Committee were stunned by Tewksbury's reversal, and unmoved by his suggestion that he might add two floors to the new Oriental for the exclusive use of nurses. The office of Sir Thomas Blamey, head of the Committee, was opposite the Oriental in Collins Street, and relations between the two sides were said to be 'about as cordial as though the street divided Tel Aviv and Jaffa'.

Impatient with post-war building restrictions that gave priority to housing, Tewksbury proposed importing all the materials and labour necessary for construction of the new Oriental. But he died too soon for his vision of a hotel 'worthy of the city and worthy of the times' to be realised. (Nor did Tewksbury – 'one of the characters of this town' – live to see Melbourne's 'dreadful' trams scrapped, another long-time preoccupation of his.)

'We've dreamed of owning the Oriental for fifteen years,' said Leon Ress, the new proprietor, in 1955. The Ress family had plans, too, for the hotel's transformation – though they weren't quite in the same league as Tewksbury's. They had eight luxury suites ready in time for the next year's Olympics, each fitted out with chiming doorbell and

Paris comes to Collins Street – the Oriental Hotel's sidewalk café. (Barry Humphries used to wonder why Parisians never spoke of 'the Melbourne end' of the Champs Elysées.)

(that scourge of travellers) a thermostat-controlled shower. Aimed squarely at American visitors, the suites came with names like 'The President' and a tariff of £10 a night (at a time when £4 was considered exorbitant for a Melbourne hotel room) – and all were booked well in advance of the Games.

The new owners, though, were more cluey than their predecessor as to ways of revivifying the Oriental without a million pounds and foreign labour. Eating and entertainment became their focus. Two years after the Olympics, the Oriental finally got its boulevard café. It may have helped that Leon Ress was a city councillor; even so, the café was on three-months' trial to begin with, and no liquor was to be served outside. The hotel's broad frontage meant there was room between the plane trees at the kerbside for nineteen little tables. 'This is wonderful,' effused the French-born Mrs Ress. 'It is just like the Champs Elysées back home in Paris.' Ergo 'the Paris end' of Collins Street. But tables and bright umbrellas hid the gunmetal parking meters for just two years before police gave the order to close the café. There was an outcry, for not only had the café given the Oriental its new signature and Collins Street East a new identity, it had also become the face of 'cosmopolitan' Melbourne, featuring on postcards and travel brochures and even, once, on British TV. But the Chief Police Commissioner was insistent: the café hindered traffic. Like the Oriental's verandah before it, it had to go.

Just like Pearson Tewksbury, though, the Ress family had plenty more ideas. Early in the '60s, the Oriental's old dining room and lounge bar were reborn as Rib Room and Harlequin Room, ritzy eating-and-meeting places in tempo with the times. And in 1965 the dining room was again overhauled, this time as a restaurant-discotheque, the Persian Room, decked out in deep-purple velvet, with gold drapes, dim lighting, and abundant dark nooks. Premier Henry Bolte strutted the strobe on opening night, 'hitch-hiking' with 18-year-old Denise Drysdale before snaring a bead curtain with his parliamentary tie-pin. With the end of six o'clock closing in 1966, the Persian Room really took off. Renamed the Casbah, it featured live music and late-night happenings such as a 'Casbah Queen' beauty contest with local pop luminaries Ross D. Wylie and Ronnie Burns as judges.

Tony Whelan, the youngest of the wreckers, was pushing thirty and still single when, in 1967, he chose the Oriental Hotel as rendezvous for a blind-date with a nurse from St Vincent's Hospital, the friend of a friend's friend. Within a year, Tony and Lyn were married, and four years later Tony was instrumental in the wrecking of the Oriental. No Whelan could afford to be sentimental (certainly not in 1972), but Tony did save a brick from the Oriental for building into his Templestowe home.

The more biddable fittings of the Oriental Hotel were sold off in 1971 at the then-standard TV auction. The electric clock in the saloon bar, which for donkey's years had ticked down the desperate minutes to six o'clock, went for $6, while the bar itself, twelve metres long, fetched a paltry $5. 'One could have re-created the entire Oriental saloon bar at home,' Keith Dunstan tallied it up, 'for $36.'

Two doors down from the Oriental, and one up from the corner, was 59 Collins Street. Though lately occupied by a pair of optometrists and a hearing-aid clinic, it was still recognisably a house – the last remnant, in fact, of Collins Street domestic architecture. Externally, the plain-faced two-storey Georgian terrace was little changed since the early 1850s, when it was built as a surgery-residence. A verandah hemmed in iron lace and a narrow portico stuck over the entrance – practical but incongruous – were the only obvious additions. The sole exception to its succession of medical tenants had been a Miss J.M. Law, dress- and habit-maker, who had the place in the 1870s.

A hundred years later, 59 Collins Street's simple lines made it the cheapest demolition on the Collins Place site. Whelan's were paid just $1,000 for the job (compared to a site average of $21,000). Next cheapest, at $10,000, was an old hotel at the Exhibition Street and Flinders Lane corner. Three storeys high, it had been the Astoria (originally the Waverley), a middle-sized residential hotel of fifty rooms. Its closure at the end of 1961 had marked a terminal dwindling of Flinders Lane's one-time reputation as Melbourne's beeriest mile. You could say the character of the thoroughfare was pre-ordained, since the town's first inns – Johnny Fawkner's and the Governor Bourke – had been situated on the Lane *before* the Lane existed. Only when Hoddle's grid was over-laid, in 1837, were the waterfront pubs found to have Flinders Lane addresses. In the 1880s the Waverley had been one of fifteen hotels strung along Flinders Lane. Since it closed, Whelan's had done-in three of the four hotels then remaining: the Cathedral, Johnny Connell's Railway (at Elizabeth Street) and the Kerry Family (at King).

Before there was a hotel at the Flinders Lane–Stephen Street corner, there'd been a house, wherein for a short time in the 1860s Madame

Carole, a 'medical mesmerist', had picked her patients' brains. The
Waverley Hotel first got its licence in 1883. Built at the same time,
next door on Collins Place, was a three-storey row named Bayview
Terrace. Beyond them, Nightingale's fancy box factory had lately
replaced the builder's yard of Norris Dike, whose name still cleaved to
the lane alongside.

There were then few tradesmen and factories on Flinders Lane
hereabouts, though that changed in the course of the '80s. On the
long stretch of land between Flinders Lane and Flinders Street – a
slope dropping steeply to the river – was a 'country house' built by
solicitor John Duerdin in the '40s. With the death of his widow in the
1880s, the old Duerdin home became a garrison officers' mess and,
later, a boarding-house. Eastward of Duerdin's yawned an expanse
of empty ground, partly quarried – one (actually, four) of the city's
last virgin allotments. Forty years later, the Herald and Weekly Times
building filled up the space and supplanted the old house, and the
all-hours racket of printing works, delivery vans, and carousing press-
men changed the character of the neighbourhood – and the custom
of the hotel at the Flinders Lane corner. The Waverley's remodelling
as the Astoria, around that time, reflected a shift in tone from Home
Counties to jazz-age.

The Astoria's corner bar, after it was de-licensed in 1961, ended
up a sandwich shop, sharing premises with the Madrid Cabaret and
a firm of window-cleaners. Just one-fourth of the former Bayview
Terrace was still standing, having been annexed, at some stage, to the
old hotel. Its fellow three terraces had given way in the '30s to the
burgeoning garage space of P.W. Tewksbury's chauffeured-car service,
which joined, in an L, with the original City Motor Service garage
around the corner in Flinders Lane.

Along the Lane, where once had been a brewery, a wine and spirit
merchant's, a carpenter's shop, and a milliner or two, were now a
series of buildings with the crusty names of Lancashire, Ascot, and
Hartnell House. Brick and reinforced concrete structures of twentieth-

Collins Place demolition, 1972, looking north across Collins Street.

century date, they housed warehouses, factories, and offices. Hartnell House (60–70 Flinders Lane), a six-storey glass-house built in the late 1950s, had replaced the long-time premises of Joseph Ellis, hardware and galvanised iron merchants. This had been Ellis's supplementary outlet from about 1880 until 1930 when his sons sold the firm's original works and head office beside the Cathedral Hotel.* Ellis's had continued to sell plumbing supplies at the top end of Flinders Lane until 1956. Still marking their long residency fifteen years later, when the wreckers set to work on Hartnell House, was the contiguous Ellis Lane. Like Henderson Lane (commemorating wine and spirit merchant, James Henderson), Freemasons Lane, and Lister Lane

---

* See city square site, Chapter 12.

(formerly Dike's), it was about to be swallowed by the king-tide of Collins Place clearances.

That no wealth of wrecker's lore emerged from these wholesale demolitions is partly a sign of the efficiency of the industry as it entered the '70s. Increased mechanisation put ever more distance between Whelan's crews and the structures they brought down. The knowledge of a building's secrets gained by a wrecker at the controls of a concrete-breaker or bobcat was necessarily less intimate than that to be had from a pick-handle's distance or the end of a shovel. Moreover, the volume of demolition committed by Whelan's through the '60s and '70s must, to some degree, have blunted them to the idiosyncrasies of individual jobs, one building's bluestone wall blurring with the concrete hide of the next. With heritage-awareness on the rise and 'progress' increasingly on the nose, there must also have been a certain defensiveness stirring among wreckers: an inclination to treat a job as a job and, if possible, to ignore its history. In those days, press coverage was likelier to cast wreckers as vandals than as plucky larrikins or frontiersmen. Nor were demolition sites as picturesque as they'd once been. There was the whine of the machines, for one thing, and the anonymous sheath of steel scaffolding. And reinforced concrete, ripped apart, conveyed none of the ruinous romance of its half-blasted equivalent in stone or brick. One way and another, the glory was fast going out of the wrecking game.

On the other side of the scaffolding, with whole city neighbourhoods disappearing, the forgetting ought to have come easier. Increasingly, though, sentiment wasn't the point. More and more, the public came to reject the old progress-is-good-for-you line, recognising instead, in the shocking contours of the city knocked flat, the bald motive of profit. From the mid-'70s, groups like the strident Collins Street Defence Movement joined with the more conservative force of the National Trust to oppose open-slather development and put pressure on authorities to draw the line.

Contemporary wrecks
Bank-packed Collins Street (south side, between Elizabeth and Queen), 1960–77

Nos. 303–339 and 351–383 all went, courtesy of Whelan's, including –

Union Bank (351 Collins Street), 1966

The marble figures in niches either side of the bank entrance were meant to symbolise Great Britain and Australia, but were better known as Ada and Elsie. Upon demolition, they went to the University of Melbourne for safekeeping, along with representative fragments of masonry – column capitols, decorative panels, urns. Flagstones from the basement were used in garden terracing at the National Trust's Como property.

St James' Buildings (bounded by William, Bourke, Church and Little Collins streets), 1966

The remaining two acres of the original Church of England land grant was cleared for the Darth-Vaderish AMP Building and plaza. Wreckers exposed a Chinese dragon painted across the wall of an attic room – exposed to the rain, it quickly faded.

Keith Dunstan called it 'probably the loveliest thing of its kind in Australia'. The last-standing fragment of St James' Buildings – the arched carriageway entrance on Bourke Street – hit the ground with 'a marvellous resonant thump'.

Board of Works building, née Sailors' Home (110 Spencer Street), 1970

No hue and cry was raised for the old Board of Works headquarters, due no doubt to the building's west-end address, its countless alterations and accretions, and to the downright hostility borne it by anyone who'd ever worked there. Described in 1946 as 'one of the most densely tenanted and obsolete, yet historic, buildings in the city', it had been earmarked for demolition ever since. But temporary solutions to the problem of overcrowding kept being found.

In 1957, Whelan's had the job of wrecking several buildings at the rear, which the Board of Works had owned and occupied in make-shift fashion since 1924. One among the several was 609–611 Little Collins Street, the former Commonwealth Coffee Palace, whose predecessor had, in 1901, been Jim Whelan's first city demolition. The painted legend, SUPERIOR ACCOMMODATION. SINGLE ROOM AND BREAKFAST 3/,

WEEKLY 17/6, was legible high up on the eastern wall until old Jim's grandsons gave the nod to knock it down.

The 1957 demolitions made way for an eight-storey building intended, not to replace, but to relieve pressure on the decrepitude in Spencer Street. It did that, temporarily, but there was no halting – or no attempt to halt – the old building's deterioration. By the late '60s it was an occupational health nightmare: the walls were cracked and juddery, one of the staircases was near collapse, the whole rabbit-warren was a fire trap. It was never meant to be so densely occupied. In 1903, when the Board of Works took occupation, the wide internal balconies were first boxed in. Then, as the Board's staff grew, the building's light-wells were reclaimed as office space and workshops, and outbuildings were added to connect up, in a kind of maze, with the buildings acquired at the rear. Only the strip of garden at the front remained, through all its long history, unencroached upon.

The old place dated back to 1864, when tens of thousands of British and foreign seamen arrived each year in Port Phillip Bay. Of them, some thousands were discharged from their vessels at the port.

The Sailors' Home in its early days.

Until they secured their next voyage, they needed a place to stay on shore – a place, ideally, where their hard-won wages wouldn't be drunk or gambled or bilked away. Hence the Melbourne Sailors' Home. Evidently the building was destined from the start to be strapped for space: just a few years after opening, it already required enlargement. For that purpose £1,200 was raised at a Sailors' Home ball during a visit by the Duke of Edinburgh in 1868.*

Besides accommodation, the Sailors' Home supplied meals, fellowship, and unbeery entertainment – there were rooms for reading, smoking and billiards. Captain Robilliard, the long-serving superintendent, was an old sea-dog, a Methodist preacher, and sole shipping agent for the port. He was the only man in Melbourne authorised to seek crewmen on behalf of sea captains. (Plenty did the job unauthorised, shanghai-ing drunken or unwilling seamen and pocketing the sailors' first month's wages-in-advance.) After the 1890s, the Home was quarter-full or less for most the year. But even if a sailor was skint, while he waited for a berth to present itself – and it could take a while, at some seasons – the Sailors' Home was *his* home. Out of thirty men lodged there in the doldrums of 1902 only one was able to pay his keep (fifteen shillings a week). All were permitted to stay, 'so long as they behave themselves' – no sure thing, since the Home's inmates ranked as 'some of the roughest even of sailor men'.

That same year, 1902, a new site was found for the Sailors' Home closer to the wharves, where Captain Robilliard might net more fish. The Melbourne & Metropolitan Board of Works bought the old building for £10,000, spent £16,000 more to double the floorspace, installed its administrative and engineering staff, and commenced the long process of demolition-by-neglect. Sixty-seven years later, Whelan's finished the job. Pulled down at the same time was the Australian Hotel, next door on Spencer Street, which fell one year short of its

---

* The ladies who were 'in a flutter of expectancy' that Prince Alfred would dance a Scotch reel, were disappointed when his Highness's piper wasn't up to the task, having 'over exerted himself at the Caledonian Gathering'.

centenary and would never have been licensed in the first place if the Sailors' Home committee had had its way.

Both buildings went to clear a site for the long-promised new Board of Works head office. Completed in 1973, it presented the Board with problems of an altogether different order. For a start, it drew criticism for the opulence of its executive offices ('Melbourne's Taj Mahal,' snorted the Labor opposition) and for the way it looked from the street. In place of garden, spindle-iron fence and mouldering brick were a rearing twenty-two storeys clad entirely in thunderhead-grey basalt. It looked, said one critic, 'as if it has been carved out of a huge monolith … like a fortress it evokes a sense of impregnable strength and autocratic power'. Its looks, though, were the least of its troubles. A year after completion, it began shedding small fragments of bluestone, and soon whole slabs of the cladding were pelting down on the street below. The building was barricaded and its flanking streets, Little Collins and Francis, closed to traffic. The bluestone, it seemed, hadn't been left to weather after quarrying, which would have let natural faults reveal themselves *before* the slabs were fixed in place. Simply re-cementing the slabs therefore wasn't the answer. It took ten years, but eventually the Board of Works building was stripped and re-clad with sheets of anodised aluminium, feather-weight compared to bluestone but somewhat similar in appearance.

The reason for extending this account of 110 Spencer Street into its modern phase is that Whelan's hadn't finished with the site just yet. To them, in 1977, went the job of removing the building's bluestone cladding. In doing so, it was in Whelan's interests to keep the slabs as intact as possible since, in part-payment for the job, the bluestone – all 33,000 square metres of it – was theirs. It was just the sort of salvage they'd have no trouble shifting: in small lots, for flagging floors and patios (including Owen Whelan's), or to big buyers like Melbourne City Council, on the look-out just then for stone to pave the Bourke Street mall and city square. For a start, though, it all went to Whelan's yard.

OLD STUFF

… we used to send some beautiful stuff to the tip, including things like wood panelling and wrought iron. Now, all of a sudden, people are becoming historically minded and they can't get enough of the old stuff.

~ Owen Whelan, 1968

The lamps either side of his front door used to light the entrance of the old Congregational Church hall and library in Russell Street. Inside, one pair of doors came from an insurance company office in the city, another from a southern-suburbs mansion. The exposed bricks in his living room were out of the workshops at the Royal Mint and the fireplace was built of St Patrick's College bluestone.* And out the back, the patio and pool-surrounds were paved with stone slabs from the Board of Works. A typical customer of Whelan's yard in the '70s, he was also the managing director.†

Owen, Myles and Tony Whelan, during that decade, all built houses that owed much to their company's 'dismantled commodity'. Inner-city renovators drew heavily on Whelan's Brunswick yard, as did the mud-

---

*   The Congregational hall (latterly Stott's Business College) was wrecked in 1968, the Royal Mint workshops and smokestack in 1970.

†   Owen replaced his father as managing director following Tom's death in 1970.

At Whelan's yard.

brick communities on Melbourne's north-east fringes. Nick Dattner was
part of the mud-brick scene at Hurstbridge in the '70s and, when it came
to sourcing building materials, he naturally went to Whelan's. There was
a lot of 'old bank stuff' surfacing at the yard about then, he recalls, besides
some glorious windows that were supposed to have come out of Willsmere
hospital at Kew. He sensed that the Whelans had 'a great affection' for

mud-brick builders. Beyond a doubt, it was the fellowship of kindred spirits. Whelan's weren't just recyclers, Nick Dattner believes, but pioneer conservationists. 'In an era when few valued our material past, here were Whelan's who did.'

As a schoolgirl, there were mornings when Beverley Flemming's father gave her the whispered instruction: 'Put on your uniform and take your lunch, but wait for me round the corner. We're going to Whelan the Wrecker's.' In the family's Ford Prefect, father and daughter would make the long, thrilling drive across town to Brunswick. At 605 Sydney Road, they'd turn in through a brick archway, park on the right and commence the day's 'scrounging'. 'It was dark and dirty,' is Beverley's memory of Whelan's yard, 'and I was very happy.'

These were the late '50s, when booty from city demolitions like Melbourne Mansions and St Patrick's Hall was beginning to proliferate again amongst the detritus of hotels and homes. Whelan's office at that time was little better than a shed, built early in the century out of salvaged stuff. In 1964 they replaced it with a new edifice that showcased the firm's thriving fortunes, as well as its sentimental side. There was a reception area now and a boardroom, smartly appointed and modern in layout. Yet the partitioning between offices was a picket fence from a North Melbourne cottage and the passageway was lined with blackwood panelling out of the old Temple Court barristers' chambers in Collins Street. The exposed ceiling beams came from the Glaciarium skating rink in South Melbourne; there were doors* from the Occidental Hotel and the CML Building, whence also originated a solid granite bench – formerly a window lintel. And in homage to the decor's provenance, one whole wall of the reception area was papered with an aerial view of nineteenth-century Melbourne.

People like Beverley Flemming and her dad, to whom Whelan's yard was a destination for a day-out, were a comparative rarity in the '50s. By

---

* When additions were made in the '70s, the doors of Whelan's new boardroom came fresh from the Board of Works building in Spencer Street.

the mid-'60s, though, hundreds of families would descend on the yard every weekend, to scavenge, sift and rootle 'as if on some mad archaeological hunt'.

> For a few shillings, week-end fossickers can pick up anything
> from a bath to a wrought-iron fence. In fact [said Owen] I
> reckon it would be possible to build a mansion from the ruins
> around here.

It was in the '70s that Nick Dattner came to know the yard. He remembers it as 'a very eccentric environment', nothing like the utilitarian set-up of rival demolishers' yards. Tivendale's and Abel Demolitions tended to deal in more straightforward building materials and timber, all laid out in the open, with no dark corners and not much in the way of surprises. At Whelan's yard, besides the piled-up building stuffs outside, there were sheds stacked with timber and iron and cannibalised fixtures of all kinds. Out of one of the sheds emerged Janet and Danny Zepnick dragging a pair of pub doors with kangaroos etched in the glass – which would shatter in the ute on the way home. (One of those 'lost treasure' stories of which every bargain-hound has their share.) The top-shelf renovator ware – bluestone, marble, architectural features – was kept, tantalisingly, 'out the back'. But what really marked Whelan's out as different, the window to the Whelan soul, was the miscellany of 'old stuff' strung up about the place on wire fences.

'You never knew what you would find,' says Nick Dattner. On one visit to Whelan's yard Nick found a pile of jarrah staves out of vats from (he thinks) a South Australian winery. He remembers clambering over the heap, sniffing the ruddy timber and thinking what use he might put it to. He bought the lot, a purchase that set his course as a maker of recycled-timber furniture. The tables made out of those old-winey staves, Nick says, smelt just beautiful.

Myles Whelan once provided an insight into the organisational principle behind Whelan's yard. It was important, he told a reporter, to keep the place tidy so that people could see what there was, 'while at the same time hiding one or two things so they can feel the thrill of discovering it for themselves'. It was a thrill Myles himself knew well. An avid collector (hoarder, some would say) of all manner of old stuff, he'd end up as patron of the Ephemera Society. Besides the thrill of discovery, though, there was something else that people looked for at Whelan's yard. As Myles explained, 'People loved to know: where did it come from? "Ohh, that came from ..." and we'd tell them.' So that, as well as a mantelpiece or a load of roofing iron or a gargoyle, the Whelan's customer bought a story to go with it. And if it wasn't strictly the truth ... well, did it matter?

CHAPTER 14

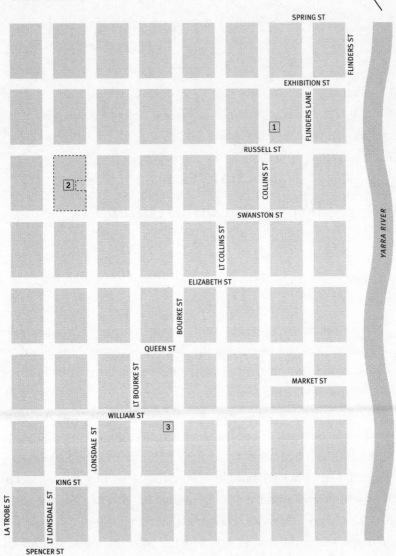

SPRING ST

FLINDERS ST

EXHIBITION ST

FLINDERS LANE

1

RUSSELL ST

COLLINS ST

2

SWANSTON ST

LT COLLINS ST

YARRA RIVER

ELIZABETH ST

BOURKE ST

QUEEN ST

LT BOURKE ST

MARKET ST

WILLIAM ST

3

LONSDALE ST

KING ST

LA TROBE ST

LT LONSDALE ST

SPENCER ST

1. *CRA Building*
2. *Queen Victoria Hospital*
3. *Shell corner*

CHAPTER 14

All Things Come to an End

CRA Building ~ Queen Victoria Hospital ~ Whelan the Wrecker

Even as the market for 'old stuff' flourished, speed was overtaking salvage as the essence of the demolition game. 'The old-time wreckers would turn in their graves,' said Owen Whelan in 1980, 'if they saw what was going to the tip.'

The tip, Whelan's own, was the old Wales quarry in Kirkdale Street, East Brunswick, close by Merri Creek. For seventy-odd years until the 1930s, it had been the source of Melbourne's best bluestone. In 1965, when Whelan's bought it, the hole was fifty metres deep, with a million-and-a-quarter cubic metres of 'air space'. They reckoned it would take them fifty years to fill it.

Ten years later the quarry was half-full. Already it had swallowed the debris of a thousand wreckings or more. (When Keith Dunstan wrote that 'Much of the glory of old Collins Street went to Whelan's,' it wasn't their yard he was talking about.) The unsaleable portion of the Board of Works' bluestone cladding joined the slate flags from Cole's Book Arcade, countless millions of bricks, and a growing preponderance of reinforced concrete rubble in what Owen Whelan called 'the grave for Melbourne'. Ashes to ashes, quarry to quarry.

By the end of the '70s, Whelan's were investigating ways to extend the life of their tip – innovations like waste-shredders and compactors that would make the remaining space go further. Another solution was to acquire a second tip, at Brooklyn in Melbourne's outer-west, and an adjacent five-acre yard which they could stack high with saleable salvage of the bulkier kind. The pressure on Whelan's tipping capacity had become critical with their move into commercial waste-disposal in 1977. As Whelan's Kartaway, they were pioneers in the field of garbage-skip hire. To begin with, they'd built the skips for their own use on demolition sites; then, seeing a demand, they extended the service to the building industry and eventually to the broader public.* The diversification turned out to be timely and ensured Whelan's buoyancy in the decade of change ahead.

Melbourne boomed in the 1980s. Late in the decade, especially, it took two hands to number off the cranes poking above the city skyline. Yet Whelan the Wrecker's plunderous presence was less dramatically felt in the CBD than at any time since the mid-'50s. At the yard, Nick Dattner noticed that the 'treasure trove aspect' waned in the early '80s, as fewer 'interesting' buildings – that is to say, fewer old buildings – were being wrecked.

As early as 1979, Myles Whelan had grumbled that the Wrecker was 'running out of old Melbourne buildings' to knock down. That shortage became more acute after 1983 when the Cain Labor government introduced heritage legislation that at last afforded real protection to the city's historic buildings and streetscapes. Any demolition in the CBD now required a planning permit, issued subject to consideration of historical significance, among other things. At the end of the '70s, Myles had backed an (unsuccessful) bid to demolish

---

* Non-Whelan's refuse had been hitherto unwelcome at their tip. In one reported incident (FLYING ARMCHAIR INJURES MAN) a tip-worker was hit on the head by an armchair dumped over the fence.

'The Mourners', Arthur Horner's comment on the state of things: 'today's developers move like armies in the night, and there is no fait quite so accompli as a flattened building'. 'I am surprised at Whelan's doing it,' said a city council spokesman in 1982 after Whelan the Wrecker demolished an historic building in Spring Street (the original Eye and Ear Hospital) without a permit.

the historic State Government offices at the corner of Collins and Spring streets. Collins Street was already so debased, he argued, that one more demolition couldn't hurt. His brother Owen, a few years later, reflected on the fate of the long-gone CML Building: 'There would have been no hope of pulling it down today. That building would have had a sticker on it, finish.'

Most of Whelan's major demolitions during the '80s were in the area of industrial obsolesence. The really big ones were the power stations at Newport and Yallourn. The dearth of steady wrecking work also led them further along the path of 'customer-directed diversification', making activities like rubbish removal and site excavation a core element of Whelan's business.

But all those cranes on the city skyline meant that new buildings were going up. They must've been taking the place of *something*: if not historic buildings, then what?

Throughout the '60s, it had towered over Melbourne: the tallest building, perched on one of the highest spots in the city. During its construction, in the first wave of skyscrapers, Robin Boyd had assured readers of the *Herald* that 'Melbourne's new towers will still be here in the 21st century.' Indeed, the Conzinc Riotinto of Australia (CRA) building had been built to last fifty years; but after twenty-five it was fit only for demolishing. Norman Lindsay would have argued that that's all it was *ever* fit for. He'd written, in the '50s, of another Collins Street 'glass house': 'There is only one finality to such abominable glass anthills and that is a bomb.' Obviously he'd never heard of Whelan the Wrecker.

Back when the CRA building was new – just three years after he'd disposed of its stately predecessor, Melbourne Mansions* – Jim Whelan (the second) had already been envisaging how his firm might pull the twenty-six storeys down. He'd been provoked, it's true, by Keith Dunstan's saying, 'It'd be practically impossible, wouldn't it?'

Jim had scoffed. 'No, it'd be easy. I'd just put a crane up the side and take it down layer by layer, like dismantling a wedding cake.' And that's pretty much how Whelan's went about it when their chance arrived, in 1987. As the first of Melbourne's skyscrapers to reach

---

*   See Chapter 8.

'Like dismantling a wedding cake'
– wrecking the CRA Building, 1987.

obsolescence, it was the biggest structure the Wrecker had yet tackled. But within less than a year they'd made 101 Collins Street 'a ghost site', ready for the next glass-house incarnation.

A couple of new Whelan faces appeared in newspaper pictures of the CRA demolition. They were Gerard and Matthew, two of Myles' *seven* sons. Now, Owen also had seven offspring, Tony had six, and it was clear that the Wrecker couldn't absorb them all. The time had come to rationalise the family business, as the previous generation of Whelans had done thirty years before. In 1988, Myles bought out his brother's and cousin's interests in Whelan the Wrecker. Tony took over the Kartaway arm of the business, while Owen, nearing sixty, remained on the Whelan's board but otherwise dedicated himself to the serious business of golf.

As the most experienced wreckers in the country, Whelan's were well-qualified to branch into the new field of demolition consultancy. Since the '60s, Myles had been a driving force in the promotion – and legislation – of safe practices within an inherently dangerous industry. Now Whelan's became increasingly involved in advising developers and construction firms on demolition issues, while Myles

Whelan's third generation: (from left) Tony, Owen and Myles.

himself was active in the area of industry training.

Still Whelan *the Wrecker* was a long way from being just a business name. Whelan's remained Melbourne's pre-eminent demolishers and boasted more than double the turnover of their nearest competitor, Australiawide. Myles gave tradition a tweak in 1990 when he introduced a new inflection to the grammar of Whelan the Wrecker signs. Besides ... IS HERE and ... WAS HERE was added the portent, WHELAN THE WRECKER IS COMING HERE. Barry Humphries, that same year, took pre-emption a step further when he toured central Melbourne with

Barry Humphries was not alone in nominating the Gas and Fuel buildings in Flinders Street (now the site of Federation Square) for the Whelan's treatment.

a sign that read WHELAN THE WRECKER SHOULD BE HERE!!, striking a pose in front of buildings he deemed wreck-worthy.

The Queen Victoria Hospital in Lonsdale Street wasn't one of them. Jim Whelan the First, you may recall, had pulled down the old Melbourne Hospital buildings in the years before World War One. The red-brick complex built in their place became the Queen Victoria Hospital (for women) in 1946, after the Royal Melbourne Hospital moved out to Parkville. By the late '70s, the Edwardian buildings were showing their age and unsuitability for modern hospital needs and the 'Queen Vic' was promised a new home out at Clayton, in Melbourne's southeast. Then began the long process of consideration and connivance as to the future of the Queen Victoria site.

The hospital filled a whole city block alongside the State Library, and its site had been eyed off and yearned over by urban planners since before that profession existed. Within the first decade of Melbourne's settlement, it had been mooted as the ideal site for a public square. That idea was now revived – and might have stood a chance of success had the site become available ten years earlier. As it was, though, by the early '80s Melbourne had a city square – albeit an unsatisfactory one – four blocks to the south. There was strong support, too, for the site's continued use as a focus for women's services in the city.

A conservation study of the Queen Victoria Hospital, commissioned by the State government in 1983, found that the five buildings along Lonsdale Street constituted 'an important and intact Edwardian streetscape' and recommended that they be retained. The site was listed for protection by the Historic Buildings Council, but just two years later the government chose a design for the site's redevelopment which would entail demolition of all but the three central buildings on Lonsdale Street – the 'Mabel Brookes', 'Queen Elizabeth' and 'Queen Elizabeth II Coronation' towers. The government's own Historic Buildings Register was selectively demolished in 1988 when most of the Queen Vic buildings were de-listed, smoothing the way for their demolition and the sale of the site for commercial development.

That's how the site once again fell into the hands of Whelan the Wrecker. Whelan's had taken a knock at it more than once since old Jim's Edwardian foray. There was the laundry block – that came down in the '60s – and back in 1948 they'd knocked down the old boiler-house with its landmark chimney stack, on Russell Street. Now they all but finished the place off.

The Queen Vic job saw the increased Whelanisation of the Wrecker, with two more of Myles' sons, Tom and Myles (Mylo), joining the firm. The outstanding architectural feature of the hospital buildings was the ornamental zinc domes (or capulettes) that crowned each corner of the facades. Amazing things, they were. With their overlapping 'scales' of sheet-zinc and boggling ventilation ports, they seemed, up close, like the carcasses of sea monsters. They weighed one-and-a-

Whelan's workers prepare to uncap one of the towers of the Queen Victoria Hospital.

half tonnes each, but (with difficulty) two of the four domes from the demolished frontages were removed intact and sold for about $1,000 each to a customer in Adelaide.

Today, just one of the three Lonsdale Street towers is still standing. Housing the Queen Victoria Women's Centre, it is dwarfed by the bulge and thrust of the QV complex that otherwise fills the block. The heritage-listed towers that flanked it fell victim first to political deal-making and then, in 1994, to the wreckers. But not to Whelan's, not any more.

'All things come to an end,' Myles Whelan was quoted as saying in January 1991. He was talking, of course, about buildings ('Demolition is the first step of progress,' he went on), certainly *not* about Whelan the Wrecker. On the contrary, the firm was gearing up to celebrate its centenary the following year. But the building boom was over, the property market in a slump and wreckers, Myles had to admit, were feeling the pinch. Whelan's had survived tough times before, though.

Survived? Hell, old Jim had started the business during the depression of the 1890s, and hadn't Whelan's emerged stronger than ever from the next one, in the '30s? 'We'll get over this,' said Myles.

But things were different this time round. Whelan's long-time and loyal bankers, the CBA, had disappeared in a merger a few years earlier and the Wrecker had switched its business to the State Bank of Victoria. Whelan's own hard times (exacerbated by interest rates of nearly 20 per cent) coincided with the collapse of the State Bank; so that, at their lowest ebb, they found themselves in the hands of the Commonwealth Bank. Always, in the past, Whelan's had felt assured that their name and reputation counted for something and would carry them through. Now though, they found themselves dealing with strangers, to whom the Whelan the Wrecker name meant nothing.

'We were in no way anywhere as financially exposed as we'd been in the past,' insisted Myles. He and his fellow Whelan's directors were confident that the Wrecker could trade its way out of the doldrums, as it had done before. They cut staff to a minimum (which was hard: Whelan's was like a big family), kept a tight rein on cash-flow, and seized any work they could find. But there wasn't much about and what there was scarcely paid: everybody else was in the same boat, making business conditions 'stupidly competitive'. And the Commonwealth Bank, determined to recoup some of the State Bank's lost millions, was disinclined to be patient. Or, as Myles put it, 'They were just brutal.'

> They took all our equipment. We were within months of paying
> it all off, but they took it. And if we haven't got equipment, we
> can't work. ... They didn't care.

When the bank squeezed off their air supply, it was the end of 1991 and Whelan's still had their sign up in the city. They were halfway through wrecking Shell Corner. The Shell oil company had a pair of eponymous buildings down at the corner of Bourke and William. The elder of the two, dating from 1933, had been one of those glorious 132-foot erections that heralded the beginning of the end of the depression. It boasted 99½ per cent Australian-made materials and was intended, said the Shell Company, as 'a gesture of confidence in the country at a critical period'. The second building, right at the corner, went up in the late '50s, in the first lusty stirrings after the post-war slump. In 1991, there were murmurs of protest at the demolition of the Shell building no. 1, the Art Deco styling of which had won architectural plaudits in its day. But the Historic Buildings Council deemed it not worth fighting for – to the relief of the hard-pressed Whelan's, desperate for something to knock down.

They were two blocks away from the site of old Jim Whelan's first city wrecking, and not seriously thinking for a minute that this might be their last. So they were stunned when the bank repossessed their demolition equipment. 'They thought they had me,' said Myles. The Wrecker was waiting on a sizeable progress payment for the Shell demolition; the bank was waiting too, until the cheque was paid in, to close their books on the company. But Whelan's pre-empted them, going into voluntary liquidation in the last week of November 1991. It made no difference to the Wrecker – they were done for – but it meant that that final payment, rather than sliding into the bank's maw, would go towards paying off creditors, of whom Whelan's employees would be first in line.

'The recession's most shocking casualty,' Keith Dunstan called it. 'It is unthinkable that a great old firm like this should disappear.' But it did, and the centenary of the 'great old firm' was marked only by a fire sale. Everything went: the remains of the plant, the contents of yard and office, and, most cruelly, the name 'Whelan the Wrecker'. 'You can't cash it at the bank,' Myles had said of his firm's good name; but, in the end, it sold for $50,000.*

More than ten years later, Myles could force a laugh as he related the awful events of 1991–92: the scuttling of the family firm in its hundredth year. 'But still,' he finished up (employing what was almost certainly an inherited Whelanism), 'it's only bloody money.'

Sure, Keith Dunstan lamented the end of Whelan's, but you can bet there were a few – a good few – defenders of Melbourne's heritage who weren't sorry to see the Wrecker undone. Ah, but how things come around.

In 2000 a developer applied for a planning permit to construct a ten-storey apartment tower at 605 Sydney Road, Brunswick – the old Whelan the Wrecker site. The yard had all been razed; only the one-time office still stood at the streetfront. The developer got his permit,† subject to umpteen conditions, including this one: 'The Whelan the Wrecker sign must be restored and must not be removed.' The clunky electric sign mounted on the front wall in 1967 now ranked as a heritage feature.

Now inviolable, it juts over the footpath still. Mind you, it's not a *real* Whelan the Wrecker sign. Just WHELAN THE WRECKER, it says, summoning memory to supply the missing words: … WAS EVERYWHERE.

---

* As an arm of Delta Demolitions, Whelan the Wrecker these days confines itself to house-wrecking and the sale of secondhand building materials from its 'Whelan's Warehouse' (with nary a dark corner) in Port Melbourne.

† The permit was subsequently withdrawn, following objections from local residents.

HISTORY MOVES FAST

Readers of the spring 1962 edition of the construction industry journal,
Building Materials, *were asked to 'Consider the concealed construc-*
tiveness of wrecking throughout the ages.' Had not the Incas, Aztecs,
Chinese, Persians, and Romans all built their cities on the ruins of the
vanquished?

> This – the perpetuation of history in layers – is the habit of
> mankind. Raze first, and raise anew.

Why, the field of archaeology had ancient wreckers to thank for its very
existence. And historians ought likewise to be grateful for the imaginative
possibilities presented by fragments, unlike intact structures which had
'the inhibiting effect of confining speculation by presenting solid fact for
all to behold'. 'So,' concluded the writer –

> wrecking has a valid, romantic tradition, which the splendid
> tradesmanship of the modern, professional practitioners with
> their explosives and bulldozers should do much to promote.

It wasn't long after that that Whelan the Wrecker took out a screen adver-
tisement at cinemas showing 'The Fall of the Roman Empire'.

Archaeologists unearth Whelan's leftovers at the College of Surgeons (former site of the Model School), Spring Street, in 2002.

For something short of a year in 1908–09, the Singer building in New York was the world's tallest. In 1967 it claimed a new record, as the tallest building demolished to that date. Its architect had predicted that his creation would be 'as lasting as the Pyramids', which made Harry Glick laugh when he heard about it. A second-generation wrecker and supervisor of the Singer building demolition, Glick was inured to such vanities. 'History moves fast,' he said – wrecker-ese for 'Get over it.'

'The ancient creed – "Cursed be he that removeth old landmarks" – has never been observed in the city.' Peter Ackroyd was writing about London, but the city could be any city. Even Melbourne. As Dame Edna Everage said of her home town in 2003, 'Melbourne is always abolishing things, pulling things down, it's a tradition here really.'

Now, it may well be true that 'After a few weeks you have to strain to remember what the old building looked like.' But the thing is – as Keith Dunstan well knew – that 'what it looked like' is rarely what matters the most. Rather, it's the sentimental substance of a place that ordains its prominence and permanence on a person's memory map. 'This – the perpetuation of history in layers – is the habit of mankind.' Of course, the *writer in Building Materials meant real, solid layers of masonry-turned-to-rubble; but it's as true, and truer, to say the same of the histories we construct for ourselves in layers of personal meaning and memory.*

Wreckers know this. As the ones who act the part of Charon, ferrying the spirits of the demolished across the River Styx, they're the last to call a dead building by its name. Stewart Dawson's, Menzies' Hotel, the Tin Shed were never really gone while there was a Whelan who remembered the wrecking of them. A wrecker lacks the excuse of a short memory – unlike the project manager of the development on the old Queen Victoria Hospital site, who could assure a journalist that 'It's a lot better than what was here before. It was just a big hole in the ground.' If you're a property developer, it's easy to believe that the history of a place began with the big hole in the ground or the site-plan stamped ALL BUILDINGS REMOVED.

An advertisement for off-the-plan apartments in Melbourne's Docklands tells potential buyers –

Today, Dock 5 is prime real estate. Tomorrow it will be Melbourne's most exclusive address and your new home.

Want to know about yesterday? Ask a wrecker.

ACKNOWLEDGEMENTS

My thanks go, in the first place, to the Whelan family: Jean and the late Myles Whelan, Owen Whelan, and Tony Whelan. Their warmth, co-operation and trust made all the difference to a writer accustomed to dealing with a more remote past.

Research for this book was undertaken largely at the State Library of Victoria where I was the blessed recipient of a Creative Fellowship in 2003–04. The Library's collections (in particular, its Whelan the Wrecker archive) and the knowledge and resourcefulness of its staff were (and are) invaluable. Especial thanks must go to Dr Dianne Reilly and Shane Carmody, as well as to my fellow Fellows.

Thanks also to: Jackie Yowell; Patty Brown; Jim and Mary Parker; Nick Dattner; Beverley Flemming; Janet Zepnick; Roger Aldridge; Shane Maloney; Catherine Freyne; Brian and Vera Wilson; Lenore Frost; James McArdle; Sandra Beaumont; Alan Bolton; Tom Molnar; Debra Vaughan; Geordie Dowell; Bill Birch; Toby Sail; Andy Brown-May; D.L. Coughlin; Adrian Robb; Merron Cullum of Cole Publications; Sigmund Jorgensen at Monsalvat; Vicki Ritchie and staff at the *Herald and Weekly Times*; Ann Jackman at St James' Old Cathedral; Jeremy Smith at Heritage Victoria; City of Melbourne Archives; University of Melbourne Archives; and Mrs Bradley, literary agent and muse.

I'm grateful to the folk at Black Inc. for their trust, hard work and good humour. Most of all, though, I thank David and Rosie, for indulging the demands of my 'interesting' life.

PICTURE CREDITS

State Library of Victoria
~ La Trobe Collection

Inside covers (from *Melbourne Guide Book*, McCarron, Bird, Melville, Mullen and Slade, Melbourne, 1st ed., c.1897); **p. 10** (from Mary Kehoe, *The Melbourne Benevolent Asylum: Hotham's Premier Building*, Hotham History Project, North Melbourne, 1998); **p. 17** (from Alexander Sutherland, *Victoria and its Metropolis: past and present*, vol. II, McCarron, Bird, Melbourne, 1888); **p. 140** and **p. 151** (from *Colonial Mutual Life Assurance Society Limited: Principal office building, 316 Collins Street*, c.1960, photographs by Wolfgang Sievers); **p. 144** (from *Industrial and Mining Standard*, 21 April 1960); **p. 196** and **p. 199** (from *Melbourne Guide Book*, 5th ed., 1911).

~ Picture Collection

p. 41 (Monahan's Building, H 39357/136); **p. 45** (Swanston Street, c.1905, H 96.200/688); **p. 57** (View from Collins Street, H 33668/51); **p. 58** (Holeproof 'Skyscrapers', photo by Edwin G. Adamson, H 98.86/9); **p. 80** (Model School, H 3682, and Model School demolition, H 3682); **p. 84** (Colonial Bank, IAN19/01/80/5); **p. 88** (Melbourne University Commerce building, photo by Lyle Fowler from Harold Paynting collection, H 92.20/562); **p. 90** (Royal Bank, photo by James Barnard Fox, H 2002.125/45); **p. 95** (top) (Royal Insurance

Building, H19649); **p. 97** (Hotel Australia, photo by Lyle Fowler from Harold Paynting collection, H 92.20/351–68); **p. 104** (Collins Place cottages, H 19968); **p. 109** (Elizabeth Street, 1916, photo by Kerr Bros., H 99.100/25); **p. 118** (64 La Trobe Street, photo by R. McInnes from *Argus* Collection, H 2002–199/671); **p. 124** (Synagogue and St Patrick's Hall, H 22992); **p. 127** (Sir Redmond Barry's residence, watercolour by John Mather, H 294); **p. 136** (Equitable Building, c.1906, H 42665/19); **p. 157** (Fish Market, photo by Airspy, H 2515); **p. 172** (detail from 'Bourke Street on a Saturday Night', IAN 31/10/77/168); **p. 178** (Eastern Market, photo by Charles B. Walker, c.1888, H 81.111); **p. 193** (Occidental Hotel demolition, photo by Lyle Fowler from Harold Paynting collection, H 94.150/63); **p. 207** (Federal Hotel, H 93.492/12); **p. 208** (Federal Hotel vestibule, photo by Wolfgang Sievers, H 98.30/376); **p. 219** (Swanston Street, 1901, photo by Gustav Damman, H 94.30/14); **p. 224** (Town Hall Chambers, photo by Anthony Pritchard, H 97.108/1); **p. 249** (Collins Street, c.1921, H 41383); **p. 253** (Oriental Hotel café, photo by Elton Fox, H 90.137/117; **p. 259 (top)** (Collins Street, c.1935, H 96.200/335); **p. 257 (bottom)** (Union/ANZ Bank, photo by Wolfgang Sievers, H 99.50/105); **p. 258** (St James Buildings, photo by John T. Collins, H 98.252/915); **p. 261** (Sailors' Home, photo by Charles Nettleton, H 82.246/2); **p. 265** (Whelan's yard, from *Herald and Weekly Times* Portrait Collection, H 38849/5801)

~ Newspaper Collection
p. 23 (*Weekly Times*, 15 April 1911); **p. 44** (*Australasian*, 3 March 1906); **p. 51** (*Herald*, 1 January 1932); **p. 141** (*Herald*, 10 October 1959); **p. 210** (*Argus*, 5 February 1913)

Herald and Weekly Times *Photographic Collection*
pages 121, 131, 169, 183, 201, 203, 217, 221, 227 (cartoon by Jeff Hook), 230, 234, 257, 275

The Age
p. 272 (cartoon by Arthur Horner)

Miscellaneous
p. 4 (courtesy of Sandra Beaumont); p. 21 (Royal Historical Society of Victoria); p. 67 (Cole Publications); p. 95 **(bottom)** (Sigmund Jorgensen, Monsalvat); p. 102 (photo by Lyle Fowler, from Harold Paynting collection); p. 226 (photo by Hewitt, from City of Melbourne Art and Heritage Collection); p. 240 (Newspix); p. 282 (Heritage Victoria, photo by Jeremy Smith)

pages 6, 16, 27, 30, 41, 72, 100, 160, 205, 223, 274 **(top and bottom)**, 277 – from the collection of Myles and Jean Whelan

pages 29, 49, 52, 73, 125, 280 – courtesy of Tony Whelan

pages 86, 139, 153 – photos by the author

cover photo/p. 233 by Brian McArdle – courtesy of Marie Shaw and James McArdle

INDEX

Page numbers in italics refer to illustrations